COLD JUSTICE

A BUCK TAYLOR MYSTERY

BOOK 14

BY

CHUCK MORGAN

Printed in the United States of America

First printing 2025

ISBN 978-1-968179-28-1 (Paperback)

LIBRARY OF CONGRESS CONTROL NUMBER

2025916445

Prologue

The funeral procession left the Cathedral Basilica of the Immaculate Conception, turned onto South Broadway and continued towards South Santa Fe. Once at South Santa Fe, it headed south until it reached South Sheridan, and then it turned into the Fort Logan National Cemetery. The mile-long procession of law enforcement vehicles from the federal government, state and local jurisdictions and a military honor guard filled the streets that wove through the cemetery. The mourners walked past thousands of simple white marble headstones that marked the final resting place of America's honored dead.

A Marine Corps honor guard led the way as six FBI agents bore the casket holding Hank Clancy. The mourners, most dressed in dark clothing and bundled up against the frigid morning, followed behind the casket as they made their way to the outdoor service area.

The morning had dawned bright and clear, but the temperature hovered around ten degrees. Buck Taylor, with a bandage covering the side of his head, followed the crowd. He had spent the night in a hotel in Denver. He left the crutches in Bax's Jeep and was helped along the walk to the cathedral and now to the service by his daughter, Cassie, and CBI Agent Ashley Baxter.

Cassie held the middle child position in Buck and Lucy's family; she fully exemplified that role. In high school, she'd played soccer, ran track and played volleyball. She lettered in all three sports. She was also the one who got in trouble for violating curfew, drinking and whatever other mischief she could find to get into. Buck was surprised when she was accepted to the University of Arizona with a full scholarship for volleyball. He was even more surprised when she was accepted into law school. Cassie was never much for regimented education.

Several years ago, she'd dropped out of law school, and her career path took a different track. She joined the Forest Service and now worked as a wildland firefighter with the Helena Hotshots. The Helena Hotshots were one of the elite firefighting teams based out of Helena, Montana. Buck was not surprised. He never saw her sitting behind a desk as a lawyer. She loved the outdoors, and she was as tough as they come.

Buck had been out of the hospital less than a week and shouldn't have been at the funeral at all, but he owed it to his dear friend Hank to be there, to honor his sacrifice and the life he'd led. He was also there for Hank's wife and family.

Hank Clancy had been a deputy director of the FBI and the deputy director in charge of the Denver Field Office. Hank had been with the FBI for almost thirty years, following a four-year hitch in the United States Marine Corps. He had been involved in many of the most famous cases in the FBI's history during his tenure and was an exceptional investigator. He was also one of Buck's oldest friends.

Their relationship hadn't always been that way, as both Hank and Buck were headstrong and driven, but that drive to solve crimes led to their long and enduring friendship. Many times over the years, they clashed over policies and procedures, but when you looked at their records of accomplishments, it was easy to see that these two men were among the best criminal investigators in the country, and even though one was a federal agent and one was an agent for the state of Colorado, they always put their differences aside and worked together. Buck was proud to have Hank as a member of his extended team, and Hank appreciated being the first person Buck called when outside help was needed.

Buck had been asked by the director of the FBI, on behalf of Hank's wife, to be one of the pallbearers, but Buck's doctor told him that was out of the question. Buck had been seriously injured when a criminal he and his team were pursuing set off an explosive device in the car she was driving. Buck, too close to the vehicle, suffered a serious head wound that tore open his scalp, a concussion, several other lacerations and soft tissue injuries from the force of the explosion. He spent a week in the ICU at the hospital in Glenwood Springs and then another week in recovery before being released. Now, a week later, he stood, leaning on his daughter, and listened as the director of the FBI spoke about Hank's impressive career.

The priest blessed the casket, the family and those in attendance: close to a thousand law enforcement officers, family and friends. The Marine Corps honor guard folded the American flag and presented it to his widow while "Taps" played.

Buck wiped the tears from his eyes and thought about how senseless the whole thing was. Hank hadn't died in a gunfight or investigating some heinous crime.

He had been stopped at a convenience store on his way home from work and was filling up his gas tank when he heard a commotion. He looked across the parking lot and saw a man and a woman having a heated argument. He watched but hadn't attempted to intervene until the man punched his wife and then punched his five-year-old son. Hank walked towards the man, who pulled out a pistol and shot his wife and son. He turned and spotted Hank, who was reaching for his own pistol, and shot him in the chest and then put the barrel in his mouth and shot himself.

The store owner, who was on the phone with the police, later said that Hank never stood a chance. It all happened so fast. Hank and the wife died at the scene, and the little boy died a day later in the hospital. It was a tragic event and took the life of an incredible man, a young woman with a future and a little boy who would never get the chance to achieve greatness.

Buck snapped out of his melancholy as the marine honor guard fired their twenty-one-gun salute. The crowd broke up and headed back to their vehicles. There was an open house at a local American Legion Hall, but Buck did not feel up to going.

"Buck," said a voice from behind him. He turned. FBI Director J. Michael Ferranti pushed through the crowd, stepped up and shook Buck's hand. "It's good to see you up and around, Buck," he said. "Last time we spoke, you were just out of recovery. How are you healing?"

Buck smiled. "Nice to see you, sir. I'm healing up as well as I guess I can. Wish I was back on the job."

Buck introduced the FBI director to his daughter and Bax, and Cassie shook the director's hand.

"Listen, Buck. You take care, and if you need anything, don't hesitate to reach out." They shook hands, and the director turned and walked away.

Buck ran into Colorado Governor Richard J. Kennedy and his boss, CBI director Kevin Jackson, and they spoke for a few minutes before Cassie looked at Buck.

"Dad, we need to get you back to the car. You're looking a little pale."

Buck nodded, and Cassie and Bax led him back to Bax's Jeep. They slid in, and Bax pulled out of the cemetery and headed for Gunnison. They had a long drive ahead of them, but Buck didn't want to spend another night in a hotel. He wanted the comfort of his bed. Cassie handed him a bottle of water and two pain pills, and Buck settled in for the drive. He was asleep before they left Denver.

Chapter One

Billy Claymore had done it. After six years of trying, he was going to be on the first ski lift chair of the season. He knew it didn't mean much. No prize or anything, maybe his picture in the local paper, but that wasn't the point. This was his year.

As soon as Billy saw the long-range weather forecast, he knew he had a shot. For the past six years, he had been beaten out by three old retired guys: Shredder Jim, Snowflake, and Mr. Snowman. He never understood how they did it, but he knew one thing. He would beat them one of these years, and this year was it.

The forecast called for up to four feet of fresh powder, and Billy made a decision. He called his friends Tim Hawthorne and Jake Woodman, and then he called his boss at the convenience store and asked for the week off. His boss hemmed and hawed but agreed, and Billy raced down to the basement and dug out his winter gear.

Arriving at the ski resort, he didn't see any of his three adversaries, so he raced over to the lift area and pitched his winter tent right at the front of the line. Tim and Jake arrived right behind him. Now they had to wait for the official opening day announcement from the resort, and he'd be all set to be on the first chair when the lift started.

The week was like a party, and even though it was cold at night, his camp stove and ultra-warm sleeping bag kept him warm. His girlfriend, Eva, brought him food every day, and at night the three would build a small campfire and sit around enjoying the evening. Tim brought his acoustic guitar, and they would sit around drinking beer and singing.

The announcement had come the night before last that the resort would open at 9 A.M. Billy and his friends were stoked. They spent some time talking to Snowflake and Mr. Snowman. It turned out that Shredder Jim had passed away during the summer. Billy almost felt bad taking this victory away from them, but not that bad.

The Grassy Mountain Ski Resort was the second highest all-natural-snow ski resort in the continental United States. Grassy Mountain Resort sat in a gorgeous tree-filled valley, nine miles southwest of the small town of Lake City, Colorado. Lake City was the sole municipality in Hinsdale County.

Hinsdale County, with an average year-round population of 788 people, was the second-least-populated county in Colorado. Except in the winter, when the resort was open. Then, the population could swell as high as ten thousand, and it put a strain on the local infrastructure.

The ski resort, on the west slope of Grassy Mountain, had started out as a local ski resort and had remained as such for years until it was discovered by resort developer Clive Bechtel. Bechtel was a billionaire industrialist and hedge fund owner, and the first time he skied the mountain, he fell in love with the place. Natural-powder ski resorts had all but disappeared in Colorado starting in the late seventies and early eighties, after a winter drought left resorts scrambling to open and stay open. Because of its location, Grassy Mountain and the valley below it never had a year with less than two hundred inches of snow, and this year would be no exception.

Bechtel invested heavily, and within twenty years, the beautiful valley was home to a plethora of multimillion-dollar homes, restaurants and shopping that would make Rodeo Drive jealous. The rich had discovered Grassy Mountain, and they had staked their claim. The money was great for the economy of the tiny county, but it left them with a problem. Where to house all the workers?

Lake City was hard to get to, especially in the winter. It sat midway between Gunnison and Pagosa Springs along U.S. Highway 149, which was treacherous in the winter, closing multiple times a year because of avalanches and accidents. Some days, it was a challenge to get there at all. Bechtel worked with the Colorado Department of Transportation, and over the past twenty years, he had invested heavily in making massive improvements to the road. He also built an airport just south of Lake City that could handle small commuter planes.

His most ambitious project was halfway completed. He had convinced the powers that be to let him build a new four-lane road from the city of Ouray to the west to the base of the mountain. This was an ambitious plan, and most people in the area didn't believe that it would ever be completed, but Bechtel was determined, and over twenty years no one had ever bet against him. He was driven, and he could be ruthless if needed.

When Billy woke up, the first thing he did was

brush away the foot of fresh powder that had fallen on his tent during the night. He cleaned up his camp, put all his gear in a safe place and then enjoyed a hot breakfast and coffee that Eva had bought for him and his friends. While they ate, they watched the workers grooming the trails and the slopes. It was like a well-rehearsed dance. Billy knew a lot of the workers, and he was always amazed that they showed no fear when grooming the slopes on some of the steepest parts of the mountain. They finished their breakfast and got their snowboards ready. The lift operators arrived and shoveled off the lift area, and they set up a yellow ribbon across the lift area in front of the first chair.

When Billy saw the photographer and reporter from the local newspaper, he knew he had achieved his dream. The resort manager, Guy Pembroke, a former Olympic downhill ski racer, made a speech welcoming everyone, then he introduced the riders of the first three chairs, and they stood together and had their pictures taken. Billy was interviewed by the reporter.

At 8:55, the lift motor revved up, and at 9 A.M. on the dot, Billy took his place on the first chair. Tim was twenty feet behind him, and Jake was twenty feet behind Tim. The lift took off, the crowd cheered and Billy waved to his audience. The ride to the top would take ten minutes, and as Billy climbed away from the base area, the silence overtook him. It was a beautiful Colorado bluebird day with lots of sunshine, and there wasn't a lick of wind. It was a perfect day to be skiing.

Billy settled in for the ride and relaxed. He looked around as he climbed higher. The air was thin, but since he'd lived here all his life, acclimating to the elevation was never a problem, and Billy was fit. He looked ahead as the lift reached the top of a small knob. From this point, it would dip, then rise to the off-loading area.

The bullet struck Billy below his left shoulder, tearing through his heart and exiting ahead of him, lost somewhere in the trees beyond. Billy slumped forward and leaned into the lift gate. He would never get to experience being the first skier on the slope.

Tim, from his vantage point in the second chair, saw Billy slump forward, and he wondered what was going on.

"Hey, Billy," he yelled. He didn't get a response. He looked around. The second bullet hit Tim in the same spot, and Tim died. Jake was lost in the scenery when he thought he heard a rumble of thunder echo across the mountain. He thought it was odd, since the sky was clear. The third bullet struck Jake, pierced his neck and exited out the front.

As the lift approached the off-loading area, the ski lift operator, Jane McBride, thought Billy looked odd the way he was slumped forward. It wasn't until the chair got closer that Jane noticed the front of Billy's snow pants had a large red spot. She spotted blood dripping from his chest onto the seat, and she screamed.

Doug Blanchard, the senior member of the ski patrol, was standing ten feet away, sipping his coffee, when he heard Jane scream.

Doug dropped his coffee and ran to her side. All she could do was point. The seat passed over the disembarking line, and Doug ran to the control panel and hit the emergency shutdown switch. He ran back to Jane.

Jane was frozen, and all she could do was stare. Doug looked over Billy's shoulder and noticed that the next two riders were not moving. It was hard to see because of the distance, but it looked like both men were bleeding.

"Oh, fuck," said Doug.

Doug had completed two tours in Afghanistan with the marines before going to work for the National Ski Patrol, and he had seen bullet wounds before. He also watched a lot of cop shows on TV, and he knew better than to touch the bodies, but he needed to see if they were alive.

He advanced the lift so the first chair was over flat ground and stopped it. He pulled out his camera and took a picture of Billy as he sat in the seat, then handed his camera to Jane to hold. He raised the guardrail, lowered Billy Claymore to the ground and checked for a pulse. There was none. He slid Billy's body to the side and advanced the lift until the second chair arrived. He repeated the same process for Tim Hawthorne and then for Jake Woodman. The results were the same. No pulse, and significant damage to each victim. He looked past the third chair to make sure no one behind them had been shot. The people in the fourth and fifth chairs had their cameras out.

He pulled the radio off his belt.

"Doug to Base."

"This is Base. Go ahead, Doug. Why is the lift shut down?"

"Base, we have a problem. We need to call the sheriff."

Chapter Two

The plaza in the resort village was designed as a safe gathering place for the residents and guests of the Grassy Mountain Resort. Designed to look like a Bavarian village in Germany, the plaza had enough room to hold several thousand people who would come to watch concerts or fireworks or just grab a coffee, sit and enjoy the company of friends and strangers. The shops, bars and restaurants covered the first floor of the building surrounding the plaza, and above on three sides were three floors of condos, town houses and apartments. The west end was open and had a great view of the mountains beyond the valley. It was the kind of place families and lone travelers could feel safe.

There were always three security guards on duty in the plaza, and today was no exception. With the arrival of opening day on the mountain, the village had filled up fast. The richest of the valley's part-time residents arrived in their own private planes or on the small commercial flights available. The planes were parked in neat rows waiting for their owners to complete their week or two of fun.

Security was tight on opening day, even though no one got into the village without a security pass. The village was exclusive, and people paid a lot of money for that exclusivity. At the end of the plaza was a bus stop where shuttle buses came and went on the hour from sunup to sundown to ferry guests to the mountain.

As the sun rose over the mountains to the east,

maintenance workers with shovels and snow throwers worked to clear the foot of snow that had fallen on the plaza overnight. Residents hated to be inconvenienced on their ski mountain by remnants of snowstorms. Snow was pushed into huge piles in alleys that were designed to accumulate snow; the drains in the concrete led to the river. A solar heating system was built into the floor of the alleys to keep the piles of snow melting.

At the same time that the ski mountain welcomed its first opening day visitors, the store owners were opening their doors to the first of many customers. Residents and guests in thousand-dollar ski outfits strolled the plaza, window shopping, sipping expensive coffee and eating pastries similar to those found in expensive shops in Europe. Even those who had never skied a day in their lives wore expensive outfits and looked the part.

An hour after the plaza shops opened, and with several hundred people strolling, sitting and sipping their coffee, the first incident occurred.

Everett Holmes, CEO of Holmes International, an international mergers and acquisitions company, and part-time resident of the village, walked out of his twelve-thousand-square-foot house, strolled along the river and entered the plaza at the west end. Everett, tall and overweight with a full head of dyed brown hair, wore expensive snow pants and an even more expensive ski jacket, even though he had never skied. He had bought the place for his four children, who had spent most of their winters growing up skiing the mountain and were now teaching their children how to ski and snowboard. He stopped and spoke with several residents, bid them a good day and made his way to the coffee shop. The bullet entered the back of his head and blew out a large piece of his face as it exited.

As he fell to the ground, Maggie Hefner, a grandmother on vacation with her family and working hard to get over the death of her husband of forty-five years a month before, stepped out of the Creamery Coffee Shop, and a bullet struck her in the chest just to the left of her sternum. She fell to the ground. Several people ran to the aid of both victims, thinking they had slipped on the concrete pavers, not realizing at first that they had both been shot.

In the center of the plaza, Steven McCormick and his ten-year-old grandson, Eddie, were walking towards the bus stop. They had just left the rental condo and were looking forward to spending some quality time on the mountain. Steven was a roughed looking man, over six feet tall and overweight. His face was lined, and he had a full gray beard. His longish hair was pulled back in a small ponytail, and it hung out under his watch cap. He was an expert skier and was looking forward to teaching his grandson how to ski the black diamond runs.

Eddie was in fifth grade back in Columbus, Ohio, and was looking forward to time with his grandparents after finishing a massive science project that won him second place at the state science fair. The ski trip was his reward. They intended to spend the entire day on the mountain while Steven's wife recovered from a migraine. Eddie's parents would arrive at the end of the week, but in the meantime, it was Eddie and his grandparents.

The bullet hit Eddie in the chest, which spun his body around, and he landed on top of his snowboard. The bullet that struck Steven entered just below his nose and severed his spinal cord as it exited the body. Steven died next to his grandson.

By this time, the people in the plaza knew something was wrong, and while some people pulled out their phones and filmed the carnage, others started screaming and running for cover. Two of the security guards ran into the plaza and yelled for people to seek shelter. They scanned the area, looking for the shooter, and one of them pulled out his radio and called for backup.

"Dispatch, Mobile Three. We need backup and emergency medical personnel to the plaza. Multiple shooting victims. I repeat. Multiple shooting victims. We do not have eyes on the shooter. Call the sheriff."

"Mobile Three, Dispatch. We are alerting all parties. Stand by."

John Finch arrived within minutes and couldn't believe what he was looking at. The paramedics and the doctor from the urgent care had arrived a few minutes before him and were running from patient to patient to see if there was anything they could do. It was obvious to the doctor that all four victims were dead, and he walked over to the hotel lobby and asked them to get him four sheets that he could use to cover the bodies.

John looked at each body and shook his head. It had been a long time since he had seen this many dead bodies in one location. He stood and was walking towards the coffee shop when his radio crackled.

"This is Dispatch. We just received a call from the mountain. They have multiple shooting victims at the top of the mountain, and they are closing the lift. Sheriff's deputy has arrived on the scene, as have paramedics."

"What the fuck?" he said to himself. John looked at his watch. Was it possible they had two shooters? The timeline didn't work in his head. He called the base lift operator.

"Kenny, this is John Finch. Tell me what's going on?"

"Hey, John. Sorry we didn't call you first. Our dispatcher called the sheriff, and then things got crazy."

"What time did the shootings take place? Dispatch said three victims?"

"Yeah, the three victims were in the first three chairs. We had just started the lift. The senior ski patroller at the top of the mountain shut down the lift and told Dispatch to call the sheriff. The deputy was already at the resort, so he responded right away. Doug is up there with him, and we are evacuating the rest of the lift riders."

"Thanks, Kenny, have Doug call me when he gets a minute."

He stood for a minute. "That makes sense." He looked at the mountains to the west.

"Hell of a shot, whoever did the shooting," said one

of his security guards.

John looked at him and nodded.

"Yeah. Listen, run back to the office, and in my lower desk drawer is a roll of yellow crime scene tape. Bring it here."

The security guard nodded and raced towards his ATV. John walked around the plaza. The security guard returned, and they taped off the plaza. The crime scene was huge.

The sheriff arrived and, after looking at the bodies, stepped away and pulled out his phone.

"I'm gonna need some help," he said as he walked away, his phone to his ear.

John pulled out his phone, dialed a number and waited. The phone was answered.

"Sir, we have several problems you need to be aware of."

Chapter Three

Deputy Toby Werthman, twenty-six years old, five foot ten and thin, was the first responder to arrive at the lift. Toby had been with the Hinsdale County Sheriff's Office for three years; he had joined right after completing his associate's degree in law enforcement from Red Rocks Community College, near Denver. He loved the mountains and was thrilled when a position opened up because of the retirement of John Mills, a thirty-year veteran of the department. The sheriff had taken a chance on the unproven young man and had not been disappointed.

Toby had been patrolling the lift parking lot when he got the call. He swung around the corner and pulled up to the lift. Guy Pembroke was waiting at the lift line, trying to avoid the crowds who were shouting questions at him. He shook hands with Toby.

"Deputy, glad you're here. I need to get you to the top of the mountain. Have you ever driven a snowmobile?"

Toby nodded. "Yes, sir." He looked at the crowd that was now screaming questions at him. "Want to tell me what's going on?"

"Not here," said Guy. "I'll explain up top."

Guy handed Toby a helmet and directed him towards two snowmobiles that were idling under the lift overhang. Toby climbed on one, Guy climbed on the other and they headed up the slope, leaving a rooster tail of snow billowing behind them.

Toby and Guy crested a knob and rode down to the lift area. Toby spotted the three bodies lying in the snow and stopped the machine. He climbed off, shook hands with Doug and kneeled next to the first body. He unzipped Billy's coat and examined the wound in his chest. The blood had congealed from the cold, so the image wasn't as bad as it could have been.

He moved to the other two bodies and did the same thing, then he walked over to Doug and Jane.

"Doug. What the hell happened?" he asked. Doug was one of the first people Toby met when he first arrived in Lake City; he was renting a room in Doug's parents' basement.

Doug took off his sunglasses and placed them on his head. "Not sure, man. Jane screamed, and I ran over and saw the first dead guy. The other two were behind him in the second and third chairs. I know I shouldn't have moved the bodies, but I had to check to see if they were still alive. They weren't."

Toby looked at Jane, who stood nearby, shaking. He introduced himself, and they shook hands. Her hands were as cold as ice, and he suggested she put her gloves on. She smiled and put them on.

"Jane, did you see or hear anything? A gunshot or loud noise of any kind?"

Jane snapped out of it when she realized he was talking to her. She stuttered, "No, I saw the first body, and I guess I screamed. Doug ran over. Everything after that is a blur. I never saw the other two until Doug pulled them out of the chairs. Oh my god. I'm gonna be sick."

Jane ran towards the warming shed and vomited.

Toby pulled his radio off his belt just as it crackled. "All units. Assistance needed in Grassy Mountain Village. Several people have been shot."

"Dispatch, this is the sheriff. Say again."

"Sheriff, I got a call from the security office in Grassy Mountain Village. Report is that four people have been shot."

"Sheriff to Toby. What's your situation?"

Toby keyed the mic on his radio. "Sheriff, I'm on top of the mountain. I've got three dead bodies up here. All have been shot. I also have a lift full of people. I need some help."

"Toby, did you say three people shot? Do you have the shooter in custody?"

"No, sir. It looks like they were shot while they were on the lift."

"Damn. Okay, son, stay there and secure the scene. I'll head to the village and see what's what. Mary Jo, call in Walt and Kevin and call the reserve deputies. Have them report to me in the village."

"Will do, Sheriff," said the dispatcher. "I'll also send paramedics."

Hinsdale County Sheriff Mike Drucker pulled his SUV through the security gate and fell in behind the Grassy Mountain Village security department ATV. The security officer led him through the main parking lot and parked near the plaza. The plaza was a large, open area surrounded by gift shops, bars, restaurants and high-end retail stores. The area was a gathering place for the residents and their guests, but at this moment four security guards stood outside the yellow emergency tape that had been strung between light poles and were keeping people out of the crime scene.

Sheriff Drucker had been the sheriff of Hinsdale County for seven years. He was six feet tall with a good build. He had a ruddy complexion from years in the high mountains, and his blond hair was turning gray. He had moved his family to Lake City after he accepted the job, and they had blended into the tight-knit community.

The sheriff slipped out of his SUV and walked up to John Finch, the director of security for the village and the resort. They shook hands. The sheriff noted the lack of bystanders, but lots of people were looking out of the guest room and residence windows that surrounded the plaza.

"What have you got, John?"

John Finch was a tall Black man with a bald head and gray mustache. He had taken the job as security director ten years before, after retiring from the United States Air Force. His brown uniform pants held a tight crease, and he tucked up his jacket to fend off the biting wind that had arrived a few minutes before.

"Four dead folks, Mike. No one saw the shooter. It all happened so fast. One of them is just a kid."

"Okay, John. Let's go take a look."

John led the sheriff under the crime scene tape, and

they approached the first body, which had been covered with a sheet from the hotel. Paramedics from the village urgent care were standing by, having declared the victims deceased. Sheriff Drucker kneeled next to the body and pulled the sheet back. The victim had been shot in the back of the head. The sheriff looked around. He wondered where the shot had come from. He replaced the sheet, and they stepped over to the next body. From the position of the body, this woman had walked out of one of the coffee shops and been hit. She had been shot in the neck. There was a large pool of blood under her head.

The sheriff moved to the next body, and from the size of the form under the sheet, he was reluctant to look at this one. The young boy, maybe twelve or thirteen, was lying on top of his snowboard. He had been shot in the chest. The body next to him was an older man who had been shot in the forehead, the bullet blowing an enormous hole in the back of his head. He replaced the sheets, stood and looked around the plaza.

"Any idea where the shots came from?" asked the sheriff.

John shook his head. "We talked to a couple of people before we cleared the plaza, and no one reported hearing any gunshots. One fella—I have his name if you want to talk to him—said he heard something in the distance that he thought might have been thunder, but he said it was very low and kind of echoed through the valley. Most of the folks we talked to said that the shots happened one right after the other. I gotta tell ya, Mike. Whoever did this is one damn skilled shooter."

The sheriff nodded and pulled out his radio. Sirens could be heard in the distance as two ambulances with paramedics arrived from Gunnison. They parked behind the sheriff's SUV and threw open the doors. The sheriff walked up to them.

"No rush, fellas. They're all dead. I need to get some pictures before you move anybody, so give me a few minutes to get organized."

They nodded and pushed their med kits back into the ambulance.

The sheriff keyed the mic attached to the shoulder of his jacket.

"Sheriff to Toby."

"Go ahead, Sheriff."

"Toby, we need to shut down the lift. Take pictures of the bodies, cover them with whatever you have available and tell the lift operators to start the lift and take everyone on it back to the start at the base. No one gets off the lift up top. Got it?"

"Yes, sir. Got it. Toby out."

He keyed the mic a second time. "Mary Jo, radio Kevin and have him go to the lift and help Toby. Also, call French over at the paper and tell him I need him ASAP to take some crime scene photos here at the plaza."

"Roger, Sheriff."

He looked at John Finch. "I'm gonna need some help. Keep this area closed and keep everyone away until the photographer gets here."

The hair on the back of his neck bristled, and he had the weirdest feeling that he was being watched. He looked around the plaza and then at the mountains that surrounded the valley. None of the mountains were close, and he wondered if this was it or if the sniper was just getting started.

He looked around the plaza and tried to figure out how this all went down.

Chapter Four

The sun had just broken over the trees, but I had been up for hours getting ready. Three days ago, I slipped into the forest and found the perfect spot. It had a great view of the ski slope, and with just a slight turn, I had an exceptional view of the plaza. These would be my kill zones.

The nights had been cold and snowy, but the old mummy sleeping bag I'd gotten from my dad was made for just such conditions. Yeah, it was heavier than the featherlight materials available today, but this old bag never let me down.

The temps overnight had dropped into single digits as I waited in the comfort of the bag to hear that the resort had announced opening day. That announcement came the night before last So, I snugged into the bag, covered up with a plastic tarp and woke up this morning to eight inches of fresh snow. I was cold, but the small propane camping stove was perfect for making scrambled eggs and coffee. Of course, the eggs came out of a bag, but they still hit the spot. I wasn't worried about anyone smelling the coffee cooking, because I was almost a mile and a half from the slope and farther from the plaza.

After finishing breakfast, I slid out of the warm bag. I didn't sweep the snow off the plastic tarp I had placed over the bag, because it was good camouflage. Anyone looking from the plaza or the slope would never see my nest.

I had chosen this spot because I could see both kill

zones without having to move. The location gave me great cover. There was a small rock outcropping that was in the trees and a small downed tree lying right across it, which gave me the perfect angle for what I intended to do.

I opened the hard side case and pulled out the rifle. It was a gift from my father. My dad is one of the best gunsmiths I have ever known, and he has built custom rifles for some very famous people. I'm not famous and don't intend to be. I just have a score to settle.

The custom-built rifle and imported optics made this one of the best sniper rifles I had ever used. It was light and chambered for .338 Lapua Magnum (LM) cartridges. It's a powerful weapon, and in the right hands, it's deadly. Those hands are mine.

I'd learned to shoot from a very early age, and by the time I graduated high school, I had won more long-range shooting competitions than the rest of the family combined. That was quite an accomplishment considering that my three brothers and two sisters were some of the best shooters I knew.

My dad had been a marine sniper, and after surviving two tours in Vietnam, he came back to the States and used the GI Bill to study gunsmithing. His specialty was building small, lightweight, concealable rifles and pistols, and his clientele included many people with sketchy pasts. He built specialty weapons for the military and some other alphabet soup agencies, but he rarely talked about them. Growing up, I was his bench tester.

Not that long ago, at a national long-range shooting

competition, I was approached by a government recruiter and offered a job. I had beaten the entire field, which included some of the best military and DOE snipers in the country. I wasn't interested. I was comfortable teaching shooting skills to kids and leading hunting expeditions from our home in Wyoming. We had the longest range in the state, and our range was in high demand, which kept the family busy running the range and the gun shop. It was a good life until that day, but I'm not going to get into that now. I need to focus on the job at hand.

I moved to the spot in my nest I had set up over the past couple of days and sighted in the rifle for the sixth time. Each time, I recorded the measurements in my logbook. I sighted the scope crosshairs on the small wind flag at the top of the lift tower. I used my spotting scope and range finder to check the measurement: 2,025 meters. Just about a mile and a quarter. I checked the wind with my handheld anemometer and clicked two clicks left. No adjustment needed for elevation.

I shifted my position and zeroed in on the plaza. I was impressed with the scope my dad had chosen. From my nest, I could see the maintenance workers clearing the snow from the plaza, and I could read their names on the jackets. Juan was doing a good job with the snow thrower. I chuckled. How easy it would be to fire a round and take him out, but I wasn't interested in hurting the people at the resort who worked for a living. I was hunting the wealthy and the powerful.

At ten to nine, I heard the lift motor start and then the host talking over the loudspeaker. I settled in and put my eye to the scope. I calmed my breathing. I watched as the rider slid onto the first lift chair and the lift moved. My focus shifted, and I aimed at the spot I had set up over the past two days. With my peripheral vision, I tracked the lift chair while keeping my eye fixed on the scope. The rider entered my field of view. I took a deep breath, let out half and held. He passed into my crosshairs, and I pulled the trigger. The rifle hardly moved. I watched the rider slump forward. I remained still as the second rider entered my field of view, and I repeated the process and watched the rider slump sideways. The third rider came into my view, and I noticed he was looking around. I wondered if he sensed what was coming. I held my breath and squeezed the trigger. The third rider leaned over the seat guardrail and didn't move.

I shifted my body to the left and focused on the plaza. I had checked the distance earlier: 2,845 meters, just about a mile and three-quarters. I spotted a man walking towards the plaza. He had crossed the lot and stepped up onto the paved area. He took ten steps, and I fired. He flopped onto the ground. I shifted and spotted a woman coming out of the coffee shop. I squeezed the trigger. She slammed into the wall behind her and slid to the ground. I shifted and spotted two people walking towards the bus stop. I fired on the smaller person and watched him spin and fall on his snowboard. My second shot hit the taller man in the face, and he fell next to the other body.

I peered through the scope as people started running, and I watched with amusement as the stupid people, instead of running and hiding, took out their phones and recorded the carnage. How easy it would have been to kill a few more, but I had completed my mission for today. I sat back, fired up my little stove and made another cup of coffee. So far, it was a good day.

Chapter Five

Buck Taylor was splitting his third cord of wood. Earlier in the day, his grandson, David Jr., and two of his friends had taken Grandma Rose's old pickup and trailer into the woods up near Monarch Pass and loaded the trailer and the truck with as much firewood as they could find. They had bogged down a little in the snow that had fallen the night before, but the truck was an old Jeep pickup, and when he put the truck in granny low, it pulled itself out of the deep snow. Grandma Rose always said that if you put four people on the hood of the old Jeep, you could drive it up a tree. David was also grateful that Buck had taught him how to drive a stick shift.

The boys had unloaded the firewood in several large piles, and then Buck went to work splitting it all. This had become his recovery process after the explosion. He had given up on physical therapy after the first week home from the hospital. It wasn't for him. He developed a better plan, and it involved being outside, which was where he belonged. He would start his morning with a hike in the woods. Each day, he added more weight to the old rucksack. On the first day, he made it to the corner of his street before exhaustion set in. Now, four weeks later, he was hiking five miles a day with a thirty-pound sack.

After his hike, he would split logs. The first weeks were hard because each time the ax hit the log, it would reverberate through the wound on the side of his head.

The wound was now healed. The stitches had been removed, and a couple of ibuprofens took care of the pain. He had stopped the painkillers after Hank Clancy's funeral because they made his brain foggy, and he hated the feeling.

Despite the 10-degree temperature and his grandson's offers to help split the logs, Buck trudged ahead. His phone chimed and he slammed the ax head into the chopping block, pulled out his phone, checked the number and put it on speaker.

"Yes, sir."

"Hey, Buck," said Kevin Jackson. "Did I catch you resting?"

Kevin Jackson was the director of the Colorado Bureau of Investigation, and Buck's boss. He had been the youngest person to ever run the bureau when he was appointed by Governor Richard J. Kennedy six years ago. He'd had a stellar career with the Colorado Springs Police Department before being tapped for the top post at CBI. He was more bureaucrat than cop, having spent most of his career on the administrative side at CSPD, but he was a seasoned investigator and was well respected in the law enforcement community, and so far, Buck was impressed with him.

Buck's grandson laughed. "Sounds like you're with one of the grandkids," said the director.

"Yeah," said Buck. "Buck dropped off a load of firewood and I'm getting it ready." David Jr. preferred to go by Buck as well, and the family called him Little Buck. Buck felt honored.

"Well, don't let them work you too hard," said the director.

Little Buck leaned into the phone. "I think it's me and my friends who are getting worked too hard."

Director Jackson laughed. "Listen, Buck. I know you were just cleared to go back to work, and I was hoping to get you back, but something came up."

"What's going on, sir?"

"I got a call from Mike Drucker over in Hinsdale County. He has multiple shooting victims on the mountain and in the Grassy Mountain Village. No ID on the shooter yet. I just hung up from the governor, and he's sending a dozen troopers to give him some backup, and he mobilized the Southwest Regional SWAT team. I need you guys down there as soon as possible."

"No worries, sir," said Buck. "The go bag is already in the Jeep. Let me grab a quick shower and I'll head out. Can you call Bax and Paul to meet me there, and I'll call Franklin?"

"Will do, Buck. I'll have my secretary find you guys a couple of rooms and text you the details. Let me know what you need when you get there."

Buck ended the call and speed-dialed a number. Franklin Williams answered.

"Hey, Buck. How's the recovery going?"

"Great, Franklin, but it looks like it's over. I'm gonna need you and your team in Lake City as soon as possible. We have reports of multiple shooting victims in two separate locations. I'm heading out in a bit, and

I'll let you know if there are any road problems. They got a lot of snow this week."

"No worries, Buck. I'll get the team rolling and we'll see you there."

"Awesome," said Buck. "I'll text you the details."

Buck put his phone away and looked at Little Buck. "Do me a favor and let your mom know I'm heading out. Could be gone for a couple of days. Don't worry about the rest of the firewood. I'll get to it when I get back."

Little Buck walked over and gave him a hug. "Should I tell Mom you're dealing with multiple shooting victims? That sounds dangerous."

Buck laughed. "No. Let's keep that between you and me. I'll call your dad and fill him in later."

"Okay," said Little Buck. "Love ya, Grandpa. Be careful."

Buck's oldest son, David, looked just like Buck when he was in his late thirties. He was taller, at six foot two, and was a little heavier, but the resemblance was almost scary. David was a patrol sergeant with the Gunnison Police Department. He was also the night shift supervisor. David had worked nights for most of his career, and he enjoyed the solitude of the small city. In his spare time, he played guitar in a local country rock band.

David's wife, Judith, had taken Buck under her wing after Buck's wife, Lucy, died a couple of years back. Judith had bought the small deli/ice cream parlor that Lucy owned, when her cancer got to be too much to keep up with the store. She had made the little shop a success. She also took care of Buck. Whenever Buck had to leave town, she took care of the house and made sure his refrigerator was stocked when he returned home. Buck had no idea what he would do without Judy.

Buck grabbed a quick shower, took his badge and gun out of the wall safe and clipped them to his belt. He grabbed his Carhartt insulated ranch jacket, turned on a couple of lights and left the house. He slid into his state-provided Jeep Grand Cherokee and headed for Lake City.

Chapter Six

Buck Taylor was six feet tall and weighed 185 pounds—very little flab for a sixty-three-year-old man. Buck's hair was salt-and-pepper, with what seemed like a lot more salt than pepper, and he wore it longer than was the fashion of the day. Buck was always pleased when he looked in the mirror since, other than getting older, he was in as good a shape as he had been when he played defensive linebacker for the Gunnison High School Cowboys, what seemed like a long time ago. Except for a couple of sore knees coming from age, Buck was in good shape, which was important in his line of work.

Buck had been married for thirty-four years before breast cancer stole the one person he cared about most in the world. He missed Lucy every day, even after all this time.

If you asked Buck, he would tell you he fell in love with Lucinda Torres on the first day of their senior year in high school. Lucy always told people that Buck stalked her their entire senior year before she gave in to shut her friends up and agreed to go to the movies with him. She had always considered him just another jock, another football player who was too full of himself.

What she found on that first date was a shy, unassuming gentleman who cared more about pleasing her than bragging about his prowess on the football field. She would tell people it was love at first sight that had taken a year to develop. After that, they were inseparable.

During senior year, Buck had been approached by several college football scouts who wanted to sign him to play for their schools. Gunnison High School was a small school back in 1978, and Buck and his family were amazed at how many schools had recruited him, but for Buck, college wasn't in the cards.

Buck hated school and spent a lot of time getting himself out of trouble instead of getting an education. When he found something that interested him, he had no problem learning all he could about the subject, but regular schoolwork just bored him. After several long, heartfelt discussions, first with Lucy and then with his parents, he joined the army after graduation. No one was surprised.

Buck spent four years after high school in the army, and by the time his enlistment was up, he had been promoted to first sergeant. He spent three years of his enlistment in the military police and took to police work. That was when he applied for a position with the Gunnison County Sheriff's Office.

Since he was already well known in the county, he had no trouble getting a job as a deputy. He proposed to Lucy the night he received the call that he had gotten the position. His life and career were set. He made the most of his time with the Gunnison County Sheriff's Office, becoming the undersheriff in charge of the Investigation Division and coming to the attention of the Colorado Bureau of Investigation.

Buck had worked with the Colorado Bureau of Investigation on several cases inside the county and had earned the respect of the investigators he had worked with.

As twilight fell on Buck's career, he knew that unless he wanted to go into politics and run for sheriff, he had reached the highest position in the sheriff's office that he could obtain. He loved his job, but when the first offer came in from CBI, he sat down with Lucy and had a long heart-to-heart talk.

He'd spent seventeen years in the sheriff's office and had always figured he would retire from that job. They had three children, two in high school and one not far behind, and he was a well-respected member of the community. Did he have the right to disrupt their lives, pick up, move someplace else and start all over? The kids had friends. Lucy owned a small deli/ice cream parlor, and they had a nice life.

He could stick it out for another ten years and retire, and they could travel and see the world as they had always planned. Twice he turned down the offer from CBI, although more and more, he felt trapped behind a desk instead of doing what he loved, which was investigating crime.

The last offer came from Tom Cole, then-director of the Colorado Bureau of Investigation. Buck always remembered that day. The Denver Broncos had just lost another game, the third one in a row, and his friends had all packed up and headed home when there was a knock at the front door.

Now, anyone who lives in a small community knows that no one ever uses the front door, and no one ever knocks. So, who could this be this late on a

Sunday evening?

Buck answered the door and was surprised to see the director of the Colorado Bureau of Investigation standing on his front porch. The director smiled and said, "Before you close the door in my face, please listen to my offer."

Buck invited him in, and he and Lucy sat on the couch and listened as the director laid out his plan. He was opening a new branch office in Grand Junction, Colorado, that would house five agents and a small forensic unit. Buck could continue to live in Gunnison but would have to report to the office in Grand Junction twice a month. Otherwise, he would be free to work from his house. There would be no disruption in his life other than spending time on the road as his investigations warranted. He would work alone but would have all the branch office's resources at his disposal.

Before Buck could say a word, Lucy said, "Buck, this is what you have been waiting for, a chance to be a real investigator again. You have to take this." That was one of the things that made him love Lucy every day. She always knew what he was thinking and understood what drove him. She had nailed it this time. Buck looked at the director and replied, "Well, I guess it's settled; looks like you have a new investigator on your team."

That was twenty-three years ago, and Buck had never looked back. He had made the most of those years and was one of the most respected and feared investigators in the state, but all that work couldn't make up for the loss he suffered.

Lucy was diagnosed with metastatic breast cancer following a routine mammogram, and they set off together on their next adventure: the quest to beat the dreaded disease. After a double mastectomy and five years of chemo, they knew their time was drawing to a close when the cancer returned several times to her brain and was no longer controlled by the radiation.

Together, they decided to stop all treatment, even though they had always told the family that the decision was Lucy's alone to make. Lucy spent the last couple of months of her life taking care of her small business and spending as much time as possible with her children and grandchildren.

The end came one spring night. Lucy had been sleeping on and off for twenty hours a day in the end. The night she died, Buck had been lying in bed next to her, reading a report, when she snuggled into his arms and rested her head on his shoulder. During the night, Buck fell asleep. When he woke up, Lucy was gone, and his world was shattered.

They say that time heals all wounds, but Buck wasn't sure that was the case when you lost your closest friend. And even now, all these years later, he missed her more and more each day.

Buck always thought back to that Sunday morning when the family had gathered for a private ceremony at the little dock along the Gunnison River to scatter Lucy's ashes. Each family member got to say a few words about Lucy, and when they finished and turned to go, they were stunned to see several hundred of their neighbors and friends standing behind them in the park. Word had gotten out about their private service, and everyone turned out to pay tribute to Lucy. The affair turned into a gigantic party with plenty of food and drinks. Lucy never wanted any kind of service, but Buck figured she would have loved this spontaneous outpouring of love.

Chapter Seven

Buck passed through the security gate for the Grassy Mountain Village and presented his credentials to the two state troopers on duty. They waved him through, and he followed the road till he saw the sign directing him to the plaza. He parked his Jeep behind the Hinsdale County sheriff's SUV, slid out and grabbed his backpack. The one-hour drive from Gunnison was uneventful, and the state had done a good job clearing the snow from last night off the highway. He called Franklin to tell him he shouldn't have any trouble making the drive. The mobile crime scene van had four-wheel drive, but it was a high-clearance vehicle, and the snow and wind played havoc with its performance in the mountains.

Buck walked up to the yellow crime scene tape and stopped. He set his backpack on the ground and looked around the plaza. Anyone who worked with Buck knew he liked to view the crime scene with his eyes before getting a briefing. He picked up his backpack, lifted the tape and stepped under.

Sheriff Drucker, standing next to the woman's body by the coffee shop, turned and spotted Buck. He excused himself from the discussion he was having with the urgent care doctor and walked towards him.

"Buck Taylor," said the sheriff. "How the hell are you doing?" He shook Buck's hand and stepped back. "You don't look much worse for wear. You doing okay?"

Buck nodded. "Mike, good to see you. Yeah. Doing

fine."

Sheriff Drucker looked at the side of his head. "Heard you got your bell rung pretty good. Also heard you are lucky to be alive."

"Yeah," said Buck. "A couple of weeks off helped with the recovery. So, what have we got?"

The sheriff walked him to the first victim. Buck kneeled next to the body and pulled back the sheet. The body was lying on its front, but Buck could see the entry wound in the back of the head, and he leaned forward and could see what was left of his face. It was not a pretty sight.

"Everett Holmes," said the sheriff. "He was the first one to get hit."

Buck covered the head and stood. The sheriff led him to the coffee shop, and he kneeled next to the second body and pulled the sheet back.

"Maggie Hefner. She was the second victim. She was walking out of the coffee shop. One round in the chest."

Buck covered the body and followed the sheriff to the middle of the plaza. Buck kneeled next to the smaller body and pulled back the sheet. One thing Buck hated about being a cop was dealing with kids who got hurt. He hated it even more when they were killed for no reason.

"Eddie McCormick, ten years old. Third person shot."

Buck turned and lifted the second sheet. The damage to the man's face was significant, and there was a huge puddle of blood and brain matter lying under the head.

"Steven McCormick, Eddie's grandfather," said the sheriff. "Never knew what hit him."

Buck stood and looked towards the mountain in the distance. "Any thoughts on where the shooter was?"

"Best we can figure is somewhere in the village or the parking area. The mountains are over a mile away, so that seems impractical, and the shooter needed time to move from the first crime scene."

"What first crime scene?" asked Buck.

"Oh, shit. Sorry, Buck. I thought you were told. This is the second crime scene. I've got three more bodies at the top of the ski lift. That was the first scene."

"Fuck," said Buck. "Let's head over and take a look."

Buck and the sheriff walked to the sheriff's SUV, and Buck pulled out his phone. He dialed a number and waited. Dr. Garrett Parkinson answered the phone.

"I'm not going to like this, am I, Buck?" asked the doctor.

"No," said Buck. "This one is gonna be a mess."

Dr. Parkinson was a semiretired emergency room doctor who picked up a couple of shifts each week at the Gunnison Valley Health Hospital. He was also a board-certified forensic pathologist who did autopsies for Gunnison County and several of the smaller counties in the area. He was a longtime friend of

Buck's.

Effective in 2024, the Colorado legislature passed HB24-1100. The act required a coroner of a county with a population greater than 150,000 who was elected on or after November 5, 2024, to be a death investigator certified by and in good standing with the American Board of Medicolegal Death Investigators or a forensic pathologist certified by and in good standing with the American Board of Pathology.

Unlike in the medical examiner system, and since the coroner did not have to be a doctor, in smaller counties, coroners would contract with a licensed forensic pathologist to handle any investigations that required an autopsy.

These forensic pathologists were trained doctors who split their time among several jurisdictions to keep costs down. Many forensic pathologists were current or former medical examiners, and several were retired, working part time to keep their hands in the game.

Buck explained the situation and what he needed, and Garrett listened without saying a word until he finished.

"Sounds like quite the mess. Let me call the transportation department at the hospital and see if they have an ambulance crew to bring the bodies back here. I'll head down right away so you can release the scene to Franklin. See you soon."

Buck ended the call and slid into the sheriff's SUV. The sheriff drove them to the foot of the mountain, about a four-minute drive from the plaza. Guy Pembroke, the ski mountain manager, was waiting at the lift with one of the resort's snowcats. Buck and the sheriff climbed inside and sat behind Guy as he negotiated the machine up the side of the mountain. The drive took longer than the lift would have taken but was a lot more comfortable considering the temperature.

Guy parked the snowcat at the warming hut next to the lift and they climbed out, and Buck stopped and looked out over the valley. He walked over to where the sheriff and Guy were standing over the three bodies. They were covered with a blue plastic tarp; Buck looked around to make sure no one else was around and pulled back the tarp.

The sheriff kneeled next to the first body. "Billy Claymore," he said. "According to his girlfriend, he was excited to be the first one up the mountain." He stood and pointed to the next body. "Tim Hawthorne, he was in chair number two, and the third fella is Jake Woodman. He was in the third chair."

Buck looked at the three bodies and then at the chairlift.

"They were shot on the lift?" asked Buck. "Who moved the bodies?"

The sheriff knew what Buck was thinking. Hopefully, they hadn't screwed up the crime scene too badly.

"The first responder was the lead member of the ski patrol. He was up here when they spotted the first body. His first instinct was to get the bodies off the lift so he could provide first aid if needed. Everyone was dead, but he had no way of knowing. He took pictures of the bodies as each chair arrived and before he took them down."

Buck nodded. "We'll need to speak with him and the lift operator, and we'll need the pictures."

"I know he shouldn't have moved the bodies, but he's a trained paramedic, and his first thought was that they might still be alive."

"No worries, Mike," said Buck. He stood and stepped over to the start of the landing area. "Any idea how far down the mountain they were shot?"

The sheriff walked up next to him. "No. The lift does a bit of a dip, and you can't see the chair until it pops up."

"Any thoughts on where the shots came from? Was anyone riding the lift down at the time?" asked Buck.

"No," said Mike. "This was opening day, and those three were the first three riders."

A short man in ballistic gear stepped up to Buck. "I think you've got a sniper, Buck."

Buck turned and reached out his hand. Sergeant Tommy White Elk grabbed it. Tommy was the team leader of the regional SWAT team.

"Tommy, how the hell are you?" asked Buck.

"Good, Buck. You look good. Heard you got banged up pretty good."

Buck smiled. "Yeah. It hurt a little when it happened. Why do you think this was a sniper?"

Tommy White Elk was assigned to the La Plata

County Sheriff's Office when he wasn't running a SWAT team. He stood five foot eight and was lean and muscular, with dark hair and dark eyes.

Tommy kneeled next to the first body. "This is a rifle wound. The shot, depending on where on the slope they got hit, could have come from the parking area, but there's limited visibility. Next spot would be the ridge on the other side of the valley, but the shooter would have to be above the houses. That's a hell of a shot. Either way, a sniper is the only thing that makes sense."

Buck looked out across the valley, and he had to agree. With where they were standing, you couldn't see the parked cars, and if they were shot from behind, then Tommy was right. That would have been a hell of a shot at that distance.

Buck called over Guy. "How many employees do you have in this area right now?" asked Buck.

Guy stepped over. "With the ski patrol and lift operators, twenty-five."

"Can you have them all report to the lower lift? I hate to do this, but we need to preserve the scene, and if it snows tonight, we're screwed. We need to see if we can find the first traces of blood."

Guy thought for a minute. "How about if we use the lift? I can put a couple of the ski patrol folks on the lift and run it slow. They should be able to see the red marks in the snow since no one has skied this area yet. It will save a lot of walking."

Buck smiled. "Okay. Let's do it."

Tommy offered three of his team members to join the search. He told Buck he would have some of his team scan the opposite ridge to see if they could see anyone.

They climbed back into the snowcat while Guy pulled out his radio and called for all the ski patrollers to meet at the lift. He slid in, started the cat and headed down the mountain.

When they arrived at the base, there were six ski patrollers, two lift operators and two SWAT officers waiting for them. They climbed out of the snowcat, and Buck approached the group.

"Hi, folks. I'm Buck Taylor with CBI. Thanks for helping us out. I need four of you to ride the lift. We need to go as slow as possible. I need you to watch the area below you. We're looking for the first signs of blood on the snow. It's a long ride, but our field of view is narrow, just under the chairs. The rest of us will work our way up the mountain. Everyone has a radio, so if you see anything, call out. Operators, when someone calls out, stop the lift right away. The sheriff and I will be on the snowmobiles, and we'll head your way."

The operators started the lift, and the first four patrollers slid onto the seats as they came around. The rest of the patrollers and the other operators started walking under the chairs and headed up the mountain.

Buck and the sheriff waited at the lift. Six minutes after they started the lift, one patroller called in a sighting. The operator stopped the lift, and Buck and the sheriff jumped onto the snowmobile and raced up the mountain. They spotted the patroller waving and came to a stop down the hill from her. She pointed to an area just off to her right, and Buck and the sheriff trudged through the snow and approached the location.

The red splatter covered an area about a foot and a half wide. Buck slowed. He looked around him and moved forward. The sheriff stepped next to him.

"Looks like blood splatter," he said.

Buck nodded. "Sure does."

The sheriff moved uphill and called back. "Got more here."

Buck looked around and located some landmarks. He pulled out his cell phone and took some pictures of the spots in the snow. He took a picture of the number 15 on the nearest lift support, which was five feet away. Buck took off his backpack, opened it and removed a DNA test swab. He dabbed the spots in a few places and put the test kit back in his backpack. He pulled out a large evidence bag and with his hand scooped the red snow into the bag. He walked to the second spot and did the same thing. He put the bags in his backpack.

He picked up the radio Guy had given him. "Buck to Guy."

"Guy here."

"Bring everyone back to the lift area. We found what we were looking for."

"Will do."

Buck waved to the patroller who spotted the blood,

and the lift started moving. He and the sheriff climbed back on the snowmobile and headed down the mountain. Back at the lift, Buck thanked everyone for their help, and he and the sheriff climbed into the sheriff's SUV and headed back to the plaza.

Tommy called his other officers and listened to their report. He turned to Buck. "My guys scanned the ridge but couldn't see anything."

"Thanks, Tommy. Let's head over to the second scene."

Chapter Eight

The sheriff pulled into the space, and Buck pushed open his door.

"What the fuck," said Buck. "Who is that guy?"

The sheriff slid out of his SUV and looked at where Buck was pointing. Standing in the middle of the plaza next to the bodies of the grandfather and young boy was a man in a shearling coat and a Stetson. He was directing two state troopers to take down the crime scene tape.

Buck walked past the tape and stopped behind the man.

"Excuse me," he said. "Who are you, and why are you in the middle of my crime scene?"

The man turned. He was Buck's height, thin, with a gray mustache and gray hair hanging over his collar.

He turned and looked at Buck. "Who the fuck are you?"

"Buck Taylor, CBI, and you are?"

"I'm Clive Bechtel. This is my resort."

Buck stared at him. "Well, Mr. Bechtel. This may be your resort, but this is my crime scene, and I need to ask you to leave."

Bechtel moved to within inches of Buck. "Who the fuck do you think you're ordering around? I need this mess cleaned up. I've got a business to run."

Buck pushed into his personal space, and Bechtel

backed up a couple of inches. "I'm asking nice right now, sir, but if you don't get behind the crime scene tape, I'm going to arrest you."

Bechtel's face grew red. "Do you know who I am, buster?"

Buck laughed. "Yes, sir. You told me, and I've found that when someone asks me if I know who they are, it turns out they're not as important as they think they are. Now, I need you to move."

Bechtel glowered at Buck. "I've got a business to run, and you're costing me money. I want that tape and these bodies gone now."

A crowd had formed outside the tape. Buck looked behind him and spotted Bax, Paul Webber and Franklin Williams approaching the tape. He turned to the sheriff.

"Sheriff, if Mr. Bechtel isn't out of this crime scene in ten seconds, I'm going to arrest him, and he'll spend tonight in your jail."

Bechtel's face was as red as a fire engine, and spittle hung from his mouth. He was furious. "I'll have your badge," he yelled.

"You're welcome to it," said Buck. "But until you get the governor to come up here and take it, I have multiple crimes to investigate, and you're in the way."

Bechtel stepped around Buck and walked to the tape. He grabbed it with both hands and pulled it. He didn't realize how strong the tape was. He pushed it away and stepped over it.

"He's gonna be trouble," said Mike. "He's not used

to being talked to like that."

"That's fine," said Buck. "I can handle him."

Bax, Paul and Franklin stepped under the tape and stepped up to Buck and the sheriff. They introduced themselves and shook hands with the sheriff.

Tommy White Elk walked up and shook everyone's hands. He turned to Buck. "Just in case, I've positioned some of my team on the roof of the condo with spotting scopes."

Buck nodded.

Paul Webber was over six foot four with a muscular physique. He had joined CBI seven years earlier after spending ten years with the Dallas, Texas, police department. His last post was as a homicide detective. Paul may have seemed like a giant, but those who knew him knew he was a pussycat. He was one of the most soft-spoken men Buck had ever met.

Paul had been instrumental in helping Buck find the hiding spot of Alicia Hawkins, a young serial killer who had returned to her hometown of Aspen, Colorado, and worked hard to fulfill a promise she made to her grandfather, an unknown serial killer from the late sixties who had murdered fifteen young women before an accident ended his career. Alicia had discovered the identity of her grandfather's sixteenth victim, a woman who was still alive and living in Aspen, and she had decided to honor her grandfather's death by killing his sixteenth victim, who would also be her sixteenth victim. If not for Buck and Paul, she would have succeeded in creating a sick legacy that would have long outlived her and inspired others.

At thirty-four years old, Ashley Baxter was the youngest agent in the Grand Junction Field Office. She'd joined CBI straight out of college, and, having had no experience in the field, she valued the time she got to spend with Buck, who became her mentor. Bax also became a kind of surrogate daughter to Buck and made sure he got enough sleep and food while they were on an investigation. She was fond of Buck, and he felt the same way about her.

Bax stood about five foot six with blue eyes and blond hair that she often kept tied in a ponytail that hung through the hole in the back of her CBI cap. Some people would describe her as husky, or what used to be called having a "mountain girl" figure. She wasn't gorgeous, but she was pretty enough to turn men's heads when she entered a room, until they spotted the badge and gun clipped to her belt. She had been with the Colorado Bureau of Investigation for eleven years and had earned the respect of her teammates.

Franklin Williams was the lead forensic tech based out of the CBI office in Grand Junction. He was a distinguished-looking Black man who stood about four inches taller than Buck but weighed about the same. He had short gray hair and a gray goatee. He had been with CBI for more than thirty years. He shook hands with Buck.

"Buck, you look a lot better than the last time I saw you. You doing okay?" asked Franklin.

Buck nodded. "Doing good, Franklin." He looked at the group. "Okay, folks. We have seven dead bodies in two locations. All shot. We have no idea where the shooter is. It is possible the shooter was in the parking lot or on the ridge on the other side of the valley. Be aware when you are out in the open that we might be dealing with a sniper, and from what I've seen, this person could have a hell of a skill set. The pathologist should be here anytime, and we're gonna lose the light. Paul, work with Garrett, and let's get the bodies off the mountain first. Franklin, have your guys set up some work lights in the plaza. There will not be much to do until we get the autopsy results. I've asked the troopers and the SWAT team to check the lot for stray shell casings in case the shots came from there. Once we have the autopsy results, let's get the ballistic gel dummy up here and see if we can find where the bullets ended up. We may never find them, but let's try. In the meantime, focus on the plaza. The bullets should be here somewhere. Bax, I texted you the rental address. Go get us checked in, open an investigation file and work with George and Mel to background our victims. Let's see if there's a reason these folks are dead. Also, have George check and see if there are any retired or active-duty military snipers living in the area. The sheriff will send you the victims' names. Questions?"

Everyone headed off, and Buck stood with the sheriff. "Who're George and Mel?" asked the sheriff.

"George Peterman and Melanie Hart are the CBI cybersecurity team based out of Grand Junction," said Buck.

Melanie Hart was about five foot two, with shoulder-length black hair; she wore black jeans and dark gray hoodies and had several piercings. Anyone meeting her for the first time would think she was a high school kid, but she had received her doctorate in computer science from MIT about a dozen years ago. She'd joined CBI right out of college.

George Peterman could have passed for her father. He was about the same height as Buck, a shade under six foot, but where Buck still weighed what he'd weighed when he played football in high school, George had added a few pounds over the years. George had joined CBI after retiring from the navy, where he'd spent his entire career working in cybersecurity. As far as Buck was concerned, George and Melanie were two of the best computer people he knew. Paul Webber was good. Ashley Baxter was better, but those two were world-class.

The sheriff pointed behind Buck, and he turned. Two ambulances from Gunnison pulled into the plaza, followed by a dark green Ford F-250. The ambulances parked, and the paramedics slid out and walked towards Buck.

Garrett Parkinson parked his truck behind Buck's Jeep, slid out and pulled a medical bag out of the back. He slipped under the crime scene tape and walked up to Buck. They shook hands.

"You look good, Buck," said the doctor. "You feeling okay?"

"Yeah. Feeling good," said Buck.

Dr. Garrett Parkinson was in his sixties but looked much younger. He was two inches taller than Buck and lean. He had a year-round tan from playing golf when he wasn't performing autopsies. He wore jeans and a black puffer jacket.

The doctor tugged his watch cap down a little snugger. "It's colder than shit here, Buck. Where do you want me?"

"We've got lights for the plaza, so I'd like you to start on the mountain before we lose the light. Paul is there waiting for you. Follow the road at the end of the parking lot and you can't miss it. Leave the one ambulance here."

"You got it, Buck."

"Hey, Garrett. Be careful. We don't have the shooter in custody, and the shots could have come from anywhere."

He nodded, turned and, followed by one of the ambulance crews, headed to their vehicles and drove towards the lift area. The second ambulance crew grabbed some body bags and positioned them next to the bodies in the plaza. It was going to be a long night.

Chapter Nine

I took a sip from the backpack water bladder and opened another energy bar. The night was getting colder, and it was time to clear out and warm up. There were more people to kill, and I wanted to be ready.

I leaned in to the spotting scope and watched the activity going on at the ski mountain and at the plaza area. This had proven to be a great spot with a good view of both areas. I watched as the cops and ambulance crews checked over the bodies and loaded them into the waiting ambulances.

It was a shame that the kid had to die, but it was important to make a statement. The publicity would not be welcomed by the company that owned the resort, but they'd had their chance to do the right thing and had refused. Whatever happened today and moving forward was their fault. I was just the instrument, the vessel sent by God to put them in the crosshairs and make them suffer.

I watched with interest as the owner of the resort got into a confrontation with the guy in the ranch jacket. He must be the boss cop, because when the owner left, he didn't look happy. I had a bead on the owner the entire time he was in the plaza. The shot would have been so easy to make, but killing him outright was not part of the plan. No, death would have been too easy for the old goat. The plan was for him to suffer. To stand by and watch as his little empire crumbled around him.

The first killings on the slope and in the plaza were

just the beginning. People were already back outside, visiting the restaurants and bars that were not connected to the plaza. They weren't concerned. The people who died in the plaza meant nothing to them. These rich people were all the same. Worry about themselves and nobody else.

I would wait until they felt comfortable again, a day or so, and then more people would die. This time they would die not just on the slopes and on the plaza, but inside their comfy, cozy mansions and high-priced condos. When the killings were done, no one in the valley would feel safe.

I had already scoped out the condos that were available. When the owners or tenants or whatever they were were feeling snug and safe, a high-speed round would blast through their gigantic windows with magnificent views and destroy something precious. Something irreplaceable. I was ready.

I finished the protein bar, drank the last of the water and cleaned up the area. Can't make it too easy for the cops. I broke down the custom-made rifle and placed it in the hard side case. It was a mile hike back to the rented SUV, and with the sun now set, I pulled out a small headlamp and attached it to my cap. It cast enough light to see the trail, but not enough that anyone in the village could see it.

I checked the area, used a pine bough to rake the snow and disappeared into the forest. Tomorrow was going to be a good day, and I needed to get an early start to get to the new nest before the sun came up. A year of planning and it was all coming to fruition. A few more days and the resort would be ruined.

There was nothing more fun than making rich people cower, and I intended to enjoy every minute. I was amazed at how indifferent I felt killing people. I had hunted animals all my life, and I always felt bad after killing a majestic animal like an elk or a bear, but after killing those people earlier today, I felt nothing. No remorse, no sympathy. They were in the wrong place at the wrong time, and I needed them to send a message. Funny how that's all they were. Not flesh and blood, not someone's family, just a message.

Chapter Ten

Buck convinced Bechtel to leave the ski lift shut down for the rest of the day. Bechtel agreed but was not happy and threatened once again to call the governor. Since there were no new incidents, he left the troopers and the SWAT team to patrol the plaza and the lift area. If they were dealing with a sniper, he didn't think that person would be operating at night. Not from the distances they had considered.

He parked in front of the VRBO house on Silver Street in Lake City. The house was a small two-story Victorian home with a white clapboard exterior, a blue metal roof and a bright blue front door with a little flower wreath hanging on a hook in the window. The sidewalk from the street to the small front porch was lined with flower beds, and the house was charming during the few months when the flowers were in bloom. Now there were piles of snow. He slid out of his Jeep and grabbed his go bag and backpack. He walked up to the door and turned the handle. The door opened, and he stepped inside.

The house was warm, and when he stepped into the small living room, he saw Bax had started a fire in the fireplace. He dropped his bag by the door and walked into the kitchen. Bax was sitting at the table, working on her laptop. She stopped when Buck walked in. He walked over and opened the refrigerator and stared in surprise. He pulled out a bottle of Coke.

"You stop at the store?" he asked as he twisted the cap and took a long drink.

"Yeah," said Bax. "We needed food and coffee. So I picked up some Coke in case you hadn't brought any with you."

"Thanks," he said. "What are you working on?"

"I just finished creating the investigation file and was sending out the email invites when you walked in."

Around the CBI office, Buck was known as a technological dinosaur. He was happiest when he had paper files and his little notebook, but the times were changing, and Buck tried to change with them.

CBI had gone digital a few years back, so instead of having a blue binder for each case, Buck just had to open a program on his laptop. The new case was assigned a case number, and Buck would list everyone who needed access to the file and send them email invites. All evidence, lab reports, photos, etc., that were part of the case would be uploaded to the file, and anyone needing access just had to open the file. That was much better than the old system, where everything had been placed in the binder by hand, and Buck would spend half his time tracking down who had the binder.

Even for a tech dinosaur like Buck, this made his life so much easier, and he had ready access to anything he needed. Buck just had to click on a file and open the chronology page, which was the first page in the file. Nothing was entered into the file without a note being entered in the chronology page first. The chronology kept track of everything that happened in the investigation.

His phone chimed as he sat at the small table. He

looked at the message. Bax waited.

"Garrett's finished looking at all the bodies. The ones from the ski mountain are on their way back to Gunnison. The ones from the plaza are being loaded. He's heading to Gunnison and figures to start the first autopsy in about two hours. He's calling in a second pathologist and two more assistants to help with the load."

Buck looked at his watch. "I'm gonna head for Gunnison to watch the first couple of autopsies. I'll grab a couple of hours of sleep at home before I come back. What room should I throw my bag into?"

"I saved the big room for you," said Bax. "First door on the left. By the way. I've got George and Mel running background on all the victims. We'll have something for you in the morning."

Buck nodded, finished his Coke, grabbed his bag and headed up the stairs. The big room was about the size of one of his spare bedrooms at home. It was comfortably furnished with light-colored walls and a stained-pine wainscot that came up about three feet off the floor. The lights were old-fashioned wood and wrought iron, and they gave the room a warm yellow glow. It was comfortable for the short term. He dropped his bag on the bed and left the room.

He put on his ranch jacket, grabbed his backpack and walked through the door. He slid into his Jeep and set off for the hospital in Gunnison.

It was full dark by the time he pulled into the hospital parking lot, grabbed his backpack, walked through the front door and took the stairs down to the morgue in the basement. He opened the door, slipped off his coat and put on a Tyvek suit and shoe coverings. He hated the hat, but Dr. Parkinson was a stickler when it came to his autopsies, especially in criminal cases. Buck grabbed a mask from the box on the desk but didn't put it on. He stepped into the autopsy suite.

Dr. Parkinson and one assistant were standing over the body of Billy Claymore. Buck noticed another younger man and one of the other assistants working at the next table. Dr. Parkinson looked up.

"Buck. Meet Dr. Jeremy Shaffer. Jeremy, Buck Taylor, CBI."

Buck nodded. "Doctor, nice to meet you."

"The pleasure is all mine," said Dr. Shaffer. "Garrett has told me a lot about you."

Buck looked at Dr. Parkinson and laughed. "Don't believe anything he tells you."

Dr. Parkinson smiled. "We were lucky. Jeremy was visiting his sister for a couple of days. She lives here in town and works at the hospital. She's a cardiac nurse. He works with the medical examiner's office in New York City. He agreed to give me a hand. I sent his pathology certification over to the state coroner a little bit ago, so he's good to perform autopsies in Colorado."

Buck stepped up to the table. The body of Billy Claymore was lying on its side. There was a solid plastic rod penetrating the body from back to front. The assistant was positioning the portable X-ray machine over the body. The doctor looked up.

"Paul asked me to get a travel path for the bullet that killed this young man. He wants to re-create it to see if he can find the sniper nest and the bullet. We're ready to take the pictures."

Everyone stepped back from the autopsy table, and the assistant hit a small button she was holding. There was a whirring sound, and she set the button down and moved to the counter. She pulled the laptop closer and clicked a few buttons. The X-ray appeared on the monitor. Dr. Parkinson looked at the path and nodded.

"That looks good. Send that to Paul."

Buck leaned in as the doctor pulled the hanging microphone closer and started the video recorder.

"Anything you can tell me so far?" asked Buck.

Dr. Parkinson looked up. "Yeah. This kid was too young to die."

Buck nodded and watched as Dr. Parkinson did a thorough examination of the exterior of the body. He picked up a scalpel and made a *Y* incision in Billy's chest.

Buck stepped over to the next table, where Dr. Shaffer was sliding a plastic rod into the entry wound in Tim Hawthorne's shoulder. Buck noticed it was in almost the same location as Billy's wound. The rod pushed out of the massive exit wound, and the doctor stopped and had the assistant take a couple of X-rays. He then removed the rod and began his exam.

Buck stepped closer. The entry wound was a nice round hole, but the exit wound was a mess, and a huge chunk of Tim's left chest was missing. Buck pulled out his phone and took pictures of both bodies as they were being examined.

"No doubt about cause of death. Any thoughts on the caliber of the round?" asked Buck.

Dr. Parkinson took some measurements. "I'd say a .308 or maybe a .30-06."

The doctor pulled down the microscope and used a probe inside the wound canal. He asked for the forceps and reached inside. Buck watched as he pulled tiny metal fragments out of the wound. He placed them in a petri dish and handed the dish to Buck.

"I don't think you're gonna find the bullet."

Buck looked at the dish under the microscope.

"It looks like pieces from a frangible round, but they're larger than I would expect to see."

"I was thinking the same thing. It almost looks like a cross between a hollow point and a frangible. Whatever it is, it came apart inside the body. That's why the exit wound is so much larger and messier than it should be. This bullet shattered on impact into a mess of tiny pieces."

"We won't get much of a comparison out of the bullets, if that's the case. Hard to find lands and grooves on pieces this small," said Buck.

"We'll gather what we can from the bodies, and there might be enough to do a metallurgic comparison," said Dr. Parkinson.

Buck took pictures through the microscope and placed the dish in an evidence bag. By the time they were finished with the first three bodies, there were very few bags to send to the State Crime Lab. Buck knew two things from the autopsies: whoever did the shooting was damn good, and they were going to have to solve this the old-fashioned way, since there was not much scientific evidence to work with.

Buck checked his watch, and at 4 A.M. they called it quits. The other four bodies had arrived, but they would wait until everyone grabbed some sleep. Buck called for the secure courier to pick up what few samples they had for the lab, waited until the courier picked up the evidence and headed home. He took a quick shower, fried up a couple of eggs and bacon and sat down in his recliner. He fell asleep holding his plate.

Chapter Eleven

My next nest gave me an ideal view of several condominium complexes. Most of the condos had huge windows overlooking the ski mountain, and I noticed that to protect the views, most people didn't close their drapes. The target selection was superb.

I arrived at the nest before dawn. The nest was in a dense area of undergrowth at the edge of the forest. I found a great spot where I could lie prone and target several of the condos with minimal movement. By the time the sun came up and people started heading towards the slopes, I had already picked out several likely victims. There was also a restaurant on the ground floor of one of the condo buildings that gave me an excellent choice of targets. I had decided that today was going to be about quantity, not quality. My plan was to hit as many targets in as short a period as possible. This was going to be fun.

The sun rose over the treetops, and the temperature warmed. The lift was still closed, but the two nearby lifts were running, and people were lining up to enjoy the fresh snow. It didn't appear that the shootings from yesterday were having an effect on skiing. That would all change today. It was time to make these people take notice.

I used my spotting scope and range finder to get the distance to the various targets and made notes in my logbook. The anemometer showed a slight breeze from behind me, and I adjusted the scope. The sun was going to be a minor problem since I was looking into it, but the coating on the optics reduced the glare, and I figured it wouldn't be a problem.

I slid the rifle over to my nest and placed it on the beanbag I had set on the rock. I snugged the stock to my shoulder and leaned into the scope. The view was superb, and at 2,400 meters I was within my comfort range, but like I said, today was about mass casualties.

I scanned the area and spotted my first targets. A man and woman were sitting at a patio table on the third floor of the building on the right. It looked like they were enjoying breakfast. There was a tall propane patio heater next to them, and they looked comfortable. I set the crosshairs on the man, took a breath and pulled the trigger. The side of his head exploded, and he fell out of the chair. The woman sat there and stared. I shot her in the chest.

I moved the rifle a few degrees to the left and spotted a woman cooking breakfast inside one of the condos. The glass would be a problem, but the rounds I was using today should blow a nice hole in the window. I tested that theory. The bullet punched through the glass, and I watched the woman slam into the cabinets behind her.

I moved the crosshairs to the restaurant. People were looking around. I picked four targets and fired. All four targets went down. That got their attention. People were running from the patio, falling over tables and chairs and one another. A server stepped through the doors, not realizing what was going on, and I shot him in his chest. Glasses and food went everywhere.

I shifted a few more degrees and zeroed in on the

two operating ski lifts. Since I hadn't spent a lot of time setting these shots up, they would be just for fun. I targeted several people in line for the lifts and squeezed the trigger. It was like shooting fish in a barrel. The people falling were enough to get the crowd moving, and from my vantage point it looked like more people were getting hurt from the stampede than from the rounds I sent downrange.

I dropped the magazine and slid an incendiary round into the first position, inserted the magazine and chambered the round. I shifted and targeted the base of one of the propane patio heaters at the restaurant. I squeezed the trigger and watched through the scope as the propane tank in the heater's base exploded and blew out the front of the restaurant. Glass, chairs, tables, plates and cups went everywhere, and several people running past were caught in the blast. The restaurant was engulfed in flames. Several emergency vehicles entered the ski area, and I slid back from my nest.

State troopers and cops in ballistic gear were running all over the parking lot. With the way the shots echoed through the valley, it would be difficult for anyone to get a good fix on my position.

I disassembled the rifle and placed it back in its case. I picked up all the brass and put it in the velvet bag I carried for that purpose. I swept the snow smooth and disappeared into the trees. It was a good morning.

Chapter Twelve

Mary and James sat on the patio of their condo, enjoying breakfast. It was a beautiful morning with clear blue skies and almost no wind. The propane heater next to the table gave off enough heat to make it comfortable. James had cooked a special breakfast before she woke up, and they sat, sipped their exotic coffee and ate their mushroom omelets. They were the picture of marital bliss, except they weren't married to each other. Mary's husband was on a two-week business trip to Dallas and had another week to go. James's wife was visiting her sister in San Diego. It was the perfect weekend for Mary and James to have a romantic getaway.

The bullet slammed into the side of James's head, and the exit wound sent pieces of his skull and brains flying over Mary. Covered in human residue, she sat there in shock. She stared at the body as it fell from the chair and landed on the patio floor. She tried to scream, but nothing came out. She was frozen in place, which made her the perfect next target. The bullet slammed into Mary's chest, and she flew out of the chair and landed on the ground a good five feet from where James lay, bleeding out on the patio floor. She lived for a few seconds and was looking at James when the darkness fell.

Sarah Cleveland was making a pan of scrambled eggs for her husband and three children in the kitchen in the condo they were renting. This was their first visit to the resort, and the kids, all excellent skiers and boarders, were looking forward to skiing and shredding on the fresh snow. They were used to skiing at resorts closer to Denver where most of the snow was man-made. This would be a new experience for them. She had just pulled the pan of bacon out of the oven and was ready to plate up the eggs when she heard what sounded like a crack in the massive front window with the view of the mountains and forests surrounding the resort. She registered the noise before something slammed into her chest and she and the frying pan of eggs went flying into the cabinets behind her. The eggs spilled from the pan as it dropped onto the counter, and she slid down the front of the cabinets and didn't move.

Several people were sitting on the patio of the restaurant that sat on the ground floor of the condo building. It was a rustic-looking place with barnwood siding, lots of dark stain and wrought iron accessories. The smell of breakfast cooking and fresh bread baking was irresistible, and there was a long line of people waiting to get in for breakfast. Several people stood and looked around, not sure what, if anything, they'd heard. Several bodies flew out of their seats as the sniper's bullets caused devastating injuries. Those not hit stood and raced out of the area, and several people were injured when they fell under the stampede.

Within moments of the restaurant attack, and before anyone in line for the lifts could react, bullets sprayed the crowd. People fell to the ground with massive wounds, and those unhurt ran for cover wherever they could find it. Several raced past the restaurant, ignoring the dead and injured. An explosion erupted from one of the heaters on the restaurant patio, and everything on the patio became a lethal weapon as chairs, tables, plates and cups flew with devastating results. Several people hit by the shrapnel fell to the ground, while others bleeding from wounds as yet undiscovered raced for places to hide. The inside of the restaurant glowed bright yellow, and black smoke filled the sky.

Bax and Paul were finishing breakfast when they heard the first of many sirens passing by on the highway headed for the resort.

"Fuck," said Paul.

"Yeah," said Bax.

They left the dishes on the table, grabbed their coats and backpacks and ran for their Jeeps. They pulled onto the highway behind a fire truck from the volunteer fire station just north of the town and put on their flashers. They turned onto the road into the resort and passed through the security gate behind the fire truck. Bax saw black smoke in the distance.

Her phone chimed, and she hit the button on the entertainment console.

"Sheriff," she said. "We're on our way. Where are we headed?"

"The base of the ski area," he responded. "Bax, it's bad. We got a dozen people injured and at least six dead, and the base restaurant is on fire. Gotta go."

Bax followed the fire truck and saw there were two other fire trucks near the restaurant. The flames wicked up the walls, and the condo above the restaurant was engulfed.

She parked her Jeep, pulled out her pistol and ran towards the sheriff. The patio area that ran between the condos and the lift was a mess with bodies and debris. People were screaming in agony, and she could see bullet wounds and burns on the victims. She stayed low and moved towards the sheriff, who was behind a steel bear-proof trash can. Paul was behind her, scanning the area.

"Sheriff, what can we do?" asked Paul.

The sheriff looked at Paul and then Bax. "Find the fucking lunatic who did this?"

Bax pulled out her phone. "Buck, we need you back here ASAP. There's been another attack, and this one was devastating."

"On my way" was all Buck got out before the call disconnected.

Buck speed-dialed a number and waited through two rings.

"Buck," said Director Jackson. "What can you tell me?"

"Besides the victims we talked about yesterday, Bax just called me and said there was a more devastating attack this morning. Sir, I'm gonna need some help. I am just leaving the autopsies of the first three victims. We've got four more from the second site, and now more victims today. Can you ask the governor to order up the National Guard mobile hospital and send us a couple more pathologists and assistants? Dr. Parkinson cannot handle this on his own."

"Okay, Buck. I'll call the governor. Where do you want the help?"

"I don't want to chance an attack on our people, so I'll find a spot in Lake City and drop you a pin."

"Buck, any idea how bad today's attack was, and any thoughts on who might be responsible? Could there be more than one attacker?"

"I'll fill you in when I get back to the resort. As far as this being a terrorist attack, that I can't say yet. I'll call you later with an update."

Buck disconnected the call and pulled out of his driveway. He hated the idea that there could be more than one person involved, and he wondered about the ultimate motive for the attacks.

Chapter Thirteen

Clive Bechtel stood and stared at the burned-out restaurant, scanned the area from the restaurant to the lift and shook his head. He couldn't believe his eyes. He spotted the sheriff talking with Bax and Paul. He moved towards them.

"This is an outrage!" he yelled. "What the fuck are you people doing to stop this?"

Paul stepped in front of Bax and confronted Bechtel. "You need to calm down, sir," said Paul in almost a whisper. He had watched Buck defuse situation after situation over the years by lowering his voice as the person confronting him raised theirs. At some point, the person doing the confronting needed to stop yelling and listen so they could hear what Buck was saying.

Bechtel looked at Paul, his face full of anger. "Who the fuck do you think you're talking to?"

Paul stared at him. "I'm talking to you, sir, and if you don't calm down, I might have to arrest you, and that would ruin my day."

Bechtel looked at him. He opened his mouth, and no words formed. He stood with his mouth agape. People didn't talk to Clive Bechtel like that. He was beside himself. He looked up at Paul.

"Why is this happening to me?" he asked.

"Why is this happening to you?" asked Paul. "Look around you. There's at least fifteen people injured and seven or eight more dead. This happened to them, not you."

Bechtel looked around. He hadn't noticed Buck standing behind him. Buck and Dr. Parkinson looked at the carnage.

"Buck," said the doctor. "I'm gonna need some help."

"Already working on that. The director is calling the governor to order up the National Guard unit we used in Grand Junction a couple of months back."

Six months prior, a brand-new drag club outside of Grand Junction was attacked on opening night. When the attack was over, there were more than seventy dead and several hundred wounded. The mobile hospital and National Guard pathologists worked with Dr. Sima Kalishe, the forensic pathologist for Grand Junction, and helped with the backlog of autopsies.

Bechtel turned and looked at Buck. "I want this maniac stopped. Do you hear me?"

Buck looked at him. "Mr. Bechtel, any thoughts on why this person is attacking your resort?"

Bechtel looked startled. "You think I have something to do with this? That's insane. This is some lunatic. Do your job and find him."

Bechtel turned and walked away from the group towards the ski lift. Buck looked at Paul and Bax.

"What the hell happened?"

"This attack was swift," said Bax. "We arrived with the EMTs. The entire attack took less than ten minutes." She pointed towards the condos. "From what we can tell, the attack started in this condo. We've got two dead on that balcony having breakfast." She pointed towards the next condo, several units over. "Next shot. The woman in that unit was standing at the stove cooking breakfast for her family. We've got seven dead at the restaurant. Those on the patio died from gunshots. Three we found inside died from the fire, which started after the attack on the lift line. Looks like the sniper took out a propane heater tank." She pointed towards the lift. "Seven dead, eleven injured. The shooter didn't even have to aim. Most of the injured were from the bullets passing through other victims' bodies."

"We did a quick look around," said Paul, "but we haven't found a single round. Franklin is going through the area with a small metal detector."

"You won't find anything," said Buck.

Franklin, dressed in Tyvek, walked up to the group. "Frangible rounds?"

"Looks that way. We found pieces of bullet fragments in the wound channels on the first three victims. Funny thing though. The pieces were bigger than those from typical frangible rounds. They were almost like a cross between a hollow point and a frangible. Still tiny, but not dustlike. Bax, call George and Mel. See if they can research the bullets. I put the pictures of the fragments in the investigation file." Bax nodded and pulled out her phone.

"Paul, did you get the X-rays from the three bodies showing the wound paths?"

"Yeah. I was about to call Franklin to break out the dummy when all hell broke loose."

Franklin nodded. "We'll get started as soon as I can finish up around here."

"Okay, but be careful," said Buck. "Until we know where the shots came from, we need to worry about the sniper."

Tommy White Elk approached Buck. "This was fast, Buck. My spotters couldn't see anyone on the ridge or near the cars. They even scanned the houses across the way for open windows. Nothing. We couldn't tell where the sound was coming from. It just bounced from wall to wall all the way down the valley. Whoever the shooter is, they are good."

Buck nodded and called the sheriff over. "Mike, has anything happened around the resort recently?"

Sheriff Drucker looked puzzled. "Like?"

"Vandalism, threats, confrontations, anything like that?"

"You think this is personal?" asked Drucker. "Bechtel is a cranky old son of a bitch, but for the most part, people in the county like what he's done here over the past twenty years. He's also pretty private. If he received any kind of threat, he wouldn't come to me about it. Let me talk to his security chief and see what he knows. You got a hunch?"

"No, just considering all the angles. We need to close the resort. As the sheriff, you can order an evacuation. Get Bechtel's people on it right away. They must have an evacuation plan in case of fire or something. Use it. We need to get all these people out of here, now."

"You worried about another attack?" asked the sheriff.

"I don't want to take that chance. See if the resort has a speaker system, and make the announcement. That includes shutting down all the shops, restaurants and bars. Thanks, Mike."

"Don't thank me yet. Bechtel's gonna have you for lunch."

Buck smiled and turned to Tommy. "Can your team go door to door through the condos and the houses and get the people moving?"

Tommy nodded and moved away from the group.

Buck waved over the state patrol captain. "The sheriff is going to order an evacuation. I need your folks to keep it orderly."

"No problem," said Captain Charles Moore. Moore had been with the state patrol for twenty years. He was tall and thin with short gray hair and blue eyes. He pushed the mic button on his collar and asked his troopers to meet up at the flagpole in the plaza.

Buck unclipped his phone and speed-dialed a number. Max answered on the second ring. "Hey, Buck. How's my favorite cop?"

Dr. Maxine Clinton was the director of the State Crime Lab and one of Buck's oldest and dearest friends. She was a matronly woman in her late sixties, about five foot five, with short gray hair. She thought she carried around an extra fifteen pounds she didn't need, but she was still a handsome woman. Married for forty years, Max had four children, eleven grandchildren and six great-grandchildren. She lived in a 150-year-old farmhouse in Pueblo, where she liked to tend her garden, sit on her porch and drink iced tea. She was also a bourbon girl and could drink most people under the table. She was loud and outspoken, but she knew her job.

Max had received her PhD in biology from the University of Colorado and worked as a biology professor for twenty years before joining CBI. She was a tough taskmaster with a belief system that didn't allow for defeat. Her goal was to give the crime investigator, no matter which department or municipality they worked for, all the information they would need to solve any crime. She held that as a sacred obligation to the victims. She was dedicated to her job and her staff, and the team at the lab worshipped her.

Buck would have been included in that group. Many times, during a challenging investigation, it was Max and her team that lit the spark that led to a breakthrough. Max was one of Buck's favorite people, and she felt the same way about him.

Buck relied on Max to get him the answers that could blow a case wide open. The people Buck worked with always joked that there wasn't anyone in Colorado that Buck didn't know. But Max was way ahead of him in that department. She had contacts worldwide and never failed to get him the answers he needed.

During one recent case, Buck was looking for

information on infrasound weapons and their effect on the body. Within a couple of hours, Buck was on the phone with a colleague of Max's, who was an expert in those types of weapons.

"Okay, Max," said Buck. "I sent you some samples early this morning. Wanted to see if you guys had time to take a look."

"Are the samples from the shooting in Lake City? The director called me early this morning and gave me a heads-up. What's going on?"

"Let's just say we're on our second mass casualty event in two days, and we're not getting much in the way of evidence. The fragments I sent you were from the wound track of one of the victims."

"Two attacks in two days," said Max. "How do you get into these kinds of situations? Oh. How are you doing?"

"I'm good, Max. All healed up."

"Good," said Max. "Don't overdo it."

"I won't. Can you get to the samples as soon as possible?"

"I'll get someone on them right away."

"Thanks, Max. I appreciate it."

She ended the call the way she always did. "You're a good man, Buck Taylor. God will watch over you."

Buck wasn't much of a religious man. He hadn't been to church in forty years. He had been raised Catholic but left the church right after confirmation. He always had too many questions about the teachings and too many people telling him he had to have faith. That wasn't the answer he was looking for. He had a lot of friends, Max among them, who had always offered a prayer when Lucy was dying. He never once rejected any of those offers, often smiling and thanking them for their kind thoughts.

Buck had realized long ago that it wasn't God and faith he had a problem with; it was organized religion. In his many years in law enforcement, he had seen too many times the aftereffects of someone's religious beliefs. It amazed him that so many people of faith could cause so much hatred and crime. But then, nonbelievers created just as much havoc.

Buck always believed there was a higher power, but he didn't believe that whatever that power was, it cared about one individual over another. His football coach always offered a prayer before each game, asking for help in defeating the other team. He always suspected the other team's coach was doing the same thing. So, how did God decide which team should win?

He knew a lot of people who said a lot of prayers for Lucy over the five years she was sick, but in the end, she still died. And she was the last person who should have gotten cancer. But Buck didn't carry any hatred. Whom could he get mad at? Whom could he blame?

Buck believed that there are spirits or a force all around us, and he always thanked them for allowing him to enjoy the hike, catch fish or see the sunrise and the sunset. It wasn't religion. It was something deeper. Something Buck didn't understand. He just accepted it. But no matter what, he always appreciated it when

Max told him God was watching over him. After all, what could it hurt?

Buck terminated the call and clipped his phone onto his belt. He looked for Paul and Franklin.

Chapter Fourteen

Buck spotted Paul and Franklin standing by the forensic van and walked over. A SWAT officer was standing next to them, scanning the area with binoculars. They opened a large wooden crate, from which they pulled a full-sized gel humanoid, or at least that's how it looked. The dummy would have made a great prop for a horror film. Six feet long and weighing 180 pounds, the dummy was used for testing ballistics. Here they were going to use the dummy to see if they could determine where the shots came from.

They laid the dummy on the stainless steel table, and Franklin pulled out a long plastic probe that was pointed at one end. Paul opened the investigation file and pulled up the X-rays Dr. Parkinson had uploaded from the Billy Claymore autopsy. They took the measurements off the monitor and transferred them to the dummy. Franklin took the probe and inserted it into the dummy at the location Paul had marked for the entry wound. He angled the probe towards the exit wound location and pushed the probe through the dummy. Once the probe pierced the exit wound location, he cut off the tip, which gave them a tube to shine a laser through.

Paul pulled a pair of laser enhancement glasses from the case on the shelf in the van and slipped them into his shirt pocket. They climbed out of the back of the van and slid into the seats. Franklin drove the van with Paul as his passenger, and Buck followed behind in his Jeep. They parked at the empty ski lift and climbed out of the van. Opening the back, they removed the dummy, carried it to the lift and placed it on the seat. Paul opened his phone and pulled up the pictures the ski patroller had taken of the position of the body and placed the dummy as best he could. He used a couple of straps to secure it to the seat.

Franklin handed Paul a high-powered laser pointer, and Paul sat on the seat next to the dummy. The lift operator started the lift. Franklin handed Buck a pair of laser glasses, and Buck followed in the second chair.

When they reached tower fifteen, Buck radioed to stop the lift, and he turned to face the mountains on the other side of the valley. He put on his glasses and waited. Paul put on his glasses and pulled the laser pointer from his pocket. He pushed the tip of the laser pointer into the tube and turned it on.

At first Buck didn't see anything as he scanned the range, then he spotted a tiny pinpoint of red light reflecting off a snowbank. He opened his backpack and pulled out his spotting scope. He focused on the snowbank and clicked the button that activated the range finder. He made a note in the notebook that he pulled from the front pocket of his backpack. He then pulled a compass from another pocket and shot a line to the spot. He made a note.

"Fuck," he said.

He lifted the radio and told Paul to shoot another line in the opposite direction, just in case they might find the bullet or fragments. Paul reversed the laser pointer in the tube and aimed it towards the exit wound. Buck spotted the red dot and followed the same procedure. They now had two points to work with. Buck radioed the lift operator, and the lift moved towards the top and back to the base.

Once back at the base, the lift stopped, and Paul and Franklin pulled the dummy from the seat, removed the tube, carried it back to the van and placed it in the wooden crate. Buck had walked back to his Jeep, pulled out an old torn and weathered topographical map book that looked like it had been in his Jeep for years and carried it to a picnic table.

Sheriff Drucker parked behind Buck's Jeep and slid out of his SUV. He walked over to Buck and watched him.

"Jesus, Buck. Talk about old-school," he said as he watched Buck orient the topographic map of the area to the west of the lift to magnetic north. He placed the compass on a spot he had marked that represented the GPS location of lift tower number fifteen. He took a ruler and drew a line from the lift to the mountains beyond. Using the ruler, he laid it on the distance scale at the bottom of the page and transferred that to the compass line. He measured off 2,007 meters and drew an X.

"That's about as close as I can get." He drew a circle around the X. "The first shot came from somewhere in this area."

The sheriff turned the map so he could read it. "Shit, Buck, that's over a mile away. So we have a sniper in the valley. That's a hell of a shot. Bet there's not many people that can do that."

Buck smiled. "I'll bet there's more than you think."

Paul, who had walked up, agreed. "Most expert hunters can hit a target a mile away. Beyond a mile, it takes a little more skill. Mile and a half to two miles, and we can narrow down the field a lot. Over two miles, and there's maybe three or four people in the world can make a kill shot from that distance."

"Sheriff, any way to get to that point?" asked Buck, pointing to the circle.

The sheriff looked at the map. "There's an old fire road runs south of there. We'd still have to walk about a mile or so, but yeah. We can get there."

"Paul," said Buck. "Why don't you come with the sheriff and me and let's see if we can find our sniper."

Buck pulled out his phone and called Bax.

"Hey, Buck."

"Bax, has Dr. Parkinson released the bodies?"

"Yeah," said Bax. "The mobile hospital arrived along with three pathologists and a bunch of helpers. I didn't think we'd want them conducting autopsies in the resort, so I commandeered the county garage parking lot. They're getting set up, and the ambulances are loading the bodies. Dr. Parkinson was heading back to Gunnison to get to the next four autopsies. I called the director and asked for a couple of National Guard choppers so we can fly some of the worst injured to Colorado Springs."

"Great work, Bax. Listen. Paul, the sheriff and I are going to try to get to where we think the first shots came from. We'll keep you posted. Cover a couple of the autopsies, and we'll hook up at dinner and look at our notes."

Buck hung up and placed a second call.

"Hey, Buck," said Mel. "What's up?"

"Hi, Mel. We've got a little more info to add to the search parameters for the shooter. The distance of the first shot was somewhere around two thousand to twenty-one hundred meters. That should narrow our focus."

"Great, Buck. I'll give that to George so he can put it in the search engine. One more thing. We've had no luck coming up with any connections on the first group of victims, and we went deep. It looks like they were all random. Bax sent me the list of the next group from today, and we'll get working on them, but my gut says the shooter is not being picky."

"I agree, Mel. I'm not sure of the motive or the objective, but I'm thinking this might be about fear or retribution against the resort." Buck had a thought. "Hey, Mel. Do me a favor and do a deep background search on Clive Bechtel. He's the owner of the resort. Let's see if there's something in his background that might make him a target."

"Will do, Buck."

The call disconnected, and Paul and Buck walked to their Jeeps. They grabbed their ballistic vests and headed for the sheriff's SUV. They climbed in, and the sheriff headed for the old fire road.

Chapter Fifteen

The sheriff turned off the highway onto the old fire road. The entrance had been blocked by shrubs, but Buck asked the sheriff to stop. He slid out of the SUV and walked to the front. Kneeling in the road, he brushed the snow aside, pulled out his phone and snapped a picture. He climbed into the SUV.

"Someone's been here in the past couple of days. Tracks are firm. We need to be careful," said Buck.

Paul, sitting in the back seat, pulled his pistol and placed it next to him. Buck did the same. The sheriff pulled forward. The road was rough, overgrown and covered with snow. They consulted the map, and when Buck figured they had gone far enough, they stopped and slid out of the vehicle.

Buck pulled out his compass and took the lead. The walk was made difficult by the snow that had piled up from the storm, but Buck noticed several spots that looked like they had been walked on. He stopped and took some pictures. There was no actual trail, and Buck was concerned they might walk right past the rock outcropping when the sheriff pointed.

"That looks like it over there."

They headed up the slope and came to a small outcropping with a dead tree lying behind it. They stopped and spread out, looking for anything that didn't belong in the picture.

Paul stopped and pulled a spotting scope out of his backpack. He placed it on the tree and sighted in on the ski lift. He raised the scope until he found tower fifteen and clicked on the range finder.

"I think this is the spot. The distance is close."

He shifted the scope to the side and focused on the plaza. He clicked on the range finder.

"Hell of a shot from here," he said. "It's over a mile and three-quarters to the plaza, but from this spot, the sniper would barely have to move."

He focused on the tower. "The lift shots took some talent. Not only from the distance, but from the fact that the target is moving uphill and away from the shooter. I wonder why the sniper stopped at three victims. With a full lift, he could have killed a dozen people. Same in the plaza. From this spot, the sniper could cover the entire plaza. This is a target-rich environment."

Buck stopped and looked at him. "That's an interesting thought. The sniper killed three at the lift, four in the plaza, then stopped. This morning, the attack was indiscriminate. What's the point?"

They looked around, but there was nothing in the area that would lead them to whoever used the area as a sniper nest. They trudged through the snow until they reached the SUV.

"Is there anything farther up?" asked Buck.

"If I remember right, it connects with the new road they're building from Ouray. Wanna check it out?" asked the sheriff.

Buck nodded. "We might as well. We're here."

The sheriff pulled ahead, and they drove for another forty minutes until they came to the highway construction site. The project had been put on hold due to the winter, but Buck was impressed. The contractors had made good progress from what he could see through the snow. It looked like they were about four miles from the base of the ski mountain.

The sheriff slid out and pushed a couple of plastic barricades out of the way, and they drove towards the construction trailer. As they pulled up, they noticed the door was ajar. The sheriff stopped, and they slid out with pistols drawn. The sheriff approached the left side and worked his way to the back of the trailer. Paul went right. He moved towards Buck, who was next to the door; Buck pulled open the door and they stepped inside, Paul going right, Buck going left.

The trailer looked like it hadn't been disturbed. There were papers and a desktop computer on the desk. There were a couple of chairs, an empty coffee maker and a long plan table along the back wall, covered in site plans.

The sheriff stepped in. "There're heavy tracks behind the trailer, and they're not filled with snow. It snowed yesterday, so someone has been here today."

Buck looked at his watch. They had an hour left of daylight. He hated the idea of going down that old fire road in the dark, but he hated losing an opportunity.

"Let's give it a half an hour and see if we can find anything, then we'll head back."

Paul and the sheriff nodded and stepped out of the trailer. Buck followed and pulled the door closed. He looked around and pointed towards a cut between two hills.

"Looks like they cleared the cut already," said Buck. "That should take us to the ski area. Let's see if there's a view from there."

Fifteen feet from the trailer, they spotted the first footprints. The boot looked small, and Buck pulled out his camera and took a couple of pictures, laying his pocketknife next to the print as a reference. They moved towards the cut.

The contractors had made more progress than Buck had realized, and when they reached the top of the rise, they had an outstanding view of the valley below. They stopped when Paul found a small berm of hard-packed snow. There were two quarter-sized round impressions on the top of the berm about eight inches apart. He pulled his spotting scope and set it on top of the two impressions and focused on the lift area. He clicked the range finder. He looked up at Buck.

"We need to call George and have him change the sniper's search criteria," said Paul.

"What have you got?" asked Buck.

"A bit over three thousand meters. We just moved into a whole different level of sniper."

Buck pulled out his phone and clicked on a speed-dial number. George answered on the second ring.

"Hey, Buck. What's up?"

"George, we need to change the search criteria for the sniper. We found the second location and were out over three thousand meters."

"That's gonna narrow things down a bit," said George. "Give me a few minutes to refine the search and call you back."

Buck hooked his phone onto his belt. "Let's look around and see if the sniper left us anything we can work with."

They spread out and worked their way around the area. The sun was low on the horizon and the temperature had dropped a few degrees, so, finding nothing of interest, they headed back to the construction shed.

"Should we get Franklin up here to sweep the shed for fingerprints or DNA?" asked Paul.

"It couldn't hurt," said Buck. "I'll bet the sniper used the shed to get out of the wind, but we might get some cast-off DNA. I'll drop him a location pin, and he and his team can drive up here in the morning."

Buck pulled out his phone, opened his GPS app and sent the location to Franklin. He put the phone away, and they walked away from the shed. Halfway back to the SUV, Buck stopped. Something on the edge of his hearing caught his attention, and as he turned, the propane tank on the front of the shed exploded, and the shed flew apart and burst into flames. Buck dove over a snowbank, and Paul and the sheriff, who were a little ahead of him, dove for cover behind the SUV.

"What the fuck?" said Paul.

Buck lay on the snow with his pistol in his hand. He looked over the pile at the burning shed, then he scanned the area, looking for the source of the sound.

Paul moved out from behind the SUV and ran towards Buck; he plopped down onto the snow. The heat from the shed was carried on the wind, and the warmth cut through some of the chill they had been experiencing. Paul watched the flames dance on the twisted ruins of the shed.

"You okay?" he asked.

Buck nodded. "Second time someone tried to blow me up. I'm gonna develop a complex." He smiled and looked at Paul.

"Bomb or sniper?" asked the sheriff, who dropped next to Buck.

"My money is on the sniper. I think I heard the shot just before the explosion," said Buck.

Paul pulled his spotting scope from his backpack and raised up over the snow. He scanned the area and slipped down the snowbank.

"But why did he wait until we were away from the shed?" asked the sheriff.

Buck was silent for a few seconds. "I don't think the sniper wanted to kill us. I think it was more like a warning that we're being watched. We need to find out why this resort was targeted."

"Fuck," said Sheriff Drucker. "Who the hell is this person, and what do they want?"

Buck looked at him. "I have no idea what he wants, but I will bet you he's not finished yet."

They stood and holstered their weapons. They watched what was left of the flames fade out and then turned and headed back to the SUV. Just before sliding into the passenger seat, Buck looked back towards the shed. He wondered what the sniper was after, and he wondered what was coming next. He slid into the SUV, and the sheriff headed down the trail towards the village. Buck sent Franklin a text to ignore the last text he had sent him with the location pin. Not much evidence would have survived the fire.

Chapter Sixteen

I was lying in the snow covered with a white plastic tarp and watching them progress through the snow on that old, shitty road. I watched with interest as the sheriff stopped his SUV and they hiked through the snow to my first spot. The cop I had seen earlier and the big guy who was with him slid out of the SUV and followed the sheriff. They were just below my nest when the big guy looked up and pointed.

I focused the spotting scope on him and wondered what he saw. I had policed all my brass, and I swept the area with some pine boughs. I wondered if he used a laser to pinpoint my shooting spot. That would be clever and more than I expected from some local dipshit cops. I was wondering if the big guy and the other guy might not be local.

I watched as they climbed the hill. Good effort on their part, since that snow under the nest was knee-deep. They reached the nest and looked around. The big guy pulled a spotting scope out of his backpack and aimed for the ski area. I put down the scope and picked up the rifle. I would hate to kill a cop. That's not what this is all about, but if he got too close, well, who could say?

He was sighting the scope, and it looked like he was sighting higher than the lift base area. Then a crazy thought came to me.

"Son of a bitch. They figured out where my kill point was. He's got one of those fancy-ass scopes with the digital range finder on it."

He was saying something to the other guy while the sheriff stood back and watched. They looked around, but it didn't look like they found anything. "Idiots, there's nothing to find, because I'm good."

I hoped that wasn't as loud as I thought it was. I needed to stop talking out loud and keep this shit in my head.

The sheriff, the big guy and the other cop headed down the trail to where the sheriff was parked. I figured they would turn around and head back down to the resort, and I was about to break down the rifle when the sheriff pulled ahead.

"Where the fuck is he going?" Dammit, that was out loud again. I had to stop doing that. Sound carries in the mountains.

I decided to hold off on breaking down the rifle for a bit and see where they were going. I kept getting glimpses of the sheriff's SUV through the trees, and when they stopped, they were parked almost right where I had parked earlier.

"How the hell did they find this spot?" I put my hand over my mouth. This had to stop.

I picked up the rifle and sighted in on the nest and then followed back to the snow berm. They slid out of the SUV and walked towards the berm. The other guy stepped over the berm and looked around. He was saying something to the others, and then they headed for that construction trailer. I scanned the trailer and spotted my mistake. The door was open. I mustn't have latched it when I left. I bet the wind blew it open. Shit.

They went inside, and I pictured them in my mind, looking around for clues. I didn't leave any, at least I didn't think I did. Fuck. I wondered if they could get DNA just from me being in the building.

I scoped the door, and they stepped out and latched it. They walked to the edge, and the big guy looked around as they split up. He leaned down and spotted something in the snow, right where I had set up. This guy must have military training. I wondered if he was a cop, or was he here as some kind of sniper expert? I rested my finger along the trigger. He called the other two over, pointed at the ground and pulled out his spotting scope. He was aiming towards the base area. What the hell did he spot on the ground? Fuck. I'll bet the snow was hard enough that it held the impressions from the bipod.

He said something to the other guy, and he pulled out his phone. My finger rested on the trigger, and I breathed slowly. Less than two seconds and I could take them all. No one would even know where to look for them. I needed to decide. The sun was setting, and I wanted to be off the mountain by dark.

The three of them turned and walked away. I watched the other guy doing something with his phone. They walked past the shed thing and headed for the berm. I decided. I wasn't gonna kill them, but I was gonna send a message. I aimed at the propane tank mounted to the front of the shed. I waited until they were all behind the berm.

I took a deep breath, held it and squeezed the trigger. The tank exploded, and then the entire shed blew apart. I scanned left and watched as the other guy dove behind the berm and the sheriff and the big guy dove behind the SUV.

The other guy looked over the berm as the big guy slid next to him. He pulled out the spotting scope and rested it on the berm. I slid under the tarp and pulled it up to make sure I was covered. I'd wait until they were gone before I would make a move. I didn't want to wait too long. I had one more stop to make tonight, and I didn't want it to get too late.

Chapter Seventeen

The sheriff's SUV was pulled to a stop, and Bax ran towards the vehicle.

"Fuck," she said. "Are you guys okay? We heard an explosion and saw a lot of smoke. Where the hell were you guys?"

Buck slid out of the SUV. "We're good. Our sniper sent us a message after we investigated his second nest. Blew up a construction trailer for the new highway. He waited until we were far enough away to not be affected by the blast."

"Fuck, Buck," she said. "That's the second time someone tried to blow you up. He's killed a bunch of people, yet he spared you guys. What's up with that?"

Buck laughed. "And yet, I'm still here. We need to dig deeper into the resort and into Bechtel. I have a feeling this is personal. Not sure how or why, but we need to dig. This is hurting Bechtel financially, and that might be the motivator."

Paul and Sheriff Drucker joined them on the sidewalk.

"So, you found both shooting locations?" asked Bax.

"Yeah," said Paul. "But we have a problem. The second shooting location exceeded three thousand meters. We're in another class of sniper."

Bax looked at him. The sun had set an hour before, and the streetlights from the plaza gave the area a soft, golden glow. Buck looked around the area.

"Lot of cars and people missing. How's the evacuation coming?" he asked.

"Good," she said. "There was a mass exodus out of here after you guys left. Lot of people are nervous."

"Shit," said the sheriff. "That's not gonna make Bechtel happy."

Bax smiled. "He's been around here twice today. Last time I told him if he didn't leave, I was going to arrest his ass. I think he got the message. Haven't seen him since."

Buck checked his watch. "Let's grab some dinner and see what we've got. Where's Franklin and his team?"

"In the condos that got shot up this morning," said Bax. "The rounds went through triple-pane glass. Wouldn't have happened if they were frangible like the others. They had to be FMJs, so Franklin and the team are chasing bullets through walls."

"What about the troopers and the SWAT team?" asked Buck.

"I've got three SWAT shooters with spotting scopes on the roof of the condo building. The rest are crashing in one of the empty units. Troopers are still going door to door and moving people out."

"Why don't you call Franklin and ask him to join us for dinner? Tell him to bring the crew. Is anything still open?"

"Yeah," said Bax. "The sandwich shop on the plaza

is open, but he was cleaning up a few minutes ago, so he's probably gone. The Mexican place down the side street is open. Since he's tucked back inside the condo building, he stayed open in case we had folks that needed to eat."

"Then Mexican it is," said Buck.

They moved as a group, and when they reached the Mexican restaurant, Franklin and his team were waiting for them. The owner, a young man named Jesus, was thrilled to see them. He had sent his waitstaff home, but he did an excellent job of getting them seated and getting their drinks. There were two other couples in the restaurant, but they left soon after Buck and the team arrived. Buck looked around.

Like most small mom-and-pop Mexican restaurants, this one was steeped in heritage. The walls were brightly painted and covered with colorful paintings and exquisite clay tiles. The booths were painted bright colors, and the light fixtures were stained glass hanging from chains. It was a lively, fun-looking restaurant, and Buck felt bad for Jesus as he looked at the empty tables.

Jesus took their orders and disappeared into the kitchen. Buck looked around the table and stopped when he saw Franklin. He had a smile on his face.

"Okay, Franklin," he said. "You look like the cat who swallowed the canary. What d'ya got?"

Franklin reached into the pocket of his Tyvek coveralls and pulled out a small evidence bag. He handed it to Buck.

"We found one of the bullets. That's the one that killed that woman cooking breakfast. After it passed through her, it went through a cabinet, through the wall, into the next condo, which was unoccupied, passed through the wall into a bathroom and smashed into the back side of the brick on the exterior of the building."

Buck examined the round and handed it to the sheriff. The bullet was smashed almost flat, and there was no way to check it for a ballistic comparison, but it looked like it was intact, which meant they could do a metallurgical test on it and determine the caliber. That was good news. It was the first clue, other than the small metal fragments Buck had already sent to the State Crime Lab.

Jesus carried a huge tray to the table and set it on the next table over. He passed out the plates to everyone and asked if there was anything else. Buck thanked him, and he disappeared into the back.

The sheriff passed the bag around the table, and it ended back at Franklin, who put it in his coverall pocket.

"I called for a secure courier pickup," said Franklin. "Should be here in an hour."

"Great," said Buck. "What else do we have? Anything?"

Bax spoke up first. "We sent the names of all the victims to George and Mel. So far, no connections, other than family ones. All the shootings appear to be random. The pathologists have completed the autopsies on everyone from today, and I spoke with Dr.

Parkinson, and he's finished with the other four victims. He told me to tell you he was taking the night off and not to call. All the other victims were airlifted to Alamosa or Colorado Springs or driven to Gunnison. We tried to interview as many as we could, and we got the same story. Standing in line, suddenly hit and bleeding. No idea where the shots came from or why they were targeted."

The team dug into the food, and the conversation turned more lighthearted. Buck finished and pushed his plate to the center of the table and sipped his Coke. He looked around the table. Everyone was dog-tired, yet none of them complained. He was proud of the teams, both his and Franklin's, and agreed with them that a good night's sleep would be welcomed with open arms. It was not meant to be.

Chapter Eighteen

The sniper, concealed in the trees behind one of the mini mansions, watched as the last of the ski slope maintenance guys left and locked up the building. All the equipment had been put away for the night. The weather report had called for a dusting of snow overnight, so no one should be around until after sunrise.

The sniper was surprised at how quickly the resort had turned into a ghost town. The parking lot was empty save for a few stragglers, and all the shops and restaurants had shut down. The only ones left on-site were the law enforcement folks. She had spotted the three guys on the condo roof and made sure she stayed out of their lines of sight.

Erring on the side of caution, the sniper waited another hour to be certain no one was coming back. The sniper, dressed in black and carrying a backpack, slipped out of the trees and ran to the building.

The large Quonset hut building was white on the outside and blended in with the snow-covered scenery. Bechtel hated having to build it, and he hated even more that he had to build it so close to the slopes in view of the houses and condos, but his maintenance director needed it to be near the slopes for ease of operation.

Inside the hut were snowcats used to groom the slopes, snow throwers, shovels, lawn mowers and snowplows for clearing the parking area and the sidewalks. The resort was a self-contained operation, and Bechtel never needed to call in anyone from outside the resort to help. That also meant that more than a million dollars of Bechtel's money was tied up in equipment and supplies.

The sniper snuck around the building to the small exterior door. The lock was no match for the lockpick tool, and within seconds, the sniper heard the lock click and the door opened. The sniper looked around to make sure no one was watching, pulled open the door and stepped into the darkened space. The space was huge, the roof over twenty feet in the air, and was crammed with equipment of all kinds.

The sniper lit the small headlamp and moved towards the mechanic's space. The space was filled with tools and equipment, but more important, the shelves were full of various chemicals needed to maintain the fleet.

The sniper opened the backpack and pulled out a small brick of plastic explosives and a digital timer. The timer was set for fifteen minutes, and the sniper placed it on the shelf. Next stop was the main floor area. Six more times the sniper removed larger bricks of explosives and attached them to the fuel tanks on the heavy equipment and to the gas tanks of the snowplows. Gasoline equipment, being the most volatile, would blow first, but the diesel in the heavy equipment needed to be heated first. It took a long time to ignite diesel fuel with an open flame unless it was hot enough, and even then it still didn't burn as well as gasoline. The sniper knew the heat from the gasoline explosions would make the diesel easier to ignite.

The sniper checked the time. Eight minutes. Time

to evacuate the area. The sniper picked up the backpack and raced to the door, opening it slowly and checking to make sure the coast was still clear. The sniper raced back to the hiding spot behind the house and waited.

The bomb by the chemicals and the bombs attached to the plows blew simultaneously. Within a minute, the diesel fuel was hot enough, and the explosives did their job. The large roll-up door at the front of the building blew off its tracks and sailed into the small parking area. It was scorched by the heat and twisted from the flight.

Flames leaped out of the entrance, and the sniper could hear the metal popping as it expanded and snapped the bolts and welds holding the walls together. Car horns and alarms were going off all around the village. The sniper moved farther up the hill to a better observation point and waited.

Within minutes, the fire department responded, and the sniper watched the teams of firefighters man their hoses and spray the building, which appeared to be melting from the intense heat. The sniper felt bad for the firefighters. It didn't take long before their coats were covered in ice and icicles hung from their helmets.

The sniper watched with interest as the cops from earlier today along with the sheriff gathered on the sidewalk and watched the building collapse.

The sniper focused on Clive Bechtel and stared. It would be so easy to put a bullet in his brain right now, but the sniper didn't feel that Bechtel had suffered enough. There would be a lot more pain to come.

The sniper grabbed the backpack and drifted into the forest and disappeared.

Chapter Nineteen

Buck settled the bill with Jesus, left a generous tip and thanked him for the excellent food and service. He stepped into the night air and zipped up his jacket. The temperatures had dipped well below freezing, and the air was crisp with a hint of moisture. Buck expected they would wake up in the morning to more snow. Bax and Paul stood with the sheriff. The village was quiet.

"Franklin leave?" he asked.

Bax nodded. "He had to meet the courier. His team was gonna get some sleep. They're staying in an empty condo."

"I think I'll do the same," said the sheriff. "Night, all."

The sheriff headed for his SUV, which was parked by the plaza. Buck looked around.

"Hard to believe," he said, "that a place so peaceful could become a scene of such carnage. I . . ."

The explosion split the air, and the night sky towards the ski slope lit up a bright orange. They felt the pressure wave as it spread through the valley.

"Holy shit," said Paul.

"What the fuck was that?" asked Bax.

They turned towards Buck, but he was sprinting down the road towards the ski lift. They ran after him. The sheriff, who had slid into his SUV, pulled the mic from the hook and called Dispatch to roll the fire trucks. The resort had its own paid fire department, and he could hear sirens coming from the back of the resort. He started his SUV and followed Buck.

Buck reached the lift area and stared in amazement. The garage that housed all the snow-grooming equipment and snowcats was engulfed. The flames were shooting a hundred feet into the air, and the heat could be felt as far away as the lift building. Buck could hear sirens in the distance.

Bax and Paul caught up with him and stopped. They stood as a fire truck roared past them and stopped near the building. The four firefighters jumped off the truck and unspooled a couple of hoses, connecting them to the fire hydrants and then running towards the flames as the hoses swelled. They stood as two teams pouring water on the fire, ice forming on their turnout gear as the mist from the hoses encircled them.

"What the hell happened?" asked the sheriff.

"My guess," said Buck. "Our sniper just added arson to the list of charges against him."

"Great," said Bax. "Just what we need, a multidiscipline criminal. Fuck!"

One of the county fire engines pulled into the lot, and the firefighters followed the same procedure.

Clive Bechtel parked his SUV behind the sheriff and ran to the group. He stood with his mouth open, wheezing, and stared at the flames. He turned to the sheriff.

"We are under attack," he yelled. "What the fuck

are you doing to stop this madman? So far, you've been worthless."

Buck turned to Bechtel, whose face was bright red. Perspiration dripped off his forehead.

"Mr. Bechtel," said Buck. "I need you to back off. Screaming at the sheriff will not solve this, and all it's gonna do is put you in the hospital with a heart attack. Whoever is doing this to you is very good, and so far, we have almost zero evidence. Without evidence, all we can do is keep looking."

Bechtel glared at Buck. "My health is none of your concern, sir. You need to focus on catching this sicko before I call the governor."

"Call whoever you want, Mr. Bechtel. He'll tell you the same thing I'm telling you. Now, you need to think long and hard and tell me who hates you so much that they would ruin everything you have built."

Bechtel laughed. "This has nothing to do with me personally. It's those crazy environmentalists who are trying to prevent me from building my road."

Buck leaned his head to the side and looked at Bechtel. "What environmentalists?"

"Those crazy fuckers," said Bechtel. "They've taken me to court five times and have lost every case, but I knew they were dangerous from the start."

"Have they threatened you?" asked Bax.

Bechtel paused. "Well. Not directly, but who else could it be? They want to destroy me."

"Mr. Bechtel, does this group have a name?"

"Not really," he responded, "but it's run by some crazy fucking lawyer. He lives in an old cabin in the valley and has been trying to stop me from expanding for years. Go arrest his ass and beat a confession out of him."

Before Buck could respond, Bechtel turned and walked towards Guy Pembroke, the ski area manager, and John Finch, the security director, who had arrived and were standing by the lift building watching the flames.

Franklin's SUV pulled to the curb, followed by the forensic van. Franklin slid out and walked towards Buck.

"Here I thought we might get some sleep. Our sniper has another skill set."

"Yeah. Gonna be another long night. Check with the fire chief and get into the building as soon as it's safe."

Franklin nodded and walked back towards his team, who were putting on Tyvek suits.

Buck stepped away from the group, walked up to Finch, tilted his head and walked off. Finch followed.

"Bechtel mentioned environmentalists causing problems. What the hell is that all about, and why am I finding out about it only now?" asked Buck.

Finch looked around. "This was not caused by environmentalists."

"And you know this how?" asked Buck.

"The environmentalists are harmless. Fuck, they're

not even a group. It's one guy. A lawyer named Griffin Hurley. He lives five miles outside Lake City. All he does is file lawsuits. He's been in the valley for forty years, and he wants to stifle any growth. He's been suing Bechtel for three years over that damn road. Lost every time, but it's costing Bechtel big money in legal fees. But I'm telling you right now. The guy is harmless."

Buck was irritated. "You still should have told us. Text me the guy's contact info. We'll go talk to him first thing in the morning."

"You got it, but I'm telling you. He's a nuisance, but this kind of crap is way out of his league."

Finch walked away, and Buck looked back at the building. The flames had been knocked down, and the firefighters were walking through what remained of the building and the equipment, putting out hot spots.

Buck walked back to Bax and Paul as his phone chimed with an incoming text. He pulled out his phone and checked the message. He showed the message to Bax, Paul and the sheriff.

"This is the environmentalist Bechtel mentioned. Finch says he's harmless, but let's go have a conversation with him in the morning."

"John is right," said the sheriff. "He didn't do this. Hurley's been a thorn in the side of this valley—the whole county, for that matter—for years. He's a lonely, grumpy old man, and all he does all day is file lawsuits. Been doing it for decades. One of those big city lawyers who had no trouble moving here but now doesn't want anyone else to move here."

"Still, it would have been nice to know, and we still need to talk to him," said Buck. "Who knows? Maybe he got tired of just filing lawsuits."

The sheriff nodded. "Meet me at the diner in town at nine A.M. and I'll take you guys to see him. He might not talk to you if you go alone, but I've known him for a long time. He'll talk to me."

The sheriff turned and walked towards the fire chief, and Buck stepped up to Bax and Paul. "Paul, stick around here and see what Franklin can find, and as soon as the sun's up, call George and have him and Mel run background on Hurley and see if he has anything on local snipers yet."

"Not much we can do here right now," he said to Bax. "Let's head to the B and B and see if we can get a couple of hours of sleep before we talk to this Hurley guy."

They moved towards their Jeeps and hopefully some sleep.

Chapter Twenty

Wow, that was a hell of an explosion. It was like watching a movie, except this wasn't movie magic, with lots of noise and smoke and flames. This was the real deal, with lots of noise and smoke and flames.

Shit, that big front door just flew and landed in the parking lot. Damn, I should have thought about getting out my camera. This would look so cool on Facebook. Bet it would get a thousand likes.

Those flames are amazing. The sky is lit up like it's daytime. I'll need to remember the name of that website that has the instructions for making the plastic explosives and the timers. Everything worked just the way it was supposed to.

Listen to that. You can hear the rivets and screws that are holding the wall together popping. I remember when we built the hut on the ranch. Damn, there must have been a million screws. I can still see Dad, Uncle Kurtis, Uncle Wayne and my brothers working on that building. It took a week before Dad could move his equipment into his new workspace. It was so much better than the old space in the basement. This space was bright and open, and when he got the lights and the heaters hooked up, it was a great place to hang out while Dad built his custom rifles and repaired rifles for the folks in the area. Dad is a master at what he does, but time has slowed him down. He still gets calls for custom rifles, but he turns down a lot more work than he used to. I think when my brother Tyler died, something in Dad died too. He's too proud to admit it, but the last time I was home, I could see it in his eyes. The enthusiasm wasn't there anymore. That spark that made people want to be around him just wasn't there. Mom took it hard, but it crushed Dad.

There're those cops from earlier today. I wonder if they got the message. I know they have a job to do, but I sure as hell ain't gonna make it too easy for them. I could have killed them, but I didn't.

Now, who's that in the fancy SUV pulling up? Ah, just what I expected. Clive Bechtel, the man of the hour. I could put a round right through his skull, but then he wouldn't get to watch me tear his world apart, piece by piece. God, is he an arrogant piece of shit. I should have killed him the first day, but what fun would that be?

I'm like a cat playing with a mouse. Licking it and carrying it around in my mouth, but keeping it alive. That the mouse knows it's going to die is the fun part. Letting it run a few steps and then using my claws to stop it and pull it back. Giving it that little taste of freedom and then snapping it back. That's what I'm doing with Clive Bechtel. I want him to watch as I take everything that's dear to him away.

The firefighters have done a good job. There's nothing but embers left. Soon the cop and his friends will enter the building to see what they can find. They might find bits of the timers, but when they send them to the ATF to look for a signature, they won't find one. Each timer, though they all worked the same way, was built with the tiniest difference, and they weren't built to mimic something someone had already done. The signature on my timers is unique, and I might even get a place in the ATF's gallery of signatures. Right alongside the Unabomber and the Oklahoma City bomber.

The fire is out, and the tall Black forensic guy and his people are entering the building. The sun will be up in a little while, and even though I'm keyed up, I still need to get some sleep. There's still a lot of work to do, and I need to be ready, mentally and physically.

Chapter Twenty-One

Buck's phone woke him before his alarm. He looked at his watch through bleary eyes and realized he had gotten three hours of sleep. He sat and picked up his phone. He grabbed the warm bottle of Coke sitting next to the bed and took a big drink. He set the bottle down on the nightstand and pushed the green button.

"Hey, George. What's up?"

"Hope I didn't wake you," said George. "Bax wanted background on the attorney turned environmentalist before you headed to his place this morning."

Buck checked his watch.

"Great, George. What did ya find out?"

"Griffin Hurley graduated Yale law school in 1978 and passed his bar exam that same year. He worked for a lot of big Denver firms, handling environmental law. He sued a lot of big companies and won a lot of money. At the height of his career, he stopped going to work and disappeared. According to his former boss, no one had any idea why he left or where he went. In 2000 he reappeared in Lake City and started suing companies all over the western U.S. for environmental damage. Won some cases, small settlements, but gained a reputation as a crazy guy and was ignored by most people in the environmental movement. So far, he has filed eleven suits against Bechtel or the resort. It looks like Bechtel's lawyers do a number on him each time, and so far, they've all been dismissed. He sued the county six times and Lake City four times. Other than that, he has no social media presence, and he's a ghost."

"George," said Buck. "Can you load the most recent filings to the investigation file? Go back, say, two years for the resort, Bechtel, the city and the county."

"What are you thinking?" asked George.

"Not sure. I don't think these shootings are about the resort. My gut says whoever is doing this is after Bechtel. I'd like to see what this guy goes after and see if any of it fits. Anything yet on Bechtel or the local snipers?"

"Mel's working on Bechtel right now," said George. "I'll have the list of snipers in about an hour."

"Thanks, George."

Buck finished the warm Coke. He threw the bottle in the trash, grabbed a quick shower and a clean shirt and headed downstairs to meet Bax.

The ground outside the B&B was covered with an inch of light, fluffy snow. Buck brushed off his Jeep, and he and Bax put their backpacks in the back and slid in. The diner the sheriff had told them about was a few blocks away, and as Buck drove, the cloud cover broke, and a few rays of sun pushed through the clouds.

Buck pulled into the small parking lot. They grabbed their backpacks and walked to the door. They pushed open the door, and the smell of bacon was overwhelming. The sheriff was sitting along the front windows, and he waved to them as they entered. They made their way to the table and pulled out two of the chairs. They sat and read the menu. The waitress, a tall, dark-haired older woman wearing glasses and a name tag that read SUE, walked over with a coffeepot. Buck held his hand over the coffee mug and asked her to bring him a Coke. She filled Bax's cup and took their orders.

Buck placed his laptop on the table and opened the investigation file. He found the files he had asked George to upload, clicked the first one and read. He pointed towards the screen.

"This guy, Hurley, sued the city because they wanted to turn an empty lot into a parking lot. That was a year ago. The case was thrown out of court."

The sheriff laughed. "Yeah, Hurley is a piece of work. He has sued or tried to sue almost everyone in town over something stupid for the past twenty years. People are so fed up with him, he rarely comes to town anymore. He lives like a hermit."

Bax was reading Buck's screen. "What's his story, Mike?"

The sheriff sipped his coffee. "Heard he quit some big firm in Denver and moved out here to find himself. Guess he made a boatload of money and bought a sixty-acre piece of ground with a shitty old house on it. He's made some improvements, but people who have seen it, me included, would call it one step up from a hovel. After he moved in, he started suing people. His first suit was to stop Bechtel from developing the ski area, then he sued to stop the resort. Then he tried suing anyone who bought or built a house or a condo in the resort. He has a real hard-on for Bechtel. Not sure why."

Buck sensed the sheriff was holding back, but he decided not to push it just yet. He set the laptop aside when breakfast arrived, and they ate quietly. Once he finished, he pushed his plate aside and reopened the laptop.

"You think Hurley is dangerous?" asked Buck.

"He never has been. When I was first a deputy, he used to come to town for city meetings, and he would get loud and obnoxious, but he never threatened anyone. I think he's just a lonely, grumpy old man with nothing to do."

Buck closed his laptop and placed it in his backpack. "Let's go see if you're right."

They each left money on the table, and Buck pointed to it when he caught the waitress's attention. She smiled and mouthed thanks. They grabbed their coats and stepped into the sunshine. According to the sign on the bank, the temperature was now a balmy 3 degrees.

They climbed into the sheriff's SUV, and he headed north. A half mile out of town, they turned onto a small dirt road that seemed to run as far as the eye could see. They passed three small ranches before they arrived at a cattle crossing with a locked gate. The sheriff pulled up next to a small box mounted to a fence post. He rolled down the window and pushed the button. Three more pushes of the button, and a crackly voice came over the speaker.

"What?" said the voice.

"Griffin, it's Mike Drucker. I'd like to come up and talk to you for a few minutes."

"You got a warrant?" asked the voice.

"It's just a conversation. Won't take but a few minutes."

"Who's in the car with you, Feds?"

"No," said the sheriff. "Two agents from the Colorado Bureau of Investigation, they're investigating some crimes that have occurred at the resort, and they thought you might be able to help."

"Help how?"

"Come on, Griffin, unlatch the gate and let us come up and talk with you for a few minutes," said the sheriff.

There was silence for a few minutes, and then the gate opened. The sheriff pulled forward and drove down the bumpy dirt road until they came to a small ramshackle house. They pulled to a stop behind an old, beat-up pickup truck. They exited the SUV, and Buck reached under his coat and unsnapped the thumb break on his pistol. He knew Bax was doing the same thing.

The door to the shack opened, and a rough-looking man stepped onto what was left of the front porch. He had long, scraggly gray hair and a long beard, and he was thin as a rail, wearing ripped jeans and a T-shirt that at one time was white. He had a pistol tucked in his waistband. The sheriff stepped forward, holding both hands in the air.

"Griffin. You doin', okay? You look a little rough today."

Griffin Hurley looked at the sheriff through bloodshot eyes. "Doin' okay. What do you want?"

"Griffin," said the sheriff. "These folks are from the Colorado Bureau of Investigation. They're investigating some crimes over at the resort, and they know you have filed a lot of lawsuits against Clive Bechtel, and they'd like to know why. Can you help them out?"

Bechtel looked at Buck and Bax. "What crimes are you investigating? Somebody finally shoot that son of a bitch Bechtel?" He smiled.

Buck stepped forward. "Why would you ask that, sir?"

"Just wonderin'," said Hurley with a sneer. "He ruined that valley, and now he wants to destroy the next valley as well."

"Why do you think that?" asked Buck.

"That road he's putting through between Ouray and the resort will give him access to three more skiable mountains and a massive amount of untapped land, ripe for development, yet nobody wants to believe me. I'm the one trying to stop him, and so far, nothing I've done legally has been allowed to proceed. I'd shoot him myself except my hands shake so bad from the Parkinson's that I'd be lucky to even hold a rifle, let alone shoot one."

Buck had noticed that he had his fingers intertwined the whole time he spoke. Now, as Buck watched, he could see the tremor in Hurley's hands.

"Mr. Hurley, I'm gonna be straight with you," said Buck. "Did you hire someone to kill Bechtel or ruin his business?"

Hurley laughed and then coughed for a minute. "Hell no. Money ran out a long time ago. You can check my bank account. I get a tiny annuity check and Social Security every month and that's it. Just enough to buy groceries. Now, it's time you got off my land."

Hurley turned around and stepped into the shack and slammed the door.

Buck turned, and they walked back to the SUV and climbed in. The sheriff turned the SUV around and headed back to the gate, which was still open. They drove through and turned onto the dirt road.

"Bax," said Buck. "Check his bank account when we get back, but I doubt he has anything to do with what's going on. Sheriff, can someone from the county check on him and make sure he's okay? He looks like he's on his last legs."

The sheriff nodded. "I'll make some calls. I saw him a couple months back, and he looked fine. Now he looks like a hermit. Poor guy."

Buck's phone chimed, and he pulled it out and checked the message. The sheriff's radio crackled, and he held his finger to his ear and listened.

"Drop us off at the diner and then head for the resort. The sniper took a shot at Bechtel."

"Fuck," said the sheriff as he clicked the mic on his collar and acknowledged the call. The sheriff stepped on the gas.

Chapter Twenty-Two

Buck and Bax parked behind the ambulance and followed the sheriff up the stairs to where one of his deputies was standing. The house was a massive log cabin sitting on the side of the mountain overlooking the resort. Several SWAT officers with binoculars stood out front watching the parking lot and the mountains beyond.

"What happened?" asked the sheriff.

Deputy Kevin Rhodes stood on the front porch. "We got the call about fifteen minutes ago. I was at the plaza, so I raced over here. The bullet came through the office window and grazed Mr. Bechtel on his right shoulder. He seems okay. The doctor is in with him now."

He looked at Buck. "Paul and Franklin are inside."

Buck nodded, and they pushed open the door and stepped inside. The great room with its honey-colored logs and huge circular fire pit was warm and inviting. The space was massive, with a tall ceiling and huge beams. The furniture was rustic, in keeping with the theme of the house. The floors were granite, and there was no deviation between individual stones. It looked like the stones had been placed and then smoothed to a perfect finish.

Buck followed the deputy down a hall and into the office. The office was was built for a man of power and influence with dark wall paneling and large windows overlooking the resort.. Bechtel sat behind a massive walnut desk as the doctor wrapped a bandage around his arm. Bechtel's face was pale. The doctor stood and looked at Buck.

"It's a deep scratch," said the doctor. "I've stopped the bleeding, but I'm going to have the ambulance take him to the hospital in Gunnison."

"I could have lost my arm!" shouted Bechtel. He looked at Buck. "You call the governor and tell him I want the National Guard here today. I want this son of a bitch caught. I could be dead right now."

Buck stepped over to the hole in the window. The bullet had passed through it cleanly. He stepped over to Bechtel.

"Mr. Bechtel, were you sitting then as you are now?"

"Probably. Who fucking cares? That madman tried to kill me."

"I don't think so," said Buck. "I think this shot was meant to scare you. With the size of this window and the fact that your body is almost completely covered by the chair, you made a great target. If the sniper wanted you dead, the bullet only needed to move another six inches, and we'd be having this conversation without you."

Franklin and Paul were standing in a corner of the room, looking at the wall. "He's right," said Franklin. "This sniper doesn't miss."

Franklin turned on the laser pointer, stuck it in the bullet hole in the wall and aimed it through the hole in the window. Paul walked over to the window with his spotting scope, focused on the spot on the nearby ridge and hit the range finder.

"One thousand five hundred eighty-five meters," he said. "With what we know about the sniper's skills, this would have been an easy kill shot."

"Paul," said Buck. "Take two of the SWAT officers and head over to the sniper's nest. See if he left us anything this time."

Paul put the scope away after identifying some landmarks on the distant ridge, and he left the office. Buck turned to Franklin.

"Can you retrieve the bullet?" he asked.

"It's in deep, but I'll try to get it with as little damage as possible."

Bechtel pushed up from his chair. "Tear the whole fucking wall down if you need to, but find out who's doing this to me." The doctor took him by the arm and led him out of the office. His body was trembling.

Buck's phone rang, and he pulled it off his belt and looked at the number. He pushed the green button.

"Hey, Mel. What's up?"

"Hiya, Buck. George wanted me to call you. He's grabbing some sack time in the back room. We've located three experienced snipers in the area. I loaded their info into the investigation file. Based on what we know, these are the guys capable of making these shots anywhere near you. These guys have the skills, but you're gonna have to see if they have the motivation. George used our friend and downloaded their unredacted military files."

Buck knew what Mel meant regarding their friend. A couple of months back, the team had been involved in an investigation into a dead state brand inspector and a bunch of dead cows. The investigation also uncovered murder, human trafficking and baby farming. It was determined that the cows were killed by airborne botulinum toxin, and the general in charge of a secret lab that had been built in the Colorado mountains to replace Plum Island in New York was concerned that this lab might have created the deadly toxin.

When the investigation stalled, the general gave Buck a sophisticated encryption-breaking software to get into secret government files. He let Buck keep the software with the promise to use it wisely. Buck knew George would use the software only if there was no other choice. He found out later that George and a colleague, while they were in the navy cybercrimes unit, were the ones who developed the software the general had given them.

"One more thing," said Mel. "We can't find any connections between the victims. As far as we can tell, these were all random. Wrong place, wrong time. We'll keep looking. Are you on speaker?"

"No," said Buck. "What's up?"

"I uploaded a lot of information on Clive Bechtel to the file. Look it over and let me know if you need me to go deeper."

"Thanks, Mel."

Buck turned to Bax. "Can you pull up the investigation file?"

Bax opened her backpack, pulled out her laptop and placed it on the desk. She opened the investigation file and then turned the laptop towards Buck. He found the file with the information on the area snipers and read their files. He slid it back so the sheriff and Bax could read them.

A few minutes went by, and the sheriff looked at Buck. "I know this guy, Taylor Robinson. He has a place up the north end of the county. I knew he served in the military, but I had no idea he was a former seal sniper."

"Why don't you and Bax go pay Robinson a visit and see if he knows anything? I'm gonna run over to Durango and see what Martin Whitcomb has to say."

"What about Roger Morrow, the third guy on the list?" asked Bax. "Should I make plans to go to Grand Junction and talk to him?"

"Unnecessary," said Buck. "I know Roger. He's a former marine scout sniper. Was damn good in his day, but his day has long passed. Roger was a sniper in Vietnam. Don't get me wrong, Roger can still outshoot anyone I know, but now he's a backup sniper for the Mesa County SWAT team."

"That may be so, but if he has the skills, shouldn't we check him out anyway?" asked the sheriff.

Buck smiled. "Roger has a degenerative condition and needs crutches to get around. No way he could get to where we were yesterday."

"Okay," said Bax. "We'll head over and visit this Taylor Robinson. Call me later, and I'll fill you in on what we find. You up for the drive? You haven't had much sleep, and you've got over three hours of driving ahead of you. Are you good?"

Buck laughed. "Don't worry, Mom. I'll take it easy. While I'm gone, organize a search. The sniper has to be hiding someplace. Get the troopers and SWAT to check every condo and every house in the resort. If you need more bodies, call the director and get the governor to send up more troopers. Every building in the resort should be empty, except for the ones our people are using. Let's see if we can find the lair."

"No worries, Buck," said Bax.

Bax stepped away so she could call the SWAT leader and the captain in charge of the troopers.

Buck headed for his Jeep. He had a long drive and had decided to spend the night in Durango. He looked up a number on his phone and dialed. He paid for one night in the hotel. He would visit Whitcomb in the morning after a good night's sleep.

He slid into his Jeep and drove towards the main gate. He turned onto U.S. Highway 149 and headed south.

Chapter Twenty-Three

Damn, that was close. They got to the house a hell of a lot faster than I expected them to. If I had more time, I might have put another bullet into his other arm.

He's sitting there shitting his pants, thinking he came close to getting killed. Had I wanted to kill him, he'd be dead. Christ, my younger brother could have made that shot. The arrogant fuck, sitting in front of that huge window in his fancy-ass office chair, never considering that he might be a target. Well, I hope that shook him up good.

The sheriff and those other cops just arrived. They're getting a briefing by the deputy. He must have been on the property already, as fast as he arrived. That big cop and the Black forensic guy were right behind him.

The doctor is working on Bechtel's arm. Big tough guy got a scratch. Probably crying his eyes out because he got a boo-boo.

Fuck! I need to get the hell out of here. That red laser dot hit the snow right next to me. Shit. I need to move. That big cop is ranging me already. I won't have much time before they send someone over here. I'll break the rifle down back in the trees, but I need to move. This is cutting it way too close. I lost focus. I can't let that happen again.

I'll head up the mountain to the spot I was going to use later tonight. There's good cover, and since my gear is there, I'll just hunker down until later. That spot will also give me a good view of anyone coming up the mountain after me. I'll be hard to see, but I have a good field of fire from that old stump. It would be a great place for a last stand, but I'm not done yet, and I have no intention of being around here to take part in a last stand. By the time they figure out where I am, I'll be long gone. A couple of days and my work here will be done.

Chapter Twenty-Four

Buck turned onto U.S. Highway 160 and headed towards Durango. The snow the weather channel had called for hadn't materialized yet, and the roads were clear. He'd made good time so far, but he still had a ways to go. The 174-mile drive would take him a shade over three hours.

The ringing on his entertainment console let him know he had an incoming call, and he pushed the talk button.

"Yes, sir."

"Buck," said Director Jackson. "Can you fill me in on what's going on? Clive Bechtel has been ringing the governor's phone nonstop. Would you believe he wants the governor to deploy the National Guard to protect his resort?"

"Yes, sir," said Buck. "He told me the same thing this morning. What I can tell you so far is that we've got nothing solid. The sniper is leaving few clues, and the closest we've been able to come is when he or she tried to blow us up."

"Wait a minute," said the director. "You were almost blown up again? What the fuck, Buck?"

"Yes, sir. I know. It was more of a warning. The sniper waited until we were far enough away from this construction trailer and then blew up the propane tank."

"Shit," said the director. "And you're all okay?"

"Fine, sir. Getting back to what we have. We have a few pieces of shrapnel from a bullet and one intact but flattened round. Franklin is gonna dig out the one from the wall in Bechtel's office. My guess is that will be flattened too. We spoke to an environmental attorney who's been suing Bechtel since this resort started, but that got us nowhere."

"So, what's the plan going forward?" asked the director.

"We got military records for three snipers who live in the region who have the skill set to pull this off. Bax and the sheriff are on their way to interview one guy who lives in the county, and I'm on my way to Durango to talk to another guy. Don't know if there's anything to these guys, but we need to look at them."

"Do I want to know how you got the military records?" asked the director.

Buck laughed. "Better you don't ask, sir."

The director laughed. "Okay, Buck. What about the third guy?" asked the director.

"You remember Roger Morrow, the SWAT sniper in Grand Junction? He's the third guy."

"Roger, Roger. Yeah, I remember him. Hell of a shooter. You're not looking at him?"

"No, sir. Roger has some muscle disease and has to use crutches to get around. No way he'd be hiking around in the places our sniper has been."

"Okay, Buck. Keep me posted so I can keep Bechtel from bothering the governor. And Buck. Be careful."

Buck disconnected the call. He took a sip from his bottle of Coke and placed it back in the drink holder, then his phone rang. He pushed the button.

"Hey, Max."

"Buck Taylor. How's my favorite cop?" asked Max Clinton.

"Good, Max. What's up?"

"Have you got a minute?"

"Yeah," said Buck. "Driving to Durango. Got about twenty minutes."

"Great," said Max. "Listen, those bullet fragments Dr. Parkinson sent down. We just got back the analysis. The bullets are a titanium alloy Ti-155A."

"Those don't sound cheap, Max. I don't think I've ever seen a titanium bullet. Are these common?" asked Buck.

"Not really," said Max. "Titanium is hard to work with, and it doesn't make a good bullet, but here's the thing. This titanium had carbon added to it. When you heat the mix to six hundred degrees Celsius, it becomes brittle. That's why the bullet shattered on impact. It's also why the fragments are larger. Typical frangible rounds are made of powdered copper alloy and tin. The tin, not to get too scientific, holds the powdered copper together until it hits something. When a frangible round hits something, it turns to dust. The larger fragments from your rounds would be capable of doing a lot of damage as the bullet comes apart."

"Would it take some specialized knowledge or equipment to make these bullets?" asked Buck.

"Yeah. This is not the bullet your average self-loader would make in his basement. The amount of titanium to carbon has to be perfect to keep the bullet from shattering in the barrel, and don't forget, titanium is not cheap. It's an odd choice for a bullet. We checked the database, and no one manufactures these. This would be a specialty item."

"What about the bullet Franklin sent you?" asked Buck.

"Nothing special there. It's a standard full metal jacketed bullet. Since it was flattened, we can't get lands and grooves, but the weight of the piece would suggest it's most likely a .308 Winchester or a .300 Winchester mag. Could also be a .338 Lapua Magnum."

"That's great, Max. Thanks as always for the help."

"You're a good man, Buck Taylor. God will watch over you." Max disconnected the call.

Buck turned off Highway 160 onto U.S. Highway 550 and drove towards downtown Durango. He had a stop to make before he checked into the hotel.

Chapter Twenty-Five

At Seventh Street, Buck turned right until he got to Main Avenue, where he turned left and pulled into the first parking space he found. Just down the street was his dinner destination. The La Bon Café.

Buck didn't speak a lick of French, but he knew one thing: the La Bon Café was neither La Bon, whatever that meant, or a cafe. What it was was a twenty-foot-wide hole in the wall, sitting between a local bookstore and a real estate office. It was a bar with about fifteen stools and six small tables along one wall. It was dark, musty and smelled like stale beer, amongst other fine cooking aromas. However, what it lost in atmosphere it made up for by having the best burgers in Durango.

Jimmy Palumbo looked up from where he was wiping the bar down after the lunch rush and blinked twice when he heard the front door open.

"Son of a gun, that looks just like Buck Taylor in the flesh. But I must be dreaming, 'cause he ain't been around in a couple of years to see his old pal Jimmy."

"Jimmy, is that you, or is that your older, fatter brother? How the hell are you, and how's it hanging?" Buck responded.

"Same as always," Jimmy replied. "About a foot long, give or take."

Jimmy laughed. He loved that line, and he bellowed every time he used it, which thankfully wasn't often. Jimmy walked around the bar and gave Buck a hug, but not his usual monster bear hug, which Buck was bracing for. Jimmy backed up and looked at Buck.

"You still hurtin'?" asked Jimmy. "Heard you came close to the big one. You okay?"

"Yeah, I'm good," said Buck. "Only hurts when I move or breathe." Jimmy laughed, and Buck gave him the short version of getting blown up.

"Shit, Buck. You need to be more careful. Man your age gets hurt easier than when we were young and studly."

They both laughed, and Jimmy walked behind the bar.

Jimmy Palumbo was a bear of a man. Six foot six and 270 pounds, a good bit of it still muscle. He had gray hair tied up in a small ponytail and a trimmed gray beard. He was dressed, as always, in jeans and a T-shirt that had a rude saying on it but was unreadable because of the full apron he wore. Jimmy and his girlfriend, Loraine, were the proprietors, bartenders and, as he liked to say, "head chefs of this fine establishment."

Jimmy was a transplant from Detroit by way of Southern California. At least, that was the story most people heard. Although no one ever got the real story, it was told, as a legend, that Jimmy once rode with the Hells Angels in Southern California and had to bug out when things got a little hot with the law. And he looked the part. He had tattoos on every piece of visible skin and a very light scar on the side of his face, that could be seen when he shaved off his beard, which hardly ever happened. However, Jimmy's appearance and his bloodstained apron made for quite a picture.

There was a soft side to Jimmy as well, which only the locals got to see. Each year around the holidays, Jimmy would open his place and serve free food to the homeless and less fortunate. A charity event never happened in town that Jimmy wasn't a part of. And if anyone suffered an illness or a disaster, Jimmy was the first one in line to lend a hand, whatever it took. Deep under all that outside bravado was a simple man with a heart of gold.

Buck grabbed a seat at the bar, and Jimmy threw a huge burger patty on the grill. Jimmy never asked you for your order. If you were sitting at the bar or a table, you were there for a burger. That's all Jimmy sold. He didn't have chicken or salads, and he sure as hell didn't have anything gluten-free or vegan. Jimmy was all meat and French fries. Sometimes this surprised the tourists, but the locals all knew the program, and at lunchtime, the bar was packed, and Jimmy would stand behind the bar at the open grill, sweating, regaling folks with tall tales and cooking up a storm. Loraine, his longtime girlfriend, was at the register, taking in cash and handing out to-go orders. They were quite a team.

Jimmy set a tall glass of Coke in front of Buck, then turned back to the grill.

"Holy shit," came a voice from the back. "Is that Buck Taylor?"

Loraine was blond and very attractive. She was five foot nine, and she filled out the T-shirt she was wearing. She set the box of burgers on one of the tables and ran to Buck with her arms out. Then she stopped and looked at him. "Is it okay? Can I hug you, or are you still sore?"

Buck slid off the stool and wrapped his arms around her. He pulled back. "Still a little sore, but that won't stop me from hugging you."

Buck repeated the story about his injuries and then Loraine turned, picked up the box of burgers, carried it behind the bar and walked to the end to refill a couple of glasses.

Jimmy stepped over. "You workin'?"

Buck and Jimmy went back a long way, and sometimes Jimmy had some useful information to share, and Buck knew he could trust Jimmy to keep quiet.

Buck nodded. "Yeah. Let's talk after I finish the burger."

Jimmy turned back to the grill. "You want cheddar cheese?" Buck nodded. Jimmy came back to the bar and set the plate down in front of Buck. The burger was a half pound of some of the best beef Buck had ever tasted, topped with lettuce and tomato and served with a mile-high pile of golden-brown fries. It looked like it could feed a family of four. Buck dug in, not realizing how hungry he was.

Buck knew that whatever he said to Jimmy would stay right here. Buck had first met Jimmy fifteen years ago during a homicide investigation. Buck had been new to CBI and was working with his mentor, Phil Mitchell, a grizzled, seasoned veteran of forty years of police work and one of the best investigators Buck had ever worked with. One night he and Phil accompanied two Denver homicide detectives to interview a known drug dealer about his involvement in a recent murder. This was only going to be an interview, and it should have been simple, but it went south in a big hurry. The guy they went to interview was waiting for the cops with a couple of his friends and had no plans to go back to prison.

As soon as they walked into the location and announced themselves, all hell broke loose. The two Denver homicide detectives were hit and seriously wounded. Buck dove for cover behind a desk, but Phil wasn't that lucky. The first round went in under his armpit, where his ballistic vest didn't cover. The second round hit him in the neck. The coroner would later say that either round would have killed him. Buck was pinned down and returning fire when this mountain of a man who looked like one badass biker came charging in, firing his weapon as he ran. At one point, a bullet raked across his cheek, leaving a deep, bloody gash, but he kept shooting.

By the time the cavalry arrived, the four bad guys were dead. Buck had been hit twice in the chest, but the vest had protected him. It still hurt like hell. The big guy who saved him wasn't wearing a vest. He was lying against another desk, with blood dripping down the side of his face and three gunshot wounds in his chest and right arm. Buck had been putting pressure on his chest wound when the ambulance arrived. Every day since, he'd thought about how Jimmy Palumbo's heartbeat kept getting weaker and weaker the harder he pressed to slow the flow of blood.

As it turned out, Jimmy was a ten-year veteran of the Denver Police Department and had been working undercover with the drug gang for the past two years. He wasn't even supposed to be at the location that night but had forgotten a gift for Loraine that he had left in the office. He had gone back for it and had just walked in the back door when he heard the detectives announce themselves at the front door and the shooting started. He had no choice but to get involved.

Jimmy was in recovery for ten days and in rehab for ten months before being told he could return to work. The doctors said that Jimmy would have bled out if it weren't for Buck. Jimmy never forgot that. By the time the rehab was over, Loraine had convinced Jimmy that maybe a change of scenery was in order. Reluctantly, Jimmy agreed, but he never once looked back. Jimmy and Loraine ended up in Durango after bouncing around Colorado for a few years, fell in love with the town and bought a small closed-down restaurant and bar.

Buck finished the burger and fries and washed it down with the glass of Coke. Jimmy walked over, picked up the empty plate and refilled the glass. Loraine was taking care of a couple of customers, so Jimmy walked back and leaned across the bar.

"So, what's going on?" asked Jimmy.

"You heard about the sniper at Lake City?"

"Yeah, it's all over the news. Hit the major networks yesterday."

"What do you know about a guy named Martin Whitcomb?" asked Buck.

Jimmy pulled back from the bar and looked at Buck. "Are you serious?"

Buck held up his hand. "Just a name that came up

when we searched for snipers with that kind of skill set. I'm just here to talk to him."

Jimmy leaned in. "Whitcomb is stone-cold, fucking nuts. Keeps to himself, but when he's provoked, he goes off like a bomb with a very short fuse. Don't go to his place tonight, and don't go alone. Wait till morning and talk to the sheriff. See if she'll send along a half dozen deputies. I'm serious, Buck. Don't go alone."

Jimmy walked away to put another burger on the grill and plated up an order.

Buck knew Jimmy didn't scare easily, so his reaction was unusual. Buck finished his Coke as more customers walked in and the bar filled up. Buck slid off the stool. Jimmy never charged Buck for anything, but Buck always left a twenty on the bar and told Jimmy to put it in the charity jar.

"I'll talk to you in the morning."

Jimmy nodded, and Buck stopped at the register and gave Loraine a hug. He stepped into the chilly night air and walked towards his Jeep. He pulled out his phone, opened his contact list and found the number he was looking for. He hit the green button.

La Plata County Sheriff Elizabeth Sinclair answered the call.

Chapter Twenty-Six

Buck checked out of his hotel, slid into his Jeep and headed south out of Durango. Five miles outside town, he spotted a La Plata County Sheriff's SUV parked on an unmarked dirt road. He pulled in behind the SUV and slid out of his Jeep.

Sergeant Stan Blackwell exited the SUV and met Buck halfway with his hand out. Buck shook it.

"Stan, good to see you," said Buck.

"Likewise, Buck. Been a minute," said Stan. "Sheriff said to meet up, that you need to talk to Martin Whitcomb. Wanna give me some idea what this is about?"

"His name popped up during an investigation up in Hinsdale County," said Buck.

"The sniper case?" asked Stan.

"Yeah," said Buck. "We don't think he's involved, but he meets the qualifications. Hoping he can give me some insight into elite snipers."

Stan studied Buck for a minute. "Okay. Let me give you some background. Whitcomb can be a nice guy, but he suffers from PTSD. When he gets angry or nervous, he becomes unpredictable. We have no way of knowing which Whitcomb will walk out of the house, so be alert. He will be armed, but don't draw your pistol. Best we put on ballistic vests. Let me approach him first."

"No problem, Stan," said Buck.

They left Buck's Jeep on the side of the road, and Buck slid into the passenger seat of Stan's SUV. Stan drove past the rickety chain-link gate that was pushed off to one side of the road and continued towards the house. As they drew near, Stan stared ahead.

"Now, that's interesting," said Stan.

"What's that?" asked Buck.

"Last time we were out here, the house was almost falling apart. Looks like he got himself a new roof and a paint job. There's also a kid's bike leaning against the porch. I wonder what that's about. Whitcomb doesn't have any kids."

A tall, thin White man stepped out onto the porch as they approached. He had long brown hair hanging past his shoulders and a thin beard. He wore jeans, a flannel shirt and a down vest. There was a pistol in a holster hanging off his belt.

Stan stopped the SUV, and he and Buck slid out. Stan gave a little wave.

"Marty," said Stan. "How you doing?" He walked towards Whitcomb while Buck stayed next to the SUV.

Whitcomb stepped off the porch. "Doing good, Stan. How ya been?"

Stan approached, and they shook hands. "Place looks good. New roof. Fresh paint. I like it."

Whitcomb smiled. "Lot's changed since the last time I saw ya."

A woman pushed open the screen door and stepped

onto the porch. She was a pretty blond and was wearing scrubs. A little girl hung off her leg.

Whitcomb turned and faced the woman. "Stan, this is Melody Greer and her daughter, Meg. We've been living together for about six months." He faced Stan. "Melody is a nurse at the VA clinic in Farmington. I met her when I took your advice and went down there to talk to someone. Been on the meds since, and Melody and I found something in each other."

Stan looked at him. "Marty, that's awesome. I'm so glad you got treatment." He stepped onto the porch, shook Melody's hand and kneeled to shake Meg's hand. He walked down the stairs and waved to Buck, who walked forward.

"Marty, this is Buck Taylor. He's with the Colorado Bureau of Investigation and was hoping you might spare a few minutes for a chat."

Marty glanced at Buck and extended his hand, and they shook. "Pleased to meet you, sir. How can I help?"

Before Buck could continue, Melody called out for them to come up onto the porch, promising lemonade. They trailed after Whitcomb and took seats at the wooden picnic table. Whitcomb looked a touch anxious until Melody appeared with cups and a pitcher of lemonade. Sitting beside him, she rested her hand on his while filling five cups.

"Marty," Buck began, "we're investigating a series of sniper attacks in Hinsdale County and—"

"I've never set foot in Hinsdale County," Marty interrupted.

Melody stroked his hand. "It's all right, honey. Let him finish."

Marty nodded, and Buck carried on. "This sniper is skilled, and our search criteria turned up three names. Yours, along with two others."

Melody kept caressing Marty's hand as he asked, "What was the range?"

"Between twenty-six hundred and over three thousand meters," Buck replied.

"Bet you're also talking to Taylor Robinson," Whitcomb remarked.

Buck looked curious. "What makes you say that?"

"We were part of an elite group of snipers. There are ten or fifteen marksmen in the country who can hit targets that far. In Colorado, it comes down to me, Taylor and either Roger Morrow or Gus Robinson. Last I heard, Roger was with SWAT in Grand Junction, which rules him out."

"Gus Robinson didn't show up on our list. Do you know where I might find him?" Buck inquired.

Whitcomb replied, "Gus passed away a couple of months ago—got Agent Orange cancer from his time in Nam. It finally did him in. Now, tell me about the shots."

"First set of shots left three dead on a ski lift. The target was almost twenty-six hundred meters away, and the targets were moving uphill, away from the shooter."

Whitcomb set his cup down and met Buck's gaze. "That kind of marksmanship narrows the list of potential shooters from ten or fifteen down to five or six."

"Would you be on that list?" Buck asked.

Scratching his beard, Whitcomb answered, "If I was on active duty, I would be, but I haven't fired a rifle in ages. Back then, I was that good."

Taking a sip of lemonade, Buck continued, "Do you know anyone who makes frangible rounds from titanium alloy?"

Whitcomb fell into deep thought. Buck waited. Then Whitcomb looked up and said, "That's specialized ammo. It's not something any gunsmith could deal with. Takes a lot of skill and the right equipment. If I were after such rounds around this part of the country, I'd seek Caleb Nelson. He manufactures some of the country's finest custom sniper rifles and has the expertise to produce titanium rounds. Note that titanium rounds are expensive as hell."

"Where can I find this Caleb?" Buck asked.

Whitcomb pulled a phone from his back pocket and scrolled through his contacts. After locating the information, he slid the phone to Buck. Buck jotted down the address on a notepad.

"Caleb runs a sizable operation south of Cody, Wyoming. He's got a top-notch gun shop where he builds his custom rifles. His rifles cost between five and ten thousand dollars. I've heard he made some that were more expensive than that. I know a few guys who have them, and they outperformed anything the military issued. Plus, Caleb has the country's longest shooting range, extending past three thousand meters. His range is private, and he's very particular about who gets permission to use it."

Buck returned the phone and added, "Just so I can complete my report, where were you this past week?"

Melody squeezed Whitcomb's hand and smiled at him. "It's okay, go ahead," she encouraged.

Looking uncomfortable, Whitcomb glanced at Melody, who smiled, then looked back at Buck. "I was at the hospital in Farmington. My appendix ruptured two weeks ago, so I spent two days there and have been recovering at home ever since."

Melody then turned to Buck and explained, "He was quite embarrassed about it. He kept insisting that kids have their appendix removed, claiming men never do. I told him he was wrong. I've seen men in their seventies and eighties go through the surgery. Still, he's been too embarrassed to leave the house since we got back from the hospital."

Melody reached over and picked up Buck's notepad and pen, wrote something and slid it back. Buck read the note and nodded.

"That's the name of the doctor," she said. "I'll call him and tell him it's okay to talk to you."

Buck nodded and put his pad and pen into the pocket of his jacket. He and Stan stood, shook hands and thanked them for the lemonade. Stan held his hand a little longer.

"Marty, I'm glad you and Melody found each other. Stay on the meds, okay?"

"No worries, Stan." He pulled Melody close. "She's my angel, and I'm not gonna do anything to screw that up."

Stan smiled, and he and Buck walked back to the SUV. Buck looked through the windshield and saw Melody on the phone. She hung up and gave Buck a thumbs-up. Stan turned the SUV around and headed for the highway. While he drove, Buck pulled out his pad, called Whitcomb's doctor and got the same story as he got from Marty. He thanked the doctor and disconnected the call.

Stan parked next to Buck's Jeep. "That went a lot better than I'd hoped," he said. "You need anything else, don't hesitate to call."

They shook hands, and Buck slid out of the SUV and climbed into his Jeep. He waved as Stan drove away, pulled out his phone and dialed Bax. Her phone went to voice mail, so he asked her to call him. He turned around and pulled out onto the highway to begin

the long drive back to Lake City. He could cross
Whitcomb off his potential suspect list, and he'd gotten
some good information from him. He hoped Bax and
the sheriff were having as good a day.

Chapter Twenty-Seven

Bax and Sheriff Drucker turned off Highway 149 onto a dirt road that disappeared into the mountains. They drove past a couple of small ranchettes, and just before reaching the mountains, they turned onto a smaller dirt road that took them over a metal cattle guard and through a small wood and chicken wire gate. They stopped in front of a log home, and two German shepherds raced from the side of the house and jumped at the door of the SUV, barking like mad and baring their teeth. Sheriff Drucker whooped the siren.

The front door opened, and a woman whistled. The dogs stopped barking, ran to the door and sat on either side of the woman. She was average height with gray hair and wore jeans and a flannel shirt. She was wiping her hands on a kitchen towel.

Bax and the sheriff slid out of the SUV and walked towards the front door, under the watchful gaze of the two dogs. The sheriff waved a greeting.

"Hey, Shirley," he said.

"Hi, Mike. What brings you out all this way?"

"Is Taylor around?"

"Yeah, he's out back in the shop," she said. "Hold on a second. I'll hit the buzzer to let him know you're coming." She reached inside the door, did something and faced the sheriff.

"Go on back, Mike. Can I get you guys anything, water, coffee, something stronger?"

They both thanked her and said they were fine. Bax followed Mike around the house to a large barn. The sheriff pulled open the door, and they stepped into a comfortable woodshop. A cloud of sawdust filled the space. Bax looked around. There was every kind of tool imaginable, and she marveled at a rolling rack that must have held a hundred clamps in every size imaginable.

A tall figure was leaning over a workbench running a router around a piece of wood. Bax stepped to another workbench and saw a dozen wooden cutting boards, many with intricately carved designs.

The router stopped, and Taylor Robinson set it on the workbench and stood up. He turned and faced the sheriff and Bax.

"Sheriff," he said.

"Hi, Taylor." He pointed to Bax. "Agent Ashley Baxter, CBI. Got a minute to talk?"

He dusted off his shirt and pants, wiped his hands on a shop towel and shook their hands.

"Thought you guys would have been here before now," he said.

Bax looked at him. "You were expecting us."

"As soon as I heard about what was going on at the resort, I figured my name would come up. I've got nothing to hide, so ask your questions." He leaned against the workbench.

Bax stepped forward. "Your name came up because your skill set matched the search criteria we set up for any local snipers. Can you tell us where you've been for the past couple of days?"

Taylor waved his hand around the room. "Right here. Got a big show coming up in Toronto next week, and I need to get at least a dozen more cutting boards finished before I leave."

Bax looked at the board he was working on when they walked in. "You do beautiful work. Do you hand-carve these yourself?"

"Yep," he said. "Started as a way to relax while I was on base during the first Desert Storm invasion. Found the work steadied my breathing, and it was great for hand-eye coordination. Pretty essential for a good sniper. Once I retired, I needed a hobby so as not to drive the wife crazy, so I built the shop and started working."

"Since you've heard about what's going on," said Bax, "any thoughts you'd like to share? Those skills you acquired in the service didn't come easy. Any thoughts on who might have the skills to pull this off and might have a beef with the resort?"

Taylor walked over to a small refrigerator in the corner and pulled out a bottle of beer. He held it up, but the sheriff and Bax refused. He walked to the workbench and sat on it, opening his beer and taking a long sip. He set the bottle on the bench.

"I heard from some folks in town that the sniper was shooting from around three thousand meters. That's a hell of a long way, and there's not many people I know could do that."

"Could you make a kill from that range?" asked

Bax.

Taylor smiled. "With a couple of weeks of practice, I could still make that shot, but not today. I haven't fired a shot in over a month, and that was just plinking around in the backyard with my grandson. Couldn't tell you the last time I pulled out my good rifle."

"You have any problems with the resort or with Clive Bechtel?" asked the sheriff. "Your property borders the resort, doesn't it?"

Taylor laughed. "Old Clive can be a pain in the ass, but since he wants to expand the resort, he's being overly nice right now. He always let me hunt on the resort property, and we had little interaction, but lately he's been downright neighborly. Drove up last week, knocked on the door and handed Shirley a dozen big cowboy rib eyes. Told her he had some cut for the fancy restaurant at the resort and had a few extras. So, to answer your question. No. I haven't had a problem with Clive in years. That's not to say we won't once he tries to get the Forest Service to agree to his expansion plans."

"You opposed to his plans?" asked Bax.

Taylor took a sip of beer. "Not really. If he's tellin' it square, there should be at least a mile and a half buffer between the expanded resort and my fence line. That resort bothers a lot of people, but I, for one, like the money it brings into the community."

"If you were going to take a shot like we're talking about. Twenty-six hundred meters, with the target moving uphill and away from you, what would you use?"

Taylor thought for a minute. He hopped from the workbench, walked over to a metal door built into the wall, entered a code in the digital lock and pulled open the door. He stepped inside. Bax and the sheriff stared. Through the open door, they could see at least a dozen rifles of different sizes and styles lining the wall.

Taylor reappeared, carrying a black matte-finished rifle that looked like something out of the future. He opened the bolt and handed it to Bax. She was surprised that for the size of the rifle, it was lighter than she expected. She held it in both hands, raised it to her shoulder and looked through the sight. She handed it to the sheriff, who did the same thing before handing it back to Taylor.

"I don't recognize the brand," she said. "Is that custom-made?"

"Yep," said Taylor. "Handmade by one of the finest custom gunsmiths in the country, probably the world. Fella by the name of Caleb Nelson. He lives up around Cody, Wyoming. Got this a lot of years ago, before he became famous and started charging up to ten grand for a gun like this."

Bax thought for a few seconds. "This gunsmith, Caleb Nelson. Would he be capable of making frangible titanium alloy rounds?"

"Is that what the sniper at the resort used?" asked Taylor.

Bax nodded.

"That's clever. Rounds like that would be hard as hell to trace. Yeah, there aren't any self-loaders who can work with titanium. Caleb would be one of a very few who can."

"One last question," said Bax. "If you were going to hire a sniper for a job like the resort, long-range, harsh conditions, who would you hire?"

Taylor was still for a minute. "Let's see. Roger Morrow is that good, but I heard he works for the cops, so he's probably not involved. Gus Robinson passed away this past summer. There's Marty Whitcomb, but I heard he's having trouble with PTSD. I'd most likely have to look out of state. You know one thing you might not be considering."

"What's that?" asked Bax.

"You most likely have the same list I just gave you, but you might also look at civilian shooters. There are some top-tier shooters out there who never served. Something to think about."

"Any you can suggest?" asked Bax.

"Nah, I don't follow shooting as a sport, but I know there's some big regional and national long-range shooting competitions happening several times a year. Might look into that."

Bax and the sheriff thanked Taylor for his help and walked back to the SUV. They slid in, and the sheriff turned around and headed back the way they came. Bax pulled out her phone.

"Hey, Bax," said Mel. "What's up?"

"Hi, Mel. Can you do me a favor and look into civilian long-range shooting competitions and see if there are any in this part of the country, see whose names pop up and then see if any of them fit our sniper qualifications?"

"No problem, Bax. You thinking our search focus was too narrow?"

"Could be. We were focused on military or past military, but I had an interesting conversation with a local sniper, and he suggested we look outside the military."

"We'll get on it right away. By the way," said Mel, "still no connections between any of the victims or any issues between any of the victims and Clive Bechtel. We'll keep digging, but I'm not holding out much hope."

"Thanks, Mel." Bax disconnected the call and looked at her messages. She clicked on the one from Buck and dialed his number.

"Hi, Buck. What's up?"

"Hiya, Bax," said Buck. "I got a name of a custom gunsmith who works with titanium, Caleb Nelson. Lives up near Cody."

"We just got the same name from Taylor Robinson," said Bax.

"How'd you like to fly up to Cody?" asked Buck.

"I'll call Mack and see if he can fly over here and pick me up."

Bax disconnected the call. The sheriff dropped her off at the diner where they met, and she slipped into her Jeep and dialed another number.

Chapter Twenty-Eight

Bax didn't waste any time. She needed a charter pilot, and she knew just who to call. Mack Price answered on the second ring. She explained what she needed, and Mack told her he was just puttering around the hangar, and he could be in the air in twenty minutes. He told her to meet him at the fixed base operator (FBO) at the resort's private airport, and he would pick her up there. Bax hung up, grabbed her backpack, ran out of the B&B and slid into her Jeep. She headed for the Grassy Mountain Resort Airport, a few miles south of Lake City.

Mack Price landed his Beechcraft King Air 250 on the runway at the airport like he was landing on a cloud. He throttled back the power and rolled onto the taxiway, stopping outside the local fixed base operator. Bax was standing at the tarmac door of the FBO, and she walked towards the plane.

Bax always enjoyed flying with Mack. He was personable and funny, and his white hair gave her a sense of security. Mack was five foot ten and rail thin. He wore his weathered leather bomber jacket with pride, having spent twenty years flying jet fighters, first in Korea and then in the early years of the Vietnam War. After his hitch in the Air Force, Mack started his own charter operation; with fifty thousand hours of flying, he was one of the most experienced pilots Bax knew.

Bax climbed into the cockpit and tossed her go bag onto the seat behind her. Mack had already entered his flight plan for the Yellowstone Regional Airport in Cody, Wyoming, so as soon as she was secure in her seat, he got clearance from the tower and taxied to the active runway. Mack went through his preflight checklist again, checked his fuel level and took off. He had to circle a couple of times to get enough altitude to get over the mountains. Mack always made flying look easy.

The weather was clear all the way to Cody, with little turbulence except as they cleared the mountains, which was typical in Colorado. The flight was quick, and in two hours, Mack was asking for clearance to land in Cody. He landed and taxied to the FBO.

Mack told her he would camp out at the FBO until she was ready to head home, and if she needed to stay overnight, he was okay with that. His next charter wasn't for another seventy-two hours, so he had time to wait for her. She thanked him with a big hug and headed out the door to her waiting rental car. She put her go bag into the SUV and headed south, following the map on her phone.

Twenty minutes later, she spotted a small farm road off the highway. There was no sign for a gun shop or a rifle range, just a mailbox that read NELSON. She turned onto the road and after a half mile stopped in a gravel parking lot in front of a good-sized building with a small sign that read CUSTOM RIFLES.

Bax slid out of the SUV, walked to the front door and pushed the button. A voice came through the security box, and she held up her badge and ID. There was a click as the door unlocked, and she pulled it open and stepped into a gun person's version of

Disneyland. The floor area was covered with shelves containing every kind of ammunition, target and shooting gear imaginable. She walked towards the counter and stopped to look at all the pistols in the counter cabinets. The walls behind the counter were lined with every sort of rifle available, including some she had never seen before.

A medium-height man stood behind the counter and watched her approach. He had silver hair and a three-day stubble on his face. He wore a pair of denim coveralls and had a gun hanging from his belt.

"What can I do for the police?" he asked.

Bax held out her hand. "Ashley Baxter, Colorado Bureau of Investigation. Are you Caleb Nelson?"

He shook her hand. "That'd be me. You're a long way from home."

Bax walked along the counter. "You've got quite the collection of hardware."

Caleb laughed. "This is just the retail stuff. Most of my business is custom-built guns, both rifles and pistols, but you would already know that before you arrived."

Bax walked over and stood in front of Caleb. "I'm not sure if you've listened to the national news, but we're investigating a sniper shooting at a ski resort in Colorado, and several people mentioned you might be able to help us?"

"Colorado. Let's see. That would be Taylor Robinson or Roger Morrow, right?"

"We heard it from Taylor and also Martin

Whitcomb," she said.

Caleb's smile filled his face. "Marty Whitcomb. God, I haven't heard that name in years. Last I heard, he was in South Carolina at a VA hospital. Got shot up in Afghanistan. You say he's in Colorado. That's great. He was an incredible shooter. The government trained him well."

"So," said Bax. "The reason for my visit. Our resort sniper uses frangible titanium alloy rounds, .300 or .308 caliber. Both men said if they were in the market for that type of round, they would come to you."

"And you were wondering what?" asked Caleb.

"We were wondering, since it's a unique round, if you remember selling rounds like that to anyone in particular."

Caleb thought for a few seconds. "You realize that even if I made them, I can't tell you who I sold them to. My clients know that when they come to me for a rifle or a custom bullet, that privacy is guaranteed. If I give you that information and my clients find out, my clientele will dry up along with my reputation. Sorry you traveled all this way for nothing."

"I could get a subpoena, but I was hoping to keep this friendly," said Bax.

"But you won't," said Caleb. "No judge, in his or her right mind, is going to make me give up confidential information. I wish I could help, but my hands are tied."

Bax looked above the rifle display on the back wall and noticed the trophies and pictures. Most of the pictures were of kids of various ages. Caleb noticed her looking,

"We sponsor several long-range shooting competitions. Those are the trophies going back twenty years."

She looked at the names on the plaques and noticed a pattern. Many of the last names were Nelson.

"Do your kids shoot long distance?" she asked.

Caleb smiled again. "Yeah. They all took it up at a young age, and it doesn't hurt that we have one of the longest rifle ranges in the country in our backyard."

Bax spotted a trophy from the year before. The name on the plaque was Abigail Nelson, and the picture next to it showed a young woman with a dark ponytail holding a rifle Bax didn't recognize. She pointed to the picture.

"I'll bet it doesn't hurt that their dad makes custom rifles."

Caleb remained quiet. A trophy on the shelf had a picture that was draped in black fabric. Bax walked over and took a closer look. The trophy was from two years before, and the young man was holding a similar rifle. The name on the trophy was Tyler Nelson.

Caleb stepped over. "That's one of my sons. He passed away a little over a year ago. Now, if you have no other questions, I've got to get back to work."

Bax thanked him for his time and walked through the store and out to her rented SUV. The trip had been a bust from an information standpoint, but she had this nagging feeling in the back of her head. She used to laugh at Buck when he would talk about the little bug that danced around in his head when something in the investigation clicked. She wondered if the bug was contagious. She pulled out of the lot. Once on the highway, she pulled out her phone and hit a speed-dial number.

"Hey, Bax," said Mel.

"Hey, Mel. I need you to do some research for me. I need everything you can find on Abigail Nelson and Tyler Nelson. They live near Cody, Wyoming."

"Okay," said Mel. "What am I looking for?"

"Not sure," said Bax. "Might be nothing, but I'm playing a hunch."

"Okay, Bax. I'll get back to you when I have something."

Bax disconnected and pulled into the airport rental car parking lot, parked the SUV, grabbed her bag and headed for the FBO. She found Mack asleep in a chair in the lobby and shook him awake. Twenty minutes later, they were back in the air headed for Lake City.

Chapter Twenty-Nine

The resort looks like a ghost town. There's all this incredible snow from the past couple of days and no one here to enjoy it. I almost feel bad for Clive Bechtel. Almost. Had he done the right thing, he wouldn't be in this situation. I set out to make his life miserable and destroy his business, and it looks like I've succeeded.

There's one restaurant open for those brave first responders. All the shops are closed, and I feel bad for the owners. They did nothing to deserve this, but in any action, collateral damage should always be expected. That's what they are. Collateral damage in my war against Clive Bechtel and his company.

Clive was expecting to expand the ski area once his road was completed, but now he'll need to reconsider. I've cost him a lot of money over the past week, and I'm not finished yet. He hasn't suffered nearly enough. He will when I get finished with him.

I walk through the plaza area and look in all the store windows. I feel like a tourist. I stay in the shadows so I can avoid the cops. As I walk down the small side alley, I glance into the condo lobby and see people eating in the Mexican restaurant. I'm glad he stayed open. I ate there when I first arrived at the resort, and the food was excellent. Now it looks like he's feeding the cops and forensic people. As I walk, I think about the condos sitting empty. Their owners and renters gone. I look around to make sure no one is watching, and I duck behind the building and spot the small room in the back where the gas line enters the building. I'm not going to break into the room just yet. I don't want to give anyone advance warning of what's about to happen. They'll experience it soon enough, and it will be spectacular.

I walk back around the building and walk through the trees towards the lift area. It's a short walk from the plaza. None of the shops or bars in the lift area are open. There is a small cart next to the lift that served coffee and homemade pastries. On my first day here, I stopped and purchased a cup and a bear claw. Both were delicious, and I asked the young woman working the stand how she came to be at the resort. She told me she had invested everything she had to purchase the cart, and she was hoping for an excellent season.

The poor woman. I feel bad for her. She thinks she will salvage the rest of the season once the sniper is caught. She has no idea that within twenty-four hours the resort will cease to exist.

I walk back to the plaza and head up to the town house I am renting. I keep the lights off as I pull a black duffel bag out of the closet and set my materials on the kitchen table. I've got a box of twenty incendiary bullets. I set aside a small box of custom-made frangible rounds. I've got half a box, twenty-five, full metal jacket rounds. My rifle is the last thing to come out of the bag, and I clean all the parts, even though I cleaned them after the last shooting, but it's force of habit. Always take care of your equipment.

Once the rifle parts are cleaned and oiled, I assemble the rifle and put it in the hard side case. I load my spare magazines and place them in plastic bags. I label each bag so I don't make a mistake and grab the wrong rounds. All the spare magazines go into the duffel bag, and I set everything by the door, ready to go. I've got a few hours, so I lie on the bed and close my eyes. My mission is almost complete, and soon I'll be able to head home, knowing that I did the right thing.

Earlier today, I walked into the almost-empty resort management office and dropped the letter in the internal mail slot on the wall. This is the one that owners and residents use when they need to communicate with the management staff. I hope that within a few hours someone will find it in the mail tub, read it and get it to Clive Bechtel, who will then call the sheriff. I doubt he will hand over ten million dollars, but if he doesn't, then come tomorrow night, all hell will break loose.

Most people would look at what I've done and think me a monster, but I am far from that. Monsters attack with no real purpose but to create mayhem. Everything I have done was motivated by love. When I started planning this adventure, I questioned what would happen if I got caught and put on trial. I believe that once my story comes out and I explain the motivation for my actions, no jury in the world would convict me.

I must have fallen asleep, because I wake to noise in the hall. Someone is knocking on a door down the hall and yelling, "Police." I hear the door open and then several people enter the town house. They must be searching the units looking for me. I don't know how far from my unit they are, but I need to get moving.

I run down the stairs, grab my gear, put on my coat and step onto the balcony. It's a ten-foot drop to the ground below, but I have no choice. The sound in the hall is getting closer. I close the balcony door. Luckily, this balcony faces the trees behind the building, so visibility from the plaza is nonexistent. I toss my bag into the trees and shoulder my rifle case. I step over the rail and crouch low. I lower myself until I'm hanging off the deck, take a breath and drop to the ground.

Fuck. I landed funny and my ankle hurts like hell, but I can't stop now. I grab my bag and limp into the forest. Once I lose sight of the building, I stop to catch my breath and assess the damage to my foot. This was not part of my plan, but I need to keep moving and get to my nest.

Chapter Thirty

Buck parked in front of the B&B, walked up the stairs and pushed open the front door. He could smell something cooking, and whatever it was smelled great. He realized he hadn't eaten since breakfast in the hotel in Durango, and he was starving. He dropped his backpack on the floor in the entry and walked into the kitchen.

Paul was standing at the stove stirring a pot. He turned as Buck entered. "Dinner in five," he said. "You good with chicken parmesan?"

"Hell yeah," said Buck as he grabbed a bottle of Coke from the refrigerator and sat at the kitchen table. "Where's Bax?" he asked.

"She's upstairs," said Paul. "I got the feeling things didn't go well in Cody."

"Anything happen here today?" asked Buck.

"All quiet so far. It's eerie. Like we're all waiting for the next shoe to drop. We know it's coming, we just don't know from where," said Paul.

"How is the building search going?" asked Buck.

"So far, nothing," said Paul. "The governor sent us six more troopers, and we've also got members of the sheriff's posse helping. They're all trained and armed. They're working through the night."

"The sniper has to be somewhere. What are we missing?" asked Buck.

"For all we know, he's living in a snow cave up in the mountains. He could hide anywhere, and it would take us until the spring thaw to find him."

Buck nodded and sipped his Coke.

Bax walked into the room, grabbed a bottle of wine off the counter and poured herself a drink. She sat at the table opposite Buck.

"That bad?" he asked, sipping from the bottle of Coke.

Bax took a sip from her wineglass. "Cody was a waste of time," she said. "The gunsmith threw up the Second Amendment as soon as I mentioned anything about customers. Wouldn't even tell me if he works with titanium." She took another sip. Buck waited.

"He told me that there isn't a judge in this part of the country that would give us a warrant to search his records, and he's right. As soon as I showed him my badge, he saw me as the enemy. Fuck."

Bax was passionate about her job, and Buck had seen her this angry on other occasions. He knew that there were no words that would make the feelings she was facing go away. He'd been there many times himself.

"So, we can't write off the gunsmith yet," said Buck.

Paul set three plates of rigatoni and chicken parmesan on the table, and all conversation stopped. They ate like they hadn't eaten in ages, and Bax poured herself another glass of wine as Paul set a beer on the table at his seat.

After grabbing seconds, Buck pushed his plate to the middle of the table and leaned back. Now that he was full, he was hoping his brain would engage and figure out the next steps.

Bax—not because she enjoyed washing dishes, but out of frustration and a need to do something with her hands—grabbed the plates and carried them to the sink. Instead of loading the dishwasher, she filled the sink with soapy water and washed as they talked.

"All right," said Buck. "Let's look at what we have."

Paul grabbed his laptop off the counter and set it on the table. He opened the investigation file and looked at the chronology. He stopped at the last item.

"Mel uploaded a background check on two people," he said.

Buck glanced at the entry and looked at Paul, who shook his head. "Bax," he said. "Did you have Mel run two background checks?"

Bax turned from the sink. She stepped behind Paul and read over his shoulder. "Yeah," she said. "It was just a weird hunch. While I was talking to Caleb Nelson, the gunsmith, I noticed several trophies on a shelf behind the counter. They were all for long-range shooting competitions. Two names were prominent. Tyler Nelson and Abigail Nelson. Abigail's trophies appeared to start in grade school and work their way up to last year. The trophies for Tyler stopped two years ago. I noticed a picture at the far end of the shelf, and I walked down to look. The picture was of a young man, and it was draped with black fabric. I was curious, so I called Mel and asked her to run background checks on both people.”

Paul opened the first file. “Abigail Nelson is twenty-eight years old and lives in Cody, Wyoming. She attended the University of Wyoming and has a degree in veterinary medicine. It looks like she has a clinic in Cody specializing in large animals. Now, this is interesting. As a senior, she set the state long-range shooting record. Twenty-nine hundred meters.” Paul looked at Bax and Buck. “That puts her on the list with the best shooters in the country.”

Paul opened the second file. “Tyler Nelson, age twenty-four. He graduated from Colorado Mountain College with a degree in outdoor recreation. He was the Wyoming state junior long-range shooting champion from fourth grade through high school. It looks like he stopped competing when he went to college.” Paul clicked a folder. “Tyler’s death certificate is on file with the state of Colorado. He died two years ago. His cause of death is listed as trauma.”

Buck pulled the laptop across the table and examined the death certificate. He looked up. “Trauma, nothing else.” He looked at Bax. “See if Mel can get us the autopsy report.”

“What are you thinking?” asked Bax.

“Tyler had a degree in outdoor recreation. He was likely a skier or boarder. When someone dies on a ski slope in Colorado, the COD is typically listed as trauma or head injury. I’d like to know a little more about what killed a twenty-four-year-old outdoor enthusiast.”

"You think he died in a skiing accident?" asked Paul.

Paul pulled the laptop back and clicked the keys. He pulled up the website for the little local paper and clicked on the archives. He checked the date on the death certificate, opened the newspaper's articles for the days surrounding the death and read the information. He looked up.

"There're no deaths listed at the resort during the week before or after that date."

He ran an internet search for Tyler Nelson and came up with the same information Mel had sent them. He scrolled through a couple of pages but came up blank.

He widened the search to include all Colorado, Utah and Wyoming ski areas and still drew a blank. As an afterthought, he pulled up the website for the *Cody Gazette,* one of the local papers in Cody, Wyoming. He opened the archives and clicked on the obituary tab.

He found a small picture and blurb about Tyler, but the obituary said nothing about the cause of death, just that Tyler died from trauma.

Buck was getting another bottle of Coke from the refrigerator when there was a knock at the door. He set the bottle on the counter and walked to the front door. Buck opened the door, and Sheriff Drucker pulled open the storm door.

He held up a piece of paper. "This was delivered to Bechtel sometime today," he said.

Buck invited him in and closed the door. He unzipped his coat and followed Buck to the kitchen.

Bax and Paul looked up from their laptops.

Buck took the papers and read for a few minutes. He finished reading and passed the papers to Bax, who read and handed Paul each page as she finished.

"What do you know about this?" asked Buck.

"Not much," said the sheriff. "Whoever wrote this was pretty specific about the details of an accident that occurred at the resort, but I called the court clerk to see if there was a lawsuit on file, and she couldn't find anything."

Paul was clicking keys while they spoke. "Well," said Buck. "Now we have to consider if this is the motivation behind the shootings, or is this someone looking to get rich? Ten million dollars is a lot of money." Buck looked at the sheriff. "You guys didn't investigate an accident?"

"No. I pulled our old files and can't find anything over the past three years. As far as the sheriff's office is concerned, the resort has a stellar safety record."

Bax handed Paul the last of the papers. Paul read the last page and clicked a few more keys on the laptop. "The accident didn't happen at the resort."

They all looked at him. "The state police accident investigation team was called by Ouray County to investigate a single-car rollover accident on Engineer Pass. The single victim, Tyler Nelson, had been thrown from the vehicle, which rolled over him. He was found at the bottom of a two-hundred-foot drop-off. Strewn around the crushed vehicle were several empty beer cans, and they found a bag of cocaine in the glove box."

"Do you know when Bechtel received this demand?" Buck asked the sheriff.

The sheriff pulled his notebook out of his jacket pocket. He flipped a couple of pages.

"The envelope was found in the office drop box, where the tenants drop off their rent checks. Since the resort staff had been off the property for the past two days, it could have been there for a while. SWAT escorted Bechtel's secretary in so she could collect any rent checks that had been dropped off before the evacuation. As soon as the secretary saw the letter, she called me. I had Franklin check the letter for prints. By then, Bechtel showed up, mad as hell that she called me instead of him. Not sure what that was all about. He told me the entire letter was a lie, and that there had never been an accident on the resort property."

Paul, who had been tapping away on his laptop, turned the screen so they could all see the monitor.

"This map was made before the new road was started between Ouray and the resort. According to the notes on the accident report, this is approximately where the rollover occurred." He overlaid a rendering of the new road on the old road. The new road covered part of Engineer Pass. "If the map of the new road is accurate, then the accident happened on the new road."

Buck stepped away, picked up his bottle of Coke and took a long drink.

He turned back to the group. "Why would anyone be driving on the new road when it didn't go anywhere? That was early in the project.”

“According to the report,” said Paul, “Tyler crashed through a barricade at the end of the road and drove until he either passed out or swerved. The pavement ended about a hundred feet from the crash site, and they assumed he lost control after driving onto the softer dirt and ran off the edge and down the cliff. According to the lab report, his alcohol level was four times the normal limit. They didn’t find traces of cocaine in his system, but the alcohol would have been enough to cause him to pass out.”

Buck walked to the kitchen door and stood looking outside into the darkness for a few minutes. He turned back to the group. “So, let’s think this through. Tyler, the son of a custom gunsmith and the brother of a long-range shooting champ, dies on a lonely stretch of road in Colorado he shouldn’t have been on. The family disagrees with the accident report and that sends their daughter to seek revenge on the resort two years later. Why? Did he work for the resort, or the construction company? Why was he on that road, drunk?”

“The letter,” said the sheriff, “says he worked on the construction project, but Bechtel says he didn’t and that there was no accident. The accident report by the troopers says that he’s lying. What else is he lying about?”

“We need to find out,” said Buck. He looked at Bax. “You need to head back to Cody and talk to the parents. You also need to find out if Abigail Nelson is at her clinic. Paul. Call the investigators for the accident team. We need everything they have. Get Mel working on getting the autopsy report. Sheriff, first thing in the morning, we need to talk to Bechtel. According to the letter, the sniper gave him a hard deadline to respond, or all hell will break loose. We have about fourteen hours left."

Buck pulled his phone from his belt and clicked on a number. The call was answered. "Good evening, Deputy Taylor. How can I help you?"

Chapter Thirty-One

Buck had no idea how she did it, but the few times he had contacted Harriet, he always got what he needed. Harriet was a voice with a touch of a Southern accent who was at the other end of a number he had been given by the U.S. Marshals Service.

A year back, Buck had been testifying in federal court in Denver during the murder trial of a survivalist drug dealer who had killed a DEA agent. One day, after court was dismissed, Buck and Jess Gonzales, the special agent in charge of the DEA's Grand Junction Field Office and one of Buck's closest friends, were talking outside the courthouse. Suddenly all hell broke loose, and people ran for cover. The marshals who were escorting the prisoner were ambushed in the parking garage, and Buck and Jess raced to their rescue.

Once the dust settled, the prisoner, a marshal and the ambushers were dead, but a lot of people in the garage that afternoon survived, thanks to Buck and Jess. To show their appreciation, the U.S. Marshals Service made Buck a full-fledged deputy marshal, and as part of that award, he was given a special number he could call anytime, day or night, and Harriet would get him whatever he needed. He had used the number twice before, and he wondered if Harriet was one woman or an entire team of women, but whatever she was, he appreciated the help.

Buck explained to Harriet what he was looking for, and she told him she would get back to him as soon as possible. Buck stepped into the kitchen. Bax was on her phone arranging a flight back to Cody, and Paul was working on his laptop. Buck tapped the sheriff on his sleeve and nodded for him to follow him. They stepped into the small living room.

"Buck," said the sheriff. "Do you believe that our shooter is a woman with no military experience?"

Buck thought for a few seconds. "I don't know, Mike, but it makes sense. Tomorrow, we need to look at the personnel records for the resort. Do you know the contractor who is doing the road project?"

"I know of them. Some big shot group out of Denver. They don't keep anyone in the county informed about what they're doing. The planning department pretty much rubber-stamped the plans. Bechtel spends a lot of money in the county. He gets what he wants. Why?"

"Suppose Tyler was working for the contractor and not the resort?" asked Buck.

"That could work, but why now? The accident was almost two years ago. What triggered these attacks now?" asked the sheriff.

"Do me a favor and give Paul the name of the contractor so he can run a background check on them, and then let's meet in the morning before we head to Bechtel's office." The sheriff turned and walked away.

The little bug in Buck's brain was stomping his feet. Not hard, but enough for Buck to notice. He felt like for the first time in a week, they might be onto something. He wasn't sure what it was, but they needed a break, and Buck would take even a little one. He checked his watch. Buck wondered what the sniper was doing right now. Could he or she be sleeping, or was he or she sneaking around the resort, setting up the next assault? So far, this attack had been well thought out and executed with military precision, which made him wonder if this could be the work of a civilian.

He had learned a long time ago that there's a big difference between shooting holes in a paper target, no matter how far the distance, and shooting holes in human beings. Buck had no prejudices, and that Abigail Nelson was a woman was of little concern. He believed women were as capable as men when it came to doing their jobs; Bax was the perfect example of a woman succeeding in what was historically a man's job, and he had put his life in her hands several times and would do it again without hesitation. He was more interested in how the sniper went from shooting paper to shooting people.

What was the motivation? Was it money, like the letter demanded, or was it something more? The sniper caused a lot of damage before the mention of money was made. Was that to prove a point? Or was it to scare Bechtel into paying? And why would Bechtel deny that an accident occurred? They had the report from the state patrol. Granted, the accident wasn't at the resort, but that road was his baby too. What was he trying to hide?

Buck sat in the recliner by the fireplace. The warmth felt good on his tired body, and before long he was sound asleep.

Chapter Thirty-Two

Marty Whitcomb woke from a restless sleep, sat up and rubbed his face with his hands. He wasn't sure what was bothering him. He had been taking his medications without fail, yet the dreams were back. He could see them as vividly as if they were a movie running on his television. Even though he'd spent his military career killing people at a distance, their faces still jumped out at him. He wondered if the meeting the day before with the sheriff's deputy and the guy from CBI had somehow awoken something deep inside that he had been working so hard to forget and hide.

He felt arms wrap around his shoulders and a warm body pressed against him. Melody nuzzled his neck with her nose. "Bad dreams, Marty? You slept like shit last night," she said, and she squeezed him tighter. "What's going on?"

"I'm not sure," he said. "I'm seeing the faces of the folks I killed. That hasn't happened since I started on the meds."

Melody let go and sat next to him on the bed. She took his hands in hers and squeezed them. "Did you take your pills last night?" she asked.

"Yeah," said Marty. "It's not the pills. It's something different this time."

"Did talking about being a sniper yesterday to the cops dredge up some old feelings?" she asked.

Marty let go of her hands and stood up. He walked into the bathroom and closed the door. She heard the usual morning sounds, and then the door opened, and Marty walked out. He picked up a pair of jeans off the floor and slipped them on, followed by an old sweatshirt. He walked out of the bedroom and walked to Meg's room. He pushed open the door and watched her sleeping. He walked over to the edge of the bed and brushed her hair back from her face.

Marty hadn't been this happy in years. He watched Meg sleep. He hated to wake her. She looked like a little angel. He hoped someday she would know how much her coming into his life meant to him. A thought hit him, and he sat on the floor and cried. He knew what was driving the dreams.

He stood and wiped his face with his hands. He walked away from the bed and closed the door. Melody was in the kitchen, pulling out everything they needed for breakfast. Marty poured himself a cup of coffee and stood next to her. She looked into his eyes.

"I think I know what I need to do," he said.

Melody cracked four eggs into the pan, listened to them sizzle and lowered the heat. She turned and faced him. His life had changed since Melody and Meg had arrived, but there was something missing. Something that meant as much to him as they did. He hoped she would understand.

Melody flipped the eggs and turned off the burner. She placed the eggs on the plates, grabbed the toast from the toaster and carried the plates to the table. Marty followed and then stopped and stared.

Sitting in his seat were his old camouflaged army boonie hat and his wrap-around sunglasses. He picked up the glasses and looked at Melody.

"I don't understand," he said.

Melody looked up from her plate. "Ever since we've been together, something has been missing from your life. I can feel it all the time, but after the conversation yesterday, I realized what it was and how important it was to you."

She took a sip of her coffee as Marty sat and stared at her.

"You've made great strides," she said, "and I'm so proud of you, but you've given up a part of your life, and as long as you don't face it, you'll never be whole. You're a sniper, Marty. That wasn't just a job title; that was you, your identity. It's time you faced up to it. I could see in your eyes when you were talking to the CBI agent that this is what's missing. You need that in your life."

"But I can't go back to the guy I was," said Marty. "I don't want to lose you and Meg." Tears rolled down his cheeks.

Melody smiled. "We're not going anywhere, and we'll be here when you get back, but this is something you need to do for you. You need to feel that adrenaline rush and feel useful. You said it yourself. There are a handful of snipers who can shoot like that, and right now those folks at that resort need one of those snipers to help them. They need one of the best. It's up to you."

They finished their breakfast, and Marty stood and picked up the plates. Melody smiled. "Leave those. Go out to the garage and grab your gear, soldier. You've got a long drive ahead of you.”

Marty walked around the table, lifted her out of the chair and wrapped her in his arms. She kissed him passionately and then pushed him away.

“Go,” she said. “We’ll see you when the job is done.”

Marty grabbed his coat off the hook, opened the door and headed for the garage. He hoped he wasn’t too late and that more people hadn’t died.

Chapter Thirty-Three

Mack Price landed on the runway at Yellowstone Regional Airport and taxied to the FBO. He stopped opposite the door and checked the sky, which was overcast and gray.

"We've got about five hours on the ground or we're gonna get stuck here."

Bax nodded as she pushed open the door and grabbed her backpack and her coat. "I'll call you if I'm delayed and you can get out of here before the snow arrives."

She climbed down from the wing and crunched across the frozen snow as she made her way to the door. She stopped at the desk and picked up the keys to the rental SUV, left the building and walked to the new GMC Tahoe. She slid in, started it and turned up the heater. She pulled up the directions she had used on her last trip and headed for the interstate.

Bax turned off the highway at the Nelson mailbox and pulled to a stop in the gravel lot. There was more snow on the ground than there had been just two days ago, and her boots made deep impressions in the snow as she walked to the door to the gun store.

Bax stepped up to the door and pushed the button. She held up her badge and ID and waited. The door clicked, and she pulled it open and walked into the store. She passed the shelves full of ammo and accessories and stepped up to the counter, where Caleb Nelson was waiting. He watched her as she approached.

"Didn't think I'd see you again, Agent Baxter," he said. "Thought I was clear about the Second Amendment."

Bax smiled at him. "You were quite clear," she said. "But that's not why I'm here."

He walked along the counter and stopped opposite her. She opened the phone in her hand and clicked on the death certificate. She turned the phone and showed him the screen. His smile disappeared, replaced by a frown.

"So what?" he asked.

"I'd like to know about your son and how he died," she said.

He turned and proceeded to the other end of the counter, where he stood motionless. He reached for the shelf above him and pulled down the picture Bax had noticed the first time she was there. He walked to Bax, stopped and laid the picture on the counter.

"He's not supposed to be dead," said Caleb. "They said he was drunk and drove off the road. Tyler never drank. He wouldn't."

"Tyler had been in college. Is it possible you didn't know everything about his life?"

"No," he said. "My boy didn't drink. He knew better."

"But his blood alcohol level was four times the normal limit. He must have had something to drink that night."

Caleb got red in the face. Tears formed in his eyes. "Tyler would never touch alcohol or drugs. He knew what could happen."

He could see that he wasn't convincing Bax. He reached into his pocket and pulled out a coin and dropped it onto the counter. Bax looked at it.

"Tyler wouldn't drink, because he saw me at my worst. I'm an alcoholic." He looked at Bax and wiped his eyes. "Been sober for eighteen years, but that doesn't erase all the terrible things I did when I drank. It almost cost me my life and my family."

"He's telling you the truth, Agent Baxter," said a voice down the counter.

Angela Nelson walked over, introduced herself and rested her hand on her husband's arm. She looked at Bax.

Angela was tall and thin, with long gray hair pulled back in a ponytail. She had bright blue eyes and wore a cross necklace.

"Tyler never drank," she said. "He saw how it affected Caleb and swore he would never drink. None of our kids drank. They put all their efforts into shooting competitions."

Bax slid the coin towards Caleb. "Tell me about the night Tyler died."

Caleb stepped away and composed himself. Angela took his place in front of Bax.

"We got a call from the Colorado State Patrol. It was just after dinner. They told us Tyler had been drinking and ran off a road that was under construction.

We were stunned, and we called our eldest, Jerry, to come watch the shop and we headed for Colorado. We had no idea he was in Ouray. We didn't know where Ouray was. It took us hours to get there. Caleb identified the body. He wouldn't let me see him. My son was crushed and broken, almost unrecognizable. We just sat in the car for a couple of hours and cried. When they called a week later, they told us about his blood alcohol level, and we told them they were mistaken. They didn't believe us." She stopped for a minute to catch her breath.

"Was Tyler working in Ouray?" asked Bax.

"We didn't know. We found out later that he was working undercover on the road project for some environmental group. We thought he was working at a ski resort."

"Do you know the name of the environmental group?" asked Bax.

"No," said Angela. She reached into her pocket and pulled out her phone. She swiped a couple of times and held up the phone.

"This arrived right after we buried Tyler." She pushed the replay button. A young female voice came over the speaker.

"Mrs. Nelson, my name is Rabbit. I was a friend of Tyler's. I just wanted to let you know Tyler didn't drink and die in the crash like they're saying. He went up to the construction trailer to confront them. The road they were building is illegal, and we had proof they were damaging the environment. Tyler was forced the alcohol and then he was beaten by the construction guys. They drove his car to where they were paving and ran it off the side of the mountain. I hope that helps. Tyler was good people, and we all liked him. He was a strong believer in the environment. I'll miss him."

The voice mail stopped, and Bax looked at Angela. "Did you try to locate this Rabbit?"

"Our lawyer tried," said Caleb. "Never found her. We called the state police investigator, but he told us that unless we had someone who could corroborate the message, there was nothing they could do."

"So, you have no idea what he was doing in Ouray. It sounds like he was investigating the roadwork. Any idea why?"

They both shook their heads. "We tried to sue the contractor and the resort, because the road belongs to the resort. A month ago, we lost our last appeal. No one cares why our son died."

"Can you forward that voice mail to me?" asked Bax.

Angela nodded. Bax handed her a business card, and she forwarded the message to Bax's email.

"Angela, how did Abigail respond to Tyler's death?" asked Bax.

Angela looked up at her. "She was sad and pissed off that no one cared. Why do you ask?"

"Your daughter is an ultra-long-range shooter," said Bax. "I see the trophies. Do you think she was pissed enough that she would take things into her own hands?"

Caleb got angry. "My daughter is an upstanding member of the community. If you think . . ."

Angela grabbed his arm, and he calmed down a little.

"You think our daughter had something to do with those shootings in Colorado?" she asked.

"We're looking at everything trying to make sense of the shootings," said Bax.

"Well, let's call her and ask her," said Angela. "She should be at the clinic." Before Bax could respond, Angela dialed the clinic number and put the phone on speaker.

"Cody West Large Animal Clinic, how can I help you?"

"Hi, Penny. It's Angela. Can I speak to Abigail for a minute?"

"Hi, Angela. I'm sorry, Abby's not here. Didn't she tell you?"

"Tell me what?" asked Angela.

"She left for vacation about a week ago. We don't expect her back until the weekend. I'm surprised she didn't tell you."

"Did she say where she was going?" asked Angela.

"No, ma'am. She arranged for Bill Turley to cover the clinic and said she needed to get away to clear her head."

Angela thanked her and disconnected the call. She looked at Caleb and then at Bax. "That's strange. She tells me everything."

"Was she aware that you lost your civil appeal?" asked Bax.

Caleb stepped back. "There's no way my little girl killed all those people over money."

"If I may?" asked Bax. "How much were you suing for?"

"Ten million dollars," said Caleb. "It wasn't about the money; it was about someone hurting our son."

"Can you give me your daughter's cell phone number?" asked Bax.

Angela opened her contact list, found the number and showed it to Bax, who entered it into her contact list.

"Are we in trouble?" asked Angela.

"I don't see why you would be," said Bax. "Where does Abigail live?"

"She lives behind the clinic," said Caleb.

"Do you have a key to her place?" asked Bax.

Caleb pulled a key ring off his belt and flipped through the keys. He found the one he was looking for, took it off the ring and handed it to Bax.

"I'd like one of you to lead me to the clinic and accompany me into the house. Would that be okay?"

"I guess," said Angela. "But I doubt you'll find anything. My daughter is not involved. I know my daughter." She stepped away and grabbed her coat from the closet.

Chapter Thirty-Four

Buck woke with a start, and it took him a minute to remember where he was. He knew one thing right away. He was too old to sleep in recliners. He stretched and worked the kinks out of his body. He noticed there were a lot more kinks to work out than there used to be, before the explosion that almost killed him. He shook his head to clear the cobwebs, walked to the kitchen and grabbed his first Coke of the day from the refrigerator. He took a big sip and sat next to Paul.

Paul looked up from his laptop. "Was gonna wake you last night, but you were out of it. You okay?"

"Yeah," said Buck. "Where's Bax?"

"Mack Price was available first thing. She left before the sun came up. Guess there's a big storm heading that way and he wanted to get in and out." He checked the time on his laptop monitor. "Should land about now."

"What are you working on?" asked Buck.

Before Paul could answer, Buck's phone chimed. He glanced at the number and pressed the green button.

"Good morning," he said.

The voice on the other end had a soft Southern accent. "Good morning, Deputy. I think I found what you were looking for."

"Can you hold for just a second, Harriet? I want to put you on speaker. I'm here with Paul Webber."

Buck switched the call over to speaker and set the phone on the table. "Okay, Harriet, please go ahead."

"Good morning, Agent Webber. As I was saying. I believe I found what you were looking for. Two years ago, a wrongful death lawsuit was filed against Bechtel Enterprises, the owner of the resort, by the family of Tyler Nelson. Also named in the suit was H and B Constructors, Inc. I did a little digging, and H and B is a joint venture company formed between Harrison Heavy Constructors, LLC, and Bechtel Unlimited, LLC. The contractor is based out of Denver. The suit was for ten million dollars. According to court records, the suit was dismissed, and the family appealed several times, and their final appeal was dismissed a month ago."

"So, the family is out of options?" asked Buck.

"It would appear so, but there's something else. I found a complaint filed with the EPA, by a group called the Colorado Conservation Alliance. The complaint alleges that the construction of a road between Ouray and the resort does not comply with the permit that was issued. The permit, according to the complaint, was issued for the construction of a two-lane road, but the developer is building a four-lane road. It also alleges that the contractor has destroyed wetlands they were required to go around. Several people were signatories on the complaint, but one of them was Tyler Nelson. I am forwarding both the lawsuit and the complaint to your investigation file."

"This is great, Harriet. Anything fishy about the contractor?" asked Buck. He could hear keys clicking in the background.

"This is interesting," said Harriet. "Several members of his crew were arrested for attacking a group of people who were picketing one of his projects. The folks were hurt, but all the charges were dropped."

"Sounds like the owner has a guardian angel," said Buck.

"It does," said Harriet. "He has been sued nine times for various infractions, and all have been dismissed. But this might help. Brian Harrison, the owner of the construction company, has an outstanding warrant. He was involved in an altercation on one of his jobs. The job was on a military base in Colorado, and as such the assault became federal. It doesn't look like it was ever followed up on. I am forwarding the warrant. The victim of the assault is a Colorado resident. I am sending a copy of the incident report."

She gave Buck a minute to look at the warrant and the report. Buck looked at the name and phone number of the guy who had been assaulted.

"Deputy, will you be needing a team?" she asked.

Buck thought for a minute. "Yes. Is Vicky's team available?" Keys clicking in the background.

"I have them on standby. Will you coordinate, or shall I?" she asked.

"I'll coordinate. And Harriet, thanks."

"Anytime, Deputy. Call if you need anything else."

The call disconnected, and Paul looked up from his laptop. "You want me to run a background check on this Harrison guy? Sounds like a real peach."

Buck nodded and entered the phone number in his phone. He heard the phone ringing, and then an older, deep voice answered.

"Hello," said the voice.

"James Gladstone?" asked Buck.

"Yeah. Who's this?"

"Sir, my name is Buck Taylor," he began, his tone measured but polite. "I'm an agent with the Colorado Bureau of Investigation. I'm following up on an incident report you filed while you were working at Fort Carson. The report says you were involved in a worksite altercation there about two years back, with a man named Brian Harrison."

There was a pause. Buck heard the faint crinkle of a recliner, the distant clattering of a television. "Fort Carson? That was a while ago," the old man grunted. His voice was dry and unimpressed. "You know, I figured the Feds would have let that one drop. They didn't much care when I filed the report."

Buck tried again: "I'm interested in hearing your side of the story, sir. We'd like to get a clear picture of what happened, who was involved, and whether this should've been followed up sooner."

There was another pause, longer this time, and Buck wondered if the man was weighing whether to hang up.

"You really with the CBI?" Gladstone asked. Buck could hear the skepticism—a lifetime of disappointment in bureaucracy echoed in those gravelly syllables.

"I can provide you with my ID number and a direct

line to CBI if needed," Buck offered. "But right now, it would help if you could walk me through what happened at that job."

Gladstone let out a slow, wheezing breath that Buck guessed was equal parts resignation and irritation. "Harrison's a hothead. Hired my crew to haul and prep a bunch of prefab panels, but he's a screamer. Cusses out anyone who isn't moving fast enough. I asked him to back off my guys. Two of his guys jumped me a little later. Beat the shit out of me right there in the open. Broke my glasses and put me on the ground."

Buck scribbled on his notepad, marking the details. "And you reported this to the military police on base?"

"Same afternoon," Gladstone said, clipped. "They took my statement, but no one ever bothered to call me after. Insurance paid out for my medical. I assumed the army handled the rest. When nothing came of it, I assumed Harrison had some highly placed friends and decided not to pursue it."

Buck nodded, even though the man on the other end couldn't see. "Did you know Harrison before that job?"

"Word gets around," Gladstone replied. "He cycles through labor like motor oil. Guys take a few paychecks and quit as soon as they can. All except the two guys who jumped me. I got the impression they were more like his enforcers. They'd been with him a long time. Why are you looking into this now?"

"We're looking into another incident that sounds similar involving Harrison, and we found your initial statement," said Buck. "There's a federal warrant out for Harrison's arrest, but it's old. Looks like it was never followed up on, but we're following up now."

There was a long sigh, then, "Two years late, but I guess better late than never."

"You said Harrison didn't engage with you, but his two enforcers did?" asked Buck.

"Yep. Used to call them Mutt and Jeff. Not sure if you're old enough to remember them? Given names are Branch Wilhite and Clevon Dawson. Both are mean as a snake."

"How come their names didn't make it into the statement, only Harrison's?"

There was silence on the phone. "Not sure. Their names were in the statement I gave the MPs. I told them that Harrison started the attack, but these two did the most damage. Like I said. Harrison seemed to have a lot of pull. Maybe he figured he'd be better off if they were never part of anything legal. I still have a copy of the statement."

"Sir, you should have my number on your screen. Can you take a picture of the statement and text it to me?"

"Sure can. It'll take me a minute to find it, but soon as I do, I'll send it."

"Thank you, sir," said Buck. "I'll let you know if anything comes of this."

Buck disconnected the call and looked at Paul.

"Background all three of them," said Buck. "I'll coordinate the arrest with the director and see if he can get me a chopper. I'm gonna meet the sheriff and talk to Bechtel."

Buck's phone chimed, and he opened the text. He forwarded the image to Harriet and in the text message asked her to get a new warrant with all three names.

He grabbed his coat and raced out the door. He had a feeling things were coming to a head. He slid into his Jeep and headed for the resort to meet the sheriff for breakfast. As he drove down the highway, his phone rang. He clicked the button on the console.

"Hey, Bax. What's up?"

"Hi, Buck," said Bax. "I found out something interesting. The family of Tyler Nelson has been trying to sue Bechtel and his contractor for years."

"We just found that out," interrupted Buck. "The final appeal was dismissed last month."

"Right," said Bax. "Tyler's mother has a recording of a phone message. Someone claimed that Tyler went to confront the contractor over environmental concerns and that he was beaten, force-fed alcohol, put in his car and run off the road. Tyler never drank, yet his BAL was off the charts. He was working for some environmental group. Nothing happened as a criminal matter, so the family sued for wrongful death. They lost their last appeal, and I think that's when his sister took matters into her own hands. I think Abigail Nelson, Tyler's sister, is the shooter. I'm on my way to her house along with her mother. She left town for a two-week vacation but never let her folks know. I called the Cody police, and I'm meeting one of their detectives and a forensic team at the house."

Buck gave her a quick debrief on the information and the documents Harriet had provided, and Bax said she would look at the suits and the complaint once she settled into a hotel.

"Good work, Bax. Did the mom agree to a search of the residence?"

"Yeah," said Bax. "She says there's no way her daughter is involved and wants to get her off my list. I won't be back tonight. I sent Mack home before the big storm hits. I might be here for a couple of days, depending on the weather."

"No worries, Bax. Do what you have to do. Let me know if you find anything interesting."

Buck hung up and hit the number one speed-dial button. The director answered right away.

"Hey, Buck. What's going on?"

"Morning, sir," said Buck. "Can you get me a chopper today? I need to coordinate an arrest in Denver with a team from the marshals."

"Who are we arresting?" asked the director.

"The contractor building the road up here and two guys who work for him. He has an outstanding warrant for an assault on a military base here in Colorado, but the Feds never followed up with an arrest. We're gonna help them out."

"What do we think he did, and how does it relate to the sniper?"

"We think that Tyler Nelson was working with an environmental group and went to confront the contractors. He died afterwards in a one-car accident on the road they were building, which was closed."

"You think the contractor murdered him and made it look like an accident?" asked the director.

"Yes, sir," said Buck. "The outstanding warrant gives us a way in. We think this all started because of Tyler's death and the family losing their appeal of the suit."

"Is this sister that good? She has no military experience," asked the director.

"Yes, sir, she is that good," said Buck.

"Okay, Buck. Let me work on the chopper. Denver is expecting snow later today, but it won't be a lot. Let me know what else you need, and I'll have it ready when you get here."

The director disconnected, and Buck stopped the car. He slid out of his Jeep and went looking for the sheriff.

Chapter Thirty-Five

Bax turned at the sign for the large animal clinic and followed Angela's SUV around the side of the building to the residence in the back. They parked next to a van with the Cody Police Department logo on the door and the words CRIME SCENE stenciled on the side. Two Tyvek-clad techs were pulling gear out of the back. Bax slid out of her rental SUV just as a Ford Explorer pulled in and parked next to her. An older Hispanic woman slid out of the Explorer and approached Bax, who was dragging her backpack out of the rental. Bax turned and faced her.

"Detective Gloria Villareal," she said as she reached out her hand.

Bax shook her hand. "Ashley Baxter, but just call me Bax. Nice to meet you." Bax zipped up her coat and noticed the snow intensifying.

"Want to fill me in on what we're doing here?" asked Villareal.

"Yeah, but let's get out of the snow." Bax slung her backpack over her shoulder, and the two women followed Angela to the door, followed by the two forensic techs. Bax stuck the key in the lock and pushed open the door, and they stepped into the foyer.

They took off their coats and placed them on the empty kitchen table just to the left of the door, and Bax introduced Angela Nelson.

Bax explained the plan. "Mrs. Nelson has given us permission to search this residence. This is the home of her daughter Dr. Abigail Nelson, a registered veterinarian. Mrs. Nelson and her husband are part owners of the property. I'm investigating the deaths of several people in Hinsdale County, Colorado, and we believe that Abigail Nelson might be involved in those shooting deaths. To further the investigation, we will look for anything that might lead us to either confirm or reject her involvement."

Detective Villareal stepped forward. She was of medium height and a little overweight, with black hair pulled back in a double braid. She wore jeans and a flannel shirt. "So, we are looking for anything that might show involvement in a gun crime. Ms. Nelson has a reputation around here and is well known for her shooting ability. We may encounter a lot of weapons and gun-related items. Can you be more specific?" she asked.

Bax smiled. "If she is involved in the shootings, then the weapon and ammunition will be with her. I'm looking for anything else that might point to her involvement. Hopefully, we'll know it when we see it. So, let's look. Angela, please stay in the kitchen and don't wander around without one of us with you."

They all put on nitrile gloves and Tyvek booties and spread out. The house was warm and comfortable and larger than it appeared from the outside. The spacious living room and kitchen formed a great room with a large eating area off the kitchen. There was a wood-burning fireplace on one wall, and the furniture looked lived in.

As they walked through the house, Bax looked at the three bedrooms and two bathrooms. One bedroom was an office, so Bax started there. She opened drawers and looked in cabinets, but most of the paperwork she found was related to the clinic. There was no laptop or phone, which she didn't find unusual. She was going through a file cabinet when Detective Villareal called to her. Bax left the office and walked down the hall. Villareal was standing in front of two doors. One she held open, and it led to the garage. She closed that door and pointed to the next door.

"Looks like it might be a basement door, but it's locked," she said.

Bax called for Angela, who came down the hall towards them.

"Angela, do you have a key for this door?" she asked.

"That goes to the basement. It's never locked," she said.

Bax turned towards the door, pulled a small pouch out of her backpack, opened it and pulled out two lockpicks. She went to work on the lock, and in a few seconds, the door was unlocked. She pushed the door open and flipped on the switch next to it. The small landing led to the steps, and she could see that the entire basement was lit. She asked Angela to remain at the top of the stairs, and she and Villareal started down.

The basement was finished and decorated, but it was the office area that caused Bax and Villareal to stop in their tracks. On the wall over the desk was an enlarged aerial view of the resort. Bax and Villareal walked closer. Each building in the picture was marked with a number, and as Bax looked, she saw the pattern.

The numbers corresponded to the attack locations for each day.

"Bax, check this out," said Villareal. She was standing next to a flat door that was propped up on two sawhorses. On the table, laid out by their corresponding numbers, were the blueprints for each building. Bax stared.

"I'd say she was planning this for a long time," said Villareal.

She pulled out a folded paper and unfolded it on the table. It was a large hand-drawn map of the resort area, but the striking thing was all the vector marks. Abigail Nelson had laid out all the shooting lanes to the various target points, including up and down angles and distances. She had plotted each kill location with precision.

One of the forensic techs had entered the basement and called them over to a wall shelf and counter on the other side of the room. The counter was covered with reloading equipment and a small electric kiln. Bax pulled a nitrile glove out of her pocket and picked up a cartridge blank with several grooves cut into the tip.

"I think these are titanium. That's what our State Crime Lab found in the bullet collected at the scene," said Bax.

"They look like hollow points," said the tech.

Bax pointed to the kiln. "We were told that when titanium is heated to a certain temperature, it becomes fragile. The grooves help it come apart in lots of tiny pieces."

"Frangible rounds," said Villareal. "Hard as hell to do any kind of analysis on."

She looked at the shelf, reached for a clear plastic box and stopped. She pulled back her hand.

"Those are incendiary rounds," she said. "The military marks theirs with red tips so they're not mistaken for normal rounds. This girl's got some skills. Titanium bullets and incendiary rounds. Holy shit."

Bax and Villareal turned when they heard a gasp from behind them. Angela had come down the stairs and was staring at the map on the wall and the stacks of blueprints. She raised her hand to her mouth and shuddered.

"Oh my god," she said. She looked at Bax. "There must be some kind of mistake. Abby wouldn't be involved in something like this." She turned away. "Her father never taught her how to reload. How did she learn all this?" She looked at Bax, pleading for an answer, but Bax didn't have one.

Bax looked at the two techs. "Okay, this space is our focus. Pictures, samples, fingerprints, DNA. We need to see if she's working alone or if she had help. Please send everything by secure courier to the Colorado State Crime Lab. I'll let them know it's coming."

"If the weather's as bad as expected, we may not get this stuff sent for a day or two," said the taller tech.

"Understood," said Bax. "In the meantime, I need to take as many photographs as I can and get them to my team."

While the techs went to work, Villareal followed Bax to the map table. Bax looked at the map with the shooting lanes laid out and took several pictures. She uploaded them to the investigation file on her phone and then looked at the map. Several red circles appeared behind some of the buildings, and she wondered what they represented. She picked up a set of blueprints and laid them on the table.

She opened the prints, page by page, and looked for something that might correspond to the circles. She found what she was looking for on the gas service plan. Circled with the same red marker was the gas valve that served the building. She looked at it for a minute.

"Find something?" asked Villareal.

"Fuck," she said. "I think she's going to do something to the gas valves in the buildings. She's gonna burn the whole resort to the ground."

One tech opened a metal cabinet that was standing against the wall and gasped. "Shit, we're gonna need the bomb squad," she said.

Bax and Villareal hustled over and stood next to the tech. Inside the cabinet were several paper-wrapped bundles of plastic explosives. Bax stepped up to the second cabinet and opened the door. On the bottom shelf was a box marked DIGITAL TIMERS. Bax flipped open the cover and looked inside.

"This box is half empty," she said. "Okay, we need to clear out of here right now. Don't touch anything else." Angela was standing in the middle of the room. She was pale and looked numb. Bax took her by the arm and escorted her up the stairs. She walked her to the kitchen.

"Are you okay to drive?" asked Bax.

Angela nodded.

"Okay. I need you to go back home and wait with Caleb. This is going to take hours to process, and you can't be here. I'll keep you posted on what we find."

Angela picked up her coat, put it on and walked out the door towards her car. She slid in and pulled out her phone. She dialed the number and waited for the voice mail announcement to end.

"Abby, I have no idea what you're involved with, but the cops are at your house, and they found all kinds of stuff in the basement. What the hell is going on? Call me."

The snow was falling for real, and there was already an inch on the ground. Bax watched Angela make a call and then drive away. She wondered how much Abigail's parents knew.

"Poor woman," said Villareal. "I guess you don't always know your own kids. I've called for bomb disposal. That's the highway patrol, and in this weather, it could be a while. We'll all stay up here. Right now, the plastic is safe, so we should be all right. I need to call my chief and fill him in. I'm going to ask for another unit. We'll need to close the clinic and evacuate the staff."

"Thanks," said Bax. "Sorry to screw up your day."

Villareal laughed. "Pays all the same, so it's all good."

Bax pulled out her phone and dialed Buck.

Chapter Thirty-Six

Buck found the sheriff in the condo building talking with the state patrol captain. They had completed the door-to-door and had found nothing suspicious. Buck told the captain to let some of his guys crash but to keep up the patrols around the plaza and the ski area. He and the sheriff walked across the empty parking lot to Bechtel's office building. They stepped into the lobby and unzipped their coats. The lobby was a lot warmer than it was outside. There was no one at the reception desk, so they walked down the hall and knocked on Bechtel's door.

"Come in," said a voice behind the door.

Buck pushed open the door, and they walked into the office. Bechtel was standing at a large window behind his desk that looked over the empty lot. He turned and faced the men. His left arm was in a sling, and he looked like he had aged several years since the first time Buck saw him in the plaza.

"Best snow in years, and no one is here. This is a fucking nightmare, and I'm losing money every day," said Bechtel.

"You don't move away from that window, you might not live to see the next snowfall," said Buck.

Bechtel sneered at him. "You said that if she wanted to kill me, she would have done it the other day, so fuck off."

Buck stepped up to the desk. "Tell us about the demand letter you received."

Bechtel looked at Buck. "Some fucking whacko trying to drive the final nail into my coffin. It's been a week. What the fuck are you doing to catch this person? I pay taxes, so you have a goddamn job. When the hell are you going to do it?"

"So, you have no idea about any accident on your property and a ten-million-dollar lawsuit that was filed against you and your contractor?"

Bechtel stared daggers at Buck. "I have lawyers and accountants to handle that shit. At least they do their jobs."

"And your lawyers and accountants wouldn't tell you about something as significant as a ten-million-dollar suit. Doesn't that strike you as a little irresponsible?" asked Buck.

Bechtel smiled.

"What do you know about the young man whose car went off the road and crashed on the road you're building?" asked Buck.

Bechtel walked to the credenza and poured himself a glass of something clear. He swallowed it in one gulp and poured another. He walked back to the desk and sat down.

"The contractor is in charge of the road-building project. Not me. If you have a complaint, go talk to them and leave me the fuck alone."

Buck smiled. "Oh, I intend to talk to your contractor, but right now I'd like to understand why you insist on lying to us."

"If you have proof," said Bechtel, "that I've done

anything wrong, either show it to me or get the fuck out of my office. And don't think I'll forget this come election time, Drucker."

"How are you going to respond to the demand letter?" asked Buck.

Bechtel laughed. "I'm not. I don't deal with terrorists. It's your job to protect me and my investment, so you send them ten million dollars. They won't get a dime out of me."

Buck's phone chimed, but he let the call go to voice mail.

"Aren't you worried about what will happen if you ignore the letter?" asked the sheriff.

"Fuck no," said Bechtel. "I wasn't handed my fortune. I started working in a factory until I eventually bought the factory and then started developing land. You think a demand letter like that scares me? Fuck, you never dealt with the mob and the cartels. I could tell you stories that will make your hair stand on end."

Buck smiled. "You're a real tough guy, huh?"

Buck stepped around the desk and looked out the window. "What are you going to do about all those empty parking spaces, tough guy?"

Buck turned and walked to the door, followed by the sheriff. He opened the door, stopped and faced Bechtel.

"I'm going to talk to your contractor, tough guy, and if I get the slightest inkling that you were involved in the death of that young man, I'll be back, and then we'll see how tough you are."

Buck slammed the door behind them as they walked to the lobby.

"A little rough on the old boy," said the sheriff.

"Yeah," said Buck with a smile. "One thing I can't stand is rich assholes who think the world owes them a living."

Buck pulled out his phone and called Bax.

"Hey, Buck."

"Hiya, Bax. What's up?"

"We found a workspace in Abigail Nelson's house filled with maps and blueprints of the resort. We also found plastic explosives and digital timers. Buck, she's our sniper."

"That was a good catch on your part. Now, all we have to do is find her," said Buck.

"We may have a bigger problem. I'm sending you a picture of the map."

Buck's phone chimed, and he opened the attachment and set his phone on the reception desk so the sheriff could see what he was looking at.

"Okay, Bax. I've got the map open, and Mike and I are looking at it. What are we looking for?"

"See those red circles on some of the buildings?"

Buck pulled his reading glasses out of his jacket pocket and put them on. He enlarged the image and leaned towards the map, and Mike pointed to the circles.

"Okay, we see them," he said.

"In comparing those to the blueprints, where we also found red circles on one page, those circles represent the gas valves for the buildings. If I'm right, Nelson is planning to use the explosives and blow up the valves. I think she wants to burn the whole place to the ground."

"Fuck," said the sheriff.

"Yeah," agreed Buck. "Okay, Bax. We'll deal with those right away. What are your plans?"

"I may be here for a while. The Wyoming Highway Patrol bomb squad is on the way, but the weather may drag out their arrival time. It's snowing like crazy, and I won't be able to get out of here until after the storm stops. We also have a few more forensic folks coming. Buck, Abigail Nelson was prepared to go to war against Bechtel, and she's not done yet."

"Well, we just left Bechtel, and he's telling us he knows nothing about an accident on his road project or a lawsuit. I think he's full of shit. I'll talk to his contractor later today. In the meantime, we'll let you go so we can figure out what to do about the explosives."

"Okay, Buck. Good luck."

The call disconnected, and Buck scanned his text messages and opened one from the director. He checked his watch.

"I've got two hours until the chopper gets here." He walked around the desk and looked across the lot.

"Can you call John Finch and see if he can meet us at the gas valve for the plaza building?" asked Buck.

"What are you thinking?" asked the sheriff.

"Unless we're already too late, we need to see if we can seal up those rooms. Have John bring the head of maintenance with him."

Buck was zipping his coat when his phone chimed with an incoming call. Buck checked the number and hit the green button.

"Buck, how the hell are you?" asked Vicky Dorsett. Vicky led a team of door kickers for the U.S. Marshals Service. Buck had worked with her team on several occasions and was glad when Harriet told him that her team was available today.

"I'm good, Vicky. Did Harriet fill you in?"

"Yeah. We're sitting on your guy's office, and I've got another team sitting on his house. What'd this guy do?"

"We don't know if he did anything yet, but he may have been involved in the death of a young man, which has led his sister to attack a ski resort."

"The one up by Lake City?" asked Vicky. "Saw the story on the news. Do we have a warrant?"

"Yeah, but it's an old warrant from a beef he got into on a military base he was working on."

"Ah, that's why it's federal. Okay. Are you expecting trouble? Why not just ask him to come in for a chat?" asked Vicky.

"According to sources, he's not the most cooperative guy around, and neither is his partner, who I just left and who is probably on the phone right now, warning him. I came on a little strong.”

Vicky laughed. “Buck Taylor, Mr. Patience, coming on strong. Would have loved to have seen that. Okay. What do you need from us?”

“Keep an eye on him. I’m texting you the warrant. If he rabbits, grab him. Otherwise, stay loose until I get there. My chopper will be here in a little over an hour, and I’ll try to set down somewhere close to you. Drop me a pin so I know where you are.”

“What’s our level of danger?” asked Vicky.

“If our info is correct, he was involved in beating a young man to death and staging an accident,” said Buck.

“What did this guy uncover that led to the beating?” asked Vicky.

“That’s what I need to find out. Unless things change on the ground, plan to go in hard.”

“Roger that,” said Vicky.

Buck and the sheriff pushed through the door and headed towards the main plaza building.

Chapter Thirty-Seven

Buck and the sheriff met John Finch, the security director for the resort, at the main plaza building. They kept looking around and did not look happy to be standing in the open. Buck pulled out his phone, opened the map that Bax sent him and showed it to John. He didn't tell him that the sniper had given them a deadline before the next attack and that they were safe for now.

"The red circles on this map correspond to red circles on the blueprints for those buildings. They show gas service entrances. We need to look at a couple of these."

"No problem," said John. "Follow me."

He led the way through a narrow alley between two buildings, and they came out on the back side of the first building on the map. John stopped at a nondescript door, pulled out a key and unlocked it. Buck stopped him before he pulled open the door.

"Let me look. We can't be too careful," he said.

Buck opened the door enough to get his flashlight beam in, and he looked around the edges of the frame. There were no obvious trip wires, so he pulled the door open further. He reached around and flipped on the light. He scanned the area and opened the door all the way. They stepped into the room.

The valve room was a typical industrial space containing a large gas line coming out of the floor and branching off into several smaller pipes that fed various spaces in the building. Buck noted that the room was clean enough to eat off the floor.

"This is the main gas for this building?" asked Buck as he looked around the valve.

"Yeah," said John. "Each building has its own gas supply. Doesn't look like anyone has been here or tampered with the valve in any way."

Buck stepped back over to the door. He noted that the door and frame were metal.

"John, can we weld these doors shut?" asked Buck.

"You want to keep the sniper out?"

"That's what I'm thinking. Might not stop her, but it might slow her down," said Buck.

The sheriff's radio crackled. "Kevin to the sheriff." The sheriff keyed his mic. "Go ahead, Kevin."

"Sheriff, I got a guy at the main entrance says he needs to speak with Agent Taylor?"

The sheriff looked at Buck. "This fella got a name?" asked the sheriff.

"Says his name is Marty Whitcomb."

Buck nodded. "Have him meet us out front," said Buck.

The sheriff relayed the message, and the group turned off the lights and exited the room. They headed back to the plaza.

An older-model pickup truck pulled into the closest parking space, and Marty Whitcomb slid out and headed towards the group. He walked up and reached out his hand.

"Agent Taylor. I was thinking about our conversation yesterday, and I'd like to see if I can help."

Buck shook his hand and introduced him to the sheriff and John Finch.

"What were you thinking?" asked Buck.

"Well. You've got a sniper problem, and even though I'm a little rusty, I'm still one of the best there is, and I'd like to see if I can spot the sniper and take him out before he causes any more harm."

"Well," said Buck. "A few things have changed since we spoke. We've discovered the identity of the sniper. Young gal named Abigail Nelson."

"Caleb's daughter?" asked Marty.

"Yeah. We found a lot of incriminating evidence at her house in Wyoming."

"What's her beef?" asked Marty.

"It looks like the family sued the resort, the owner and the contractor for the wrongful death of her brother, and the case just lost its final appeal. The brother died in a single-vehicle accident on a road being built between Ouray and the resort. The family disagreed with the state patrol accident report."

"Shit," said Marty. "The daughter is one of the best long-distance shooters in the country. Won all kinds of awards and beat out some incredible snipers. We need to put an end to this."

Buck thought about it for a minute. He didn't like

the idea of involving a civilian, but he also knew that if they were going to stop the sniper, Marty might be their best choice.

"Sheriff, it might be a good idea to have our own sniper, but I don't want to use a civilian. You think you could deputize Marty?"

The sheriff smiled. "I think we can make that happen. We'll head back to the office, and I'll get him papered up and issued a badge. First, I think we should finish looking at the rest of the valve rooms."

"We'll catch up," said Buck. "I'll give Marty the lay of the land."

The sheriff and John turned and walked towards the next building, and Buck turned to Marty. "I don't want to make it too obvious, so let's keep this debrief casual. Each time the sniper was active, we found a nest on that ridge on the other side of the resort. I would assume the next attack will come from there as well. Without looking around too much, give me your thoughts."

Marty stole quick glances around the area. They walked towards the ski lift area, and Marty spent some time estimating distances and angles. He led Buck back to the plaza, and they stepped into the Mexican restaurant. The place was empty, so they grabbed a table and sat.

The owner of the restaurant started towards them, and Buck waved him off. He headed back to the kitchen.

"I think the best spot for a clear view is on the ridge

behind this building about halfway towards the ski area. I can come through the woods off the main road and find a suitable spot with some good cover. The best thing would be for me to set up as soon as I'm done with the sheriff. We might be too late already. If I were the sniper, I would already be in position, but if I can stay hidden, we might be okay."

"What do you need from us?" asked Buck.

"Nothing. I've got my gear in the truck. I'll get the sheriff to drop me off on the road, and I'll come over the ridge. If he has a spare radio, that would be helpful."

"Are you sure you want to do this?" asked Buck.

Marty was silent for a minute. "Melody and I had a long talk last night, and she thinks this is what's been missing from my life. A sense of purpose. This might just give me that purpose."

"Okay, Marty. Let's find the sheriff and get you that badge."

Buck pulled up the map on his phone, and they headed for the next building. They caught up with the sheriff at the fourth building on the list.

"All good?" asked Buck.

"So far," said Finch. "I've got one of my guys coming down with a portable welder, and he'll start welding the doors shut."

"Excellent," said Buck.

"Sheriff, I need to meet my ride to Denver," said Buck. "I'll leave Marty in your hands."

Buck heard a chopper coming up the valley. He shook hands all around and ran to his Jeep to grab his backpack and ballistic vest. The chopper, owned by the state patrol, landed. Buck ran towards it, climbed aboard and settled back for the ride. He hated helicopters, but this one was much more comfortable than a military bird. He put on the headset, pulled up his text messages and showed the pilot the location pin Vicky had sent him. The pilot nodded, and Buck tapped out a text to Vicky to let her know he was in the air.

Chapter Thirty-Eight

Marty slipped into his white camo gear and pulled his rifle from the back of his SUV. He assembled the rifle and added extra magazines to his ballistic vest under his white coat. Climbing into the passenger seat of the waiting cruiser, he watched the sheriff steer onto the snow-packed road towards the mountain resort.

After ten minutes, he checked the coordinates he had written on his folded map and asked the sheriff to pull over. The sheriff handed him a radio, and he set the channel and placed the earbuds in his ears. He keyed the mic and did a radio check with the dispatcher. He responded and placed the radio in his white backpack. He shook hands with the sheriff.

"I'll check in every hour," he said.

"Good luck," said the sheriff.

Marty slid out of the SUV, slapped a magazine into the rifle and disappeared into the forest. The sheriff continued to the resort.

Marty took his time working his way over the ridge. He crested the ridge, pulled out his handheld GPS under the dying light of dusk and confirmed his bearing: the resort lay half a mile below, nestled in a valley of slate-gray rooftops and drifting smoke.

He was on a good line to reach his destination, but from this point on stealth was required. He looked down on the resort village below and checked his time. He was a little behind his schedule, but he was feeling good. He slung his rifle over his shoulder and, staying low, crawled towards the sniper nest he had pinpointed earlier.

The sun was low in the sky, and he was exhausted by the time he reached the nest. He sat against the rock outcropping and pulled an energy bar and a bottle of water from his backpack. He devoured the energy bar and drank most of the bottle of water. From this point on, he would move as little as possible, if at all.

He pulled his white rubber-coated binoculars and a spotting scope out of his backpack and set them in an opening between two boulders. Lying prone, he slid the rifle into the opening and settled in. Once he was comfortable, he pulled his hood over his head and slid the mask over his face. He disappeared into the drifting snow.

He used his white binoculars to scan the resort below, and he spotted one of the maintenance men welding the door to one of the valve rooms—sparks flying from his welding torch, the arc's blue light dancing on the metal seam. Then Marty pivoted his viewfinder to the distant ridge on the resort's far side, sweeping left to right, searching for anything that didn't belong. Satisfied there was no immediate threat, he let the twilight settle around him.

It wasn't long after full dark that something slid into his peripheral vision. He reached for the binoculars and scanned the area. He was about to put them down when a shadow crossed his field of vision. He shifted his line of sight and spotted a dark-clad figure moving through the trees. He watched as the figure approached the valve room door but lost the shadow in the trees.

Marty could make out a small beam of light through some openings in the trees but was too far away to do anything. The beam of light went out, and the shadow raced into the trees. Marty keyed his mic and kept his voice low.

"Marty to the sheriff."

"Go ahead, Marty."

"You got someone checking the welds on the valve room doors?" he asked.

"Could be one of the maintenance guys. Why?"

"Just spotted someone by the valve room to the left of my position. Couldn't see what they were doing because the line of sight was blocked. Can you get someone to check? But be careful."

"Will do, Marty," said the sheriff.

Marty set down the radio and scanned the parking area beyond the building. Nothing was moving, so he settled in again and waited.

Hours passed. The cold deepened. Then, a split-second flash flickered among the trees beyond the lot. It lasted a second, but Marty's senses kicked into high gear. He focused the spotting scope on the area where he saw the flash and waited.

Twenty minutes after the flash, he spotted a dark shadow where there shouldn't have been one. It appeared in an area he had just scanned a few minutes before. He pulled his eyes from the scope and rubbed his face. It had been a lot of years since the last time he spent this much time looking through a scope, and he wondered how badly the time off had affected his skills. He refocused on the rock outcropping, but the shadow was gone.

To be safe, Marty marked the spot. He couldn't risk using a laser range finder for fear that the sniper would see the red light, so he used his experience and his rifle scope to get an approximate range. It was a tough job in the dark.

He peered through the rifle's reticle, gauged the distance against the known height of a flagpole in the plaza and watched the flag to estimate the wind. In the dim light, he jotted quick notes in his cloth-covered notebook and ran ballistic calculations in his head: bullet drop, wind drift, air density. He adjusted the scope. He wasn't sure if he had seen the sniper or not, but at least he had a place to start.

The snow was increasing, but the wind had stayed the same. He felt comfortable that unless conditions changed, his calculations were solid. He kept his eye glued to the scope. He spotted movement heading towards the valve room door and aimed his scope towards the door. The trees blocked his view.

"Marty to sheriff."

"Go, Marty."

"I've got movement again near the valve room door," said Marty.

"Yeah. That would be me," came the response. "Our friend left us a couple of surprises. The welds worked, but she left a bomb next to each door. They would have made a mess and might have had the same effect as if she had gotten inside. Who knows? I can't wait for the bomb squad, so I'm taking each package to a secure location, so if they go off they'll cause minimal damage. The one I removed was set to go off at ten A.M."

"Great. That gives us a timeline," said Marty. "I think the sniper is in position on the opposite ridge. I am sending you estimated coordinates if you want to flank her."

"Thanks, Marty. Stay frosty."

Marty slid the radio deeper into his coat to keep the batteries warm and focused his riflescope on the nest on the opposite ridge. Now it was all a waiting game.

Chapter Thirty-Nine

This lock should be a piece of cake. You would think a resort like this would have better locks on sensitive areas like gas valve rooms. Pretty fucking stupid. Just one more click. There we go.

Why the hell won't the door open? Shit. Someone welded the door shut. What the hell. Why would they do that unless they knew what my plans were? But that's not possible. No one knows but me. Unless, shit. How the hell did they figure out who I am?

They would have had to search my house to find the information. I knew I should have gotten rid of all that paperwork before I left the house. But that must mean they've talked to my parents. If they do anything to my parents, I will make their lives a living hell.

Hah, they think they're so smart welding the doors shut. That's okay. I've got enough plastic explosive in each package to blow through the door and still rupture the pipes. They thought this would slow me down. They couldn't be more wrong. I'll put the package against the door, and when these go off, they won't know what hit them.

An icy shiver just ran down my spine. I feel like someone's watching me, but there's no one around. I'm just spooked because the rules of the game have changed. I'm no longer an unknown hunter. But now that they know who I am, they know what I'm capable of. They've seen all the long-range shooting trophies in my dad's shop. That's good. It will put an extra layer of fear into them, knowing that I can kill them from anyplace in the valley and there isn't a thing they can do about it. Advantage me. Scared people do stupid things. I don't. This is going to make the hunt more challenging, but I'm almost finished. Tomorrow morning, this will all end. And no matter how it ends, I win. I know Tyler will watch over me, but no matter what, I know he will be proud of me, and that's all that matters.

I need to get the rest of these packages placed and then head for the mountain. I'm gonna have the best seat in the house for the finale, and the entire world will know what these people did to my brother and my family.

Chapter Forty

The chopper landed in a small parking lot about a mile from the offices of Harrison Heavy Constructors, LLC, the contractor who was building the road for Clive Bechtel.

Vicky Dorsett slid out of the waiting black SUV. She was five foot seven and had a muscular physique, which was accented by the black T-shirt she wore. She had short black hair and dark eyes. Vicky was the leader of a team of U.S. Marshals Service door kickers. The door kickers were exactly what they sounded like. They were the people who kicked in doors when an arrest was imminent. Buck had worked with Vicky and her team several times, and he appreciated their professionalism and skills.

Buck climbed out of the chopper, ducked under the spinning blades and met Vicky as she stood next to the SUV. They shook hands.

"Buck," she said. "Good to see you again. How are you doing? All healed up?"

Buck laughed. "After spending two hours in the chopper, I think I should have rested up some more. Otherwise, I'm doing okay."

Buck looked in the SUV. "Where's the rest of the team?"

"We had to split up, because we weren't sure if Harrison was at home or at his office. So, my guys are sitting on the house. I've got a second team sitting on the office. They spotted Harrison entering the office about twenty minutes ago. I just texted Ari to meet us at the office."

Buck nodded, and they slid into the SUV. Vicky drove onto the street. "How do you want to handle this?" she asked.

Buck thought for a minute. "I like to try a soft approach. See if he'd be willing to talk to me. Not knowing how many guys are with him and how they'll respond, we might need to escalate into something more forceful."

"You know he's gonna bitch that the warrant is old and was taken care of," she said. "And his lawyer will stop him from having any conversation about what happened on the road since it's not included in the warrant."

"Yeah, I know. This is going to get hairy," said Buck. "It's our only play. I sent Harriet some information and asked her to update the warrant for two more of his crew."

Buck opened his phone to the background information Paul had pulled and showed her the pictures.

She looked up. "Nasty-looking fuckers," she said. She forwarded the information to her team and handed Buck back his phone.

"Well, let's go see if they're at the office with Harrison," she said.

Vicky pulled the SUV to a stop alongside a second black SUV, posted on the opposite corner of the construction office. The building, a windowless, sheet-metal-sided warehouse, was the administrative outpost of Harrison Heavy Constructors, LLC,. Snowflakes drifted on the icy wind that blew in from the north. Dark clouds showed on the horizon. All around the yard, huge yellow construction equipment slumbered in lines, and Buck could see numerous storage containers, pipe racks and prefab offices enclosed by the tall chain-link fence topped with concertina wire. There were a dozen places to hide, a hundred ways to kill or die within reach.

"Fuck," Buck said. He felt his pulse quicken. "They could hole up anywhere, and we could siege this place for a week and not flush them out."

Vicky Dorsett's hands were calm on the wheel, but her eyes were sharp. "We'll get them out. We always do."

Ari Schoenberger materialized from behind the SUV, accompanied by a mountain of a man in a black hoodie and tactical pants—Chicago. Ari shook Buck's hand, his grip dry and tight. His arms were covered in tattoos, and Buck had noticed the first time they worked together that the tats appeared to be the story of his military career. Buck had been impressed.

"You look good," Ari said. His voice was deep, with a New England lilt. "Heard you got knocked around. Glad you're upright."

Chicago stepped around the SUV and extended his hand. Buck shook it, and his hand disappeared into Chicago's hand. Chicago was six foot eight or nine and weighed 350 pounds. He had shoulder-length dark hair and a scraggly beard, and the muscles under his T-shirt had muscles of their own.

When they first met, Paul Webber had asked Vicky why they called him Chicago. Dorsett, who'd said the same thing several hundred times, explained, "He was born in Chicago into a Russian family. His family had a tradition, and he was named after his two great-grandfathers, who had unpronounceable names. Couple that with the fact that no human can pronounce his last name. It's just easier to call him Chicago."

Chicago stepped around the SUV. "Buck, nice to see you. Heard about your situation, glad you came through it okay."

Buck smiled. For a big man, Chicago was soft-spoken and polite. They shook hands, and Buck nodded.

"So," said Ari, holding up the pictures on his phone. "We know this guy Dawson is here. We spotted him go into the office earlier. The other guy we haven't seen, and neither has the team on the other side of the building. Other than Harrison and Dawson, we've seen no one else enter the building, but there are several vehicles in the lot."

Buck's phone chimed, and he checked the text. "Harriet updated the search and arrest warrants to include Wilhite and Dawson. Not sure if you've had time to read their bios, but these two guys are bad news. Keep your heads on a swivel."

Vicky radioed the team behind the building and told them to get into position and hold while Buck made a soft approach, but to be ready to go in hard if needed.

The second team leader responded they were ready to go.

Buck and Vicky slid into the SUV and pulled out, followed by Ari and Chicago. They passed through the gate surrounding the property and stopped next to the office. The second SUV drove around to the side of the office and parked, and Ari and Chicago took up positions on the side near the door.

Buck and Vicky climbed out of the SUV and approached the office door, which was locked. Buck pushed the button on the door camera and waited.

"Yeah. What do you want?" came a voice from the camera.

Buck held up his ID to the camera. "U.S. Marshals Service. We'd like to speak with Brian Harrison, please."

"Sorry, nobody here by that name. Have a nice day."

Buck glanced at Vicky, and he pushed the button again. The same voice said the same thing again.

"We have a warrant to search the premises," said Buck. "Please open the door or we will have to use force to enter the building."

"Piss off, cop. We ain't opening the door for nobody," said the voice.

Vicky nodded and motioned to Buck. They both pulled back, flattening against the wall as Ari taped a thumb-sized charge of C-4 with a remote detonator beside the lockset. He unclipped his phone and opened an app, entered some information and held his finger over the detonate button. He pointed at Vicky.

Vicky called the back team. "Prepare for hard entry." They moved away from the door and faced away from the explosion. "In three, two, one."

The charge popped, not so much a bang as a ringing concussion. The door handle flew somewhere into the building and the door swung inward, slamming into something solid. The building shook. In the same breath, a muted explosion bit from the rear of the building, a coordinated breach from team two.

Several shots rang out, hitting the doorjamb, before they could enter. Ari popped the top on a flash-bang and threw it through the door. Vicky followed his with one of her own. They turned away and covered their ears. There were two loud explosions accompanied by the light of a hundred suns as the flash-bangs went off.

Ari moved low and passed through the door. "U.S. Marshals. Warrant," he yelled as he dove to the right side of the door. Chicago was right behind him, ducking his head and shouldering his way into the narrow vestibule. Buck and Vicky followed, hugging the left wall and searching down the hall with muzzles up.

"Chicago, with me," Vicky yelled, and they moved left, the big man's body taking up the entire doorframe as they cleared room after room—break lounge, file room, conference nook—all empty.

Ari had already reached the door to Harrison's private office, Buck close behind. He could hear rapid whispering inside. "Dawson and Harrison," he mouthed to Buck.

Buck nodded. He focused his breath. Ari kicked the door, stepped to the side and threw in a flash-bang. The flash-bang detonated, and inside the office two men were thrown to the floor by light and noise. Ari and Buck moved into the room, covering the sprawled bodies.

The office had dark-paneled walls that were covered with framed photos. The desk was a live edge burled with a high shine, and there were several trophies on a credenza along one wall.

"Don't fucking move!" Buck shouted. His gun was aimed at the chest of a thick-armed bald man face down on the floor. Next to him, a thinner man with greasy hair, eyes bright with fear, whimpered and flinched at each sound.

Behind them, Vicky's voice: "Clear!" Chicago's: "Clear!"

Ari zip-tied the men with fast, practiced hands. "Clevon Dawson, Brian Harrison, you're under arrest for an assault you were involved in at Fort Carson, and also for resisting arrest and assaulting federal agents."

Harrison and Dawson looked at the marshals and then at each other. They looked confused as they tried to shake off the effects of the flash-bang.

The gunfire at the rear of the building faded. A female voice came over the radio. "Back secure. Wilhite tried to run. He's down. We're calling for an ambulance."

"Not bad for a soft approach," Vicky said, nudging Ari, who was already texting the successful update to the office. "Three injured, nobody dead."

Buck and Ari separated Dawson and Harrison, and Buck sat Harrison in the office chair. Ari led Dawson to the entry waiting area, where Chicago had already patched a shallow scrape on his forearm with a cartoon-printed Band-Aid. Vicky stepped into the office with Buck and stood in the corner.

Buck walked over to the wall behind the desk and studied the pictures. Many showed Harrison shaking hands with public officials at construction sites, and several showed him standing next to uniformed military officers. Buck looked closer at a photo of seven men in military camo posing with their weapons.

Buck spotted a younger Harrison in the photo. He was a bull of a man. Short, with muscles that came from hard work, not a gym. He had a bald head and no neck. He wore a flak jacket that was open and exposed his naked chest.

Buck stepped back towards the chair Harrison was in.

Harrison glared at Buck. "This is a bullshit arrest. That assault was cleared up."

Buck pulled his Miranda warning card from his back pocket and read Harrison his rights. Vicky filmed the interview with her phone.

Buck was about to read the warning when a deputy marshal Buck hadn't met stepped into the room and walked over to Vicky. He whispered something in her ear, and she turned off her phone.

"Stay here and watch the prisoner," she said. "Buck, come with me."

Buck looked at her, confused. She left the office, and Buck followed.

"What's going on?" he asked.

Vicky didn't respond. She led him towards the office area and out into the warehouse and repair center. The fluorescent lights overhead flickered, casting a faint yellow hue over the workspace. Large shelves full of tools and parts lined the walls, while workbenches scattered throughout the space held engines and machinery in various stages of repair. The concrete floors were stained with oil and grease, and the scent of gasoline and cleaning fluid filled the air.

Paramedics had arrived and were working on Wilhite and two Hispanic men who were lying on the ground. Buck and Vicky stepped around them and approached a tall Black deputy who was standing in front of another door, which looked like the door to a walk-in freezer. Vicky introduced Buck to Jasmine Corbin, and they shook hands.

Jasmine pulled open the metal door, and Buck and Vicky stared in disbelief.

Inside, stacked floor to ceiling, were crates of various weapons. Buck stepped into the room and read the labels on the crates. He walked around the space. He turned to Vicky.

"These crates are from military bases all over the place."

Buck lifted the top off one crate on the floor and picked up a rifle. He made sure the chamber was clear and checked the nomenclature on the tag attached to the barrel.

"This is an XM250," he said, turning it over in his hands. "This is part of the next-generation squad weapons program. This is state-of-the-art firepower."

Vicky took a picture from the door and then one of Buck holding the weapon. Vicky stepped deeper into the room, phone already up and clicking. She photographed the crate labels, the racks, Buck with the weapon, even a scope wrapped in foam beneath another case. She opened a crate herself, this one labeled HVAC, and found a stack of military-issue pistols, each with the blue dot showing armory inspection, all packed in foam cut to shape. Her hands shook as she took the photos.

"How much is this worth?" she asked.

Buck's mind tabulated: the value of a prototype weapon, the cost of a pallet, the black-market price for hardware that wasn't supposed to exist.

"Millions," he said. "Tens of millions, depending on what's in the boxes."

He tried to imagine the logistics: How had all of this moved from a secure military base, through the boring world of construction contracting, and into a freezer room in suburban Denver?

Jasmine poked at a stack of sealed envelopes taped to the side of one crate. She pulled out some papers.

"Shipping manifests," she said, handing one to

Buck. The destination address had been whited out and replaced with a fake, but the sender address?

Buck recognized it. "This stuff is supposed to be at Fort Carson," he muttered.

Jasmine leaned closer to Buck. "You realize what this means, right?" she whispered, voice taut. "This isn't just some army surplus skimming. This is supply chain infiltration. Warfighter sabotage, maybe even treason." Her eyes flicked back and forth, as if some secret microphone might be hidden in the insulation.

Vicky dialed a number and waited.

"Hey, Vicky," said a man's voice.

"Hi, Rich. I'm sending you some pictures." She hit send on her phone and waited.

"What am I looking at? Looks like an XM250. What's with all the crates? Where are you?"

"I'm at a construction warehouse in Denver. This room is full of these crates and more. Thought you might be interested in why a construction contractor who works on military bases has a warehouse full of next-gen weapons."

The voice on the line whistled. "You're kidding me. Whose name is on the receiving paperwork?"

"None. The address was changed with White-Out. Sender is Fort Carson. Is there any internal investigation on missing weapons at Carson?"

There was a pause, then Rich's voice returned, lower. "Nothing official. Nothing anyone wants to own."

"Can you post someone there until I can get a team of MPs from Fort Carson up there?" asked Rich.

"You may want to rethink using Fort Carson MPs," said Vicky.

"Why's that?" asked Rich.

"The guy we came to arrest owns the company. The warrant is for a two-year-old beef he got into with a subcontractor on the base. The warrant was never followed up on, and a lot of information is missing from the arrest report."

"Fuck," said Rich. "Okay, I'll make some calls. Secure the area, and I'll be in touch." The call disconnected, and Vicky shoved her phone in her pocket.

"Who was that?" asked Buck.

"Guy I know from army CID. He's stationed at Fort Huachuca in Arizona," she said.

"Good call on telling him not to use Fort Carson personnel," said Buck. "That could explain why no one followed up. Let's go talk to our new friend."

Chapter Forty-One

Taylor Robinson was fixing some broken fence posts at the back end of his property where it abutted the resort. He knew it was close to dinner, so he put his tools away and stopped to drain the last of the coffee from his thermos into the tin cup. He'd slipped onto the seat of his ATV when his phone rang. He pulled it from his jacket pocket, expecting the call to be from his wife, but was surprised when he saw the number.

"This is Taylor," he said.

"Taylor, Clive Bechtel. It's been a while since we've spoken."

"Hi, Clive. What can I do you for?"

"That's what I always liked about you, Taylor, straight to business. Listen, I've got a proposition for you. Got a few minutes to talk?" asked Clive.

"Sure. What's going on?"

"I guess you heard that I've been having some problems here at the resort," said Clive. "I know you're a hell of a hunter, and I'm glad we've been able to work out a suitable arrangement for you to hunt on the resort property over the years. Well, I'm wondering if you might do me a favor. You know this property better than I do, and what I'd like you to do for me is hunt down this sniper that's affecting my business and kill him."

Taylor sat there, stunned, and sipped the last of the coffee in his cup. "Clive?" asked Taylor. "Did you just ask me to come onto your property and kill somebody?"

"Sure, guy. It would be just like hunting elk, except this sniper is costing me a fortune. Now, to sweeten the deal, I'd offer to pay you, let's say, one million dollars cash, if you can kill this person before tomorrow when the sniper's deadline runs out."

"You're serious, Clive?"

"Hell yeah, son. I'm damn serious. The sheriff and those folks from CBI aren't doing anything to stop this sniper, so I figure it's time to bring in one of my people to solve the problem. I know your history, so this shouldn't be hard for a man of your talents. Am I right?"

Taylor shook his head. He was having trouble wrapping his mind around the conversation. Now, one million dollars would be a nice payday, but it had been years since he'd had a man in his crosshairs. He never wanted to go back to those days.

"I don't know, Clive. That's a lot of money, but I quit that business a long time ago. Never planned on going back," said Taylor.

"Look, pal, I get it, but I know you're hurting for money. Does your wife know how much you owe that gambling website you're always on? And I know you went to the bank in Durango looking for a loan and they turned you down. You are flat broke and deep in debt. I'm giving you a chance to get out from under and walk away with enough cash to keep the ranch. I need someone with your skills, and I need them today, before this crazy sniper destroys everything I've built.

What do you say, we make it a million and a half? Would that help get your mind in the right place?" asked Clive.

Taylor was angry. He had no idea how Clive knew his personal business, and it pissed him off. He was silent for a few seconds. "I don't kill people for money, Clive. Goes against everything that means anything to me, and I resent you throwing that shit in my face."

Clive laughed. "Don't be stupid, Taylor, and get off your high horse. The government paid you to kill people, so don't play that self-righteous crap with me. I'm offering you the same job the government did, but the pay is a hell of a lot better."

Taylor kicked the dirt. He knew Clive was right, and if he didn't find the money someplace, he was going to have to sell the ranch. He knew his wife would never understand.

"Okay, Clive," said Taylor. "One dead sniper for a million and a half in cash. I'll get my gear together and see what I can do to find this fella."

"I thought you'd come around. Thanks, Taylor."

The call disconnected, and Taylor sat for a minute. What the fuck had he just agreed to? He'd just accepted a murder-for-hire job. He must be out of his mind. But then again, the government didn't pay him near that much to kill people, so why shouldn't he make money off his talents?

Taylor started the ATV and headed for the barn. He walked into the house and kissed his wife, who was standing at the stove, and told her he had a few things to do in the barn before he came in, but it wouldn't take long. He slipped out of the kitchen and walked to the bar, closing the door behind him.

He walked to a wood-paneled door that matched the paneling inside the barn and entered five digits into the lockbox on the wall. He heard a click and pulled open the door. The room inside was lit by a single light bulb hanging from a cord in the center of the room, and he flipped the switch, bathing the room in light. He walked over and removed his M4 carbine from the rack and held it in his hands.

The M4 had been one of his favorite rifles when he served as a sniper in the military, and he still used it for hunting elk every year. He looked through the scope and felt better about the choice he had made. He put the rifle in a leather scabbard and added four full magazines to the bag. He pulled down a backpack and loaded his camo jacket, pants and boots, night vision goggles, a headlamp and an extra flashlight. He pulled a small med kit off the shelf and added that to the pack along with a second camo hat and gloves. He grabbed the pack and the scabbard, walked out of the room to his ATV and tied everything to the carrier on the back. He walked back and locked the door, thinking about what he would do with a million and a half dollars. He headed to the house for dinner.

He was quiet during dinner, and after cleaning up the kitchen and watching a little television, his wife retired early. Taylor waited until he knew she would be asleep, checked on her, grabbed his coat, hat and gloves, slipped on his boots and left by the kitchen door. He strode to the barn, opened the door and slipped inside. He opened the back door, which faced away from the house, fired up the ATV and passed through the door. He closed the door, climbed onto the seat and headed across the field to the gate he used to access the resort property during hunting season.

Taylor knew in his mind that he could succeed, even though it had been a long time since he had been on an assignment; he knew he kept his skills up by hunting every year, and he knew he was also among the most elite snipers in the world. He knew he wouldn't fail.

He stopped the ATV at the small break in the barbed wire. During hunting season, he would drive through the opening and head another mile onto the resort property, park next to a small stream and pitch his tent. He didn't want the noise from the ATV alerting his prey, so he parked the ATV and moved on foot. It would take a little longer, but it would be safer.

He grabbed his rifle and backpack, slung them over his shoulders and moved through the opening. The snow had picked up, and with a lot of snow already on the trail, it made for a slow slog to get to where he felt might be a good place to hide.

He crossed over the small stream and moved into prime hunting ground. He didn't realize how out of shape he was. He thought back on some of his missions in Afghanistan during the First Gulf War and how he could travel for hours without getting winded. He stopped to take a breather and drank some coffee from his thermos.

He noted that there was no moon and that the stars filled the sky. He always felt better on moonless nights.

If he couldn't see, then neither could the enemy. He hoped that proved to be the case tonight.

Taylor came over a small rise and spotted the lights of the resort in the valley below. He moved up onto the unfinished road and noticed the burned-out construction trailer. As he walked by, he noticed there was still warmth in the embers. His mind moved to high alert.

He moved past the edge of the road and dropped into a slight dip in the terrain. He crawled on his belly until he reached the top of a berm, dropped his pack and unsheathed his rifle. He rested the rifle on the pack and scanned the area through the scope. He wished he had one of those next-generation night vision scopes, but his old scope and his skill would have to do.

He scanned the buildings and then the area along the ski lift and spotted nothing that looked out of place. Keeping his eyes on the scope, he waited for the sun to come up. He shook off the cold and thought about how nice a little fire would be, even though he knew that was impractical. Clive was paying him good money, and he'd just have to get used to the discomfort. Just like the old days.

Chapter Forty-Two

Buck and Vicky stepped into the office and relieved the deputy who stood guard. Brian Harrison sat in the ladder-back chair with his hands cuffed behind his back. He scowled at Buck as he pulled up a second chair and sat next to him.

Buck had made patience an art form. There was a story going around CBI that Buck had gotten a murderer to confess by sitting in the interrogation room for hours and not saying a word. Over the years, the story expanded, and the time grew longer or shorter depending on who was telling the story. Either way, it was always told as a tale of respect.

Vicky sat behind the desk, raised her phone and opened her video app. She held it so she got both Buck and Harrison in the picture. Buck leaned forward, keeping enough distance between himself and Harrison that he could counter any move Harrison might make. Harrison glared at him.

Buck pulled his laminated Miranda warning card out of his back pocket and read Harrison his rights. When he finished, he asked Harrison if he understood his rights, and did he want his attorney present.

"This is a bullshit arrest," said Harrison. "You've got nothing on me."

Buck laughed, which caught Harrison off guard.

"Let's see," said Buck. "We have assault, resisting arrest, assaulting federal agents and, oh yeah, let me think. That's right. A room full of stolen military weapons. That alone should be good for thirty or forty years behind bars.”

“Fuck you,” said Harrison. “You can’t prove I had anything to do with stealing those weapons. Look around, asshole. See all those pictures on the walls? I’ve got a lot of highly placed friends, and I’m gonna have your ass.”

Buck looked around the room. “You’ve got a lot of pictures of those friends, but look around. You see any of them standing here with you right now?”

Buck sat back in his chair. “Now, all this other stuff aside, what I want to know is why you killed an environmentalist on the road you were building for Clive Bechtel.”

Harrison opened his mouth and then paused. “What the fuck are you talking about? I never killed an environmentalist. That’s bullshit. That kid was drunk and ran off the road he shouldn’t have been on. You can’t pin that on me.”

Buck smiled. “We already have.”

Buck was hoping to knock Harrison off-balance, and his tactic seemed to work. Harrison was pissed, and now he was confused. And he was talking without asking for his attorney. Harrison was fine fighting about the weapons and the assaults, but he was not about to get nailed for murder.

“We have a video of the assault,” said Buck. “One of his associates was in the woods and videotaped you and Dawson beating the shit out of the kid and then forcing alcohol down his throat. I guess you didn’t know that the guy never touched alcohol.”

“There’s no way you got a video of me beating the kid, because I wasn’t there,” said Harrison, then he stopped and caught himself.

Buck stood and looked at Vicky. “Stay with Mr. Harrison here. I’ll be right back.”

He turned and walked towards the door. The paramedics were just rolling out the gurney with Branch Wilhite on it, and Buck intercepted them.

“You fellas want to give me a minute?”

The two paramedics stepped away from the gurney and stood off to the side. Buck leaned towards Branch.

“Hurts like a son of a bitch, don’t it?” he said. He pulled out his phone and clicked on his audio recording app. He placed it on the gurney. He pulled out his Miranda card and read Wilhite his rights. Wilhite acknowledged he understood them and that he didn’t need a lawyer, because he had done nothing wrong.

“Okay, Branch,” said Buck. “So, we have a little problem that I’m hoping you can help me out with. Now, I don’t care about the weapons and the resisting arrest stuff, but what I do care about is why you killed an environmentalist and smashed his car into a ravine.”

Branch looked at Buck, and his eyes got as big as saucers.

“You see, Branch, your boss just gave you up. Said he had nothing to do with it, and it was all you and Dawson. He said he wasn’t even there when the kid showed up.”

"What the fuck?" yelled Branch. "I had nothing to do with hurting that kid. That's crap."

"Well, your boss is in his office right now, giving us a statement, and he is implicating you."

Tears rolled down his cheeks. "I tried to get them to stop, but they were out of control."

"Who was out of control, Branch?" asked Buck.

"Brian and Dawson. It was like they went crazy. I was in the trailer when the kid pulled up. They jumped him before he even said what he wanted. They picked up scrap pieces of rebar and just wailed on him. Beat him senseless. Then Dawson came into the trailer and grabbed a bottle of whiskey off the desk, and they poured it down his throat. He was unconscious. I couldn't believe all the blood. Then Dawson threw him in his car and drove away, and the boss followed."

"Well, see, Branch, that's my dilemma, because your boss is telling my associate the same story about you and Dawson. Guess we'll have to arrest you all for murder and see who the court wants to believe."

Buck picked up his phone and turned away from the gurney.

"I have proof," said Branch.

Buck stopped and turned. He stepped next to the gurney. "You have proof?" he asked.

"Yeah, but I want a deal. I'll even tell you about the weapons and how that works, but I want no charges for the murder."

"What kind of proof do you have?" asked Buck,

placing his phone back on the gurney. "I'll need to see it before I can recommend any kind of deal to the DA."

"Pull my phone from my back pocket," said Branch. His one arm was in a sling and his other was cuffed to the gurney. Buck pulled his phone out and held it for him. Buck held the phone to his face, and it chimed as it opened.

Branch told Buck which buttons to push, and a video popped up on the screen. Buck pushed the play button and watched. The video was good, and Buck could see the brutality of the attack. He stopped the video, opened Branch's email app and sent the video to his email.

"Where did you get this?" asked Buck.

"The boss was concerned that those environmentalists were damaging our equipment, so I put a couple of cameras in the trees around the site. The boss must have forgotten they were there, but after what they did to that kid, I thought it might be a good idea to keep copies of the videos. Guess I was right, huh?"

"All right, Branch. You go with these folks to the hospital, and I'll talk to the DA and see what we can work out."

Branch nodded, and Buck walked back towards the office. He sat in his chair and looked at Harrison. He pulled out his phone and slid it over to Vicky, who picked it up and hit the play button. She watched the video and watched Harrison fidget in his seat. She turned it off and handed the phone back to Buck.

Buck smiled at Harrison. "Well, Mr. Harrison, looks like you're gonna need those friends, after all. Brian Harrison, you're being arrested for the murder of Tyler Nelson, along with a whole slew of other charges. I would urge you to keep your mouth shut."

Vicky turned off the phone recording app and stepped around the desk. She nodded towards the door, and Chicago walked in, grabbed Harrison by the arm and lifted him from the chair. Harrison stared at Buck but kept his mouth shut.

"Looks like you got what you needed," said Vicky. "I'll run you back to the chopper so you can get back and stop a sniper. I'll take care of our friends Harrison, Dawson and Wilhite."

She smiled at Buck.

"What?" he asked.

"You are one lucky son of a bitch, Buck Taylor."

Buck nodded, and they headed for Vicky's SUV.

Chapter Forty-Three

Paul ran the video one more time and hit stop on his laptop. "I'm still not sure what you're hearing."

George laughed on the other end of the phone. "It's not what we're hearing, it's what we're seeing. Just before Dawson disappears out of the frame to go to the trailer and get the bottle of whiskey, Harrison pulls out his phone. He talks for a minute, puts his phone away and says something to Dawson, which leads Dawson to the trailer. Who do you think Harrison was calling?"

Paul sat for a minute. "You think he was calling Bechtel for instructions?" he asked.

"Or to tell him what he was going to do, but I think you're right," said George. "Mel is getting a cell tower dump. It won't tell us what was said, but it will tell us whose phones were active. Since this was during the offseason, there shouldn't be that many calls going through the tower at the resort. Do we have Harrison's phone number?"

Paul looked at his email. "Yeah. Buck sent it with the video. I'm sending it to you now along with Bechtel's number."

Paul waited as he ran the video several more times, looking for nuances that had been missed. He didn't see any, but the attack on Tyler Nelson was brutal.

Mel came on the line. "Okay, Paul, I had to pull some teeth, but I got the dump. There were a handful of numbers bouncing off that tower, but two of them were Bechtel and Harrison, and according to the time stamp on the video, they were the only ones talking then. Harrison was in contact with Bechtel. I'm going to go to the judge and ask for an emergency phone dump for both phones. We're gonna be waking some people up, but so be it."

"That's great, Mel. You guys did awesome. I'm gonna see if the sheriff can get us a warrant for Bechtel's phone. Maybe he saves his call logs."

Mel laughed. "It's possible. Depends how much of a tech dinosaur he is. We'll call you when we have the phone logs."

Paul disconnected and dialed another number.

"Paul," said the sheriff.

"Hi, Mike. Couple of things. Buck got a video of the assault on Tyler Nelson."

"What? How?" asked the sheriff.

"Seems the contractor installed video cameras because of vandalism and didn't take them down. One of his men kept the videos as insurance if they ever got nailed for it. That happened this afternoon. We also got a cell tower dump, and the only people talking at that exact time were Harrison and Bechtel. We need a search warrant to seize Bechtel's phone and laptop. You got someone we can wake up?"

"Yeah, give me a few minutes. The judge might still be awake."

The sheriff disconnected the call and leaned back in his chair. He ran the video one more time and felt repulsed by the amount of violence they had perpetrated on that young man. He stood and walked to the counter and poured himself a cup of coffee. He'd started a new pot when his phone chimed.

"Mike," he said.

"I'll pick you up in fifteen minutes," said the sheriff. "Bring the video."

Paul disconnected the call, finished his coffee and grabbed his things. He was waiting outside the rental house when the sheriff pulled up, and he slid into the front seat, dropping his backpack on the floor. Five minutes later, the sheriff parked in front of an old Victorian-style house that looked like it needed some loving care. They slid out and walked up the front walk as the door opened and the judge invited them in.

Inside, the house was warm and comfortable with a fire burning in the fireplace in the living room. The judge wasn't the best housekeeper, and there were numerous books on the tables and court file folders on the couch. Despite the clutter and disarray, there was a sense of comfort and familiarity, as if the house had seen its fair share of stories and secrets.

Judge Harold Werthman had a full head of white hair, was stoop-shouldered and walked with a limp, but you could still feel his commanding presence. He asked them to follow him to the kitchen, and as they walked, Paul stopped to look at a picture on the wall. The picture showed a younger version of the judge, thin and standing ramrod straight, next to Deputy Toby Werthman. Toby was holding his POST police training certificate and wore a shiny new badge.

The judge turned and noticed Paul looking at the picture. He walked over.

"That was a proud day. A proud day indeed. Toby is my grandson. His parents died in an auto-elk accident when he was four. The wife and I raised him from that day on. I wish my wife could have seen him graduate from the academy. She passed away a few months before that picture was taken."

The judge wiped a tear from his eye and walked into the kitchen. It was large, a true country kitchen. The cabinets were solid wood and looked like they were as old as the house, and the open upper shelves held a collection of exquisite plates, cups and bowls. The sweet smell of warm vanilla and freshly baked chocolate chip cookies filled the space. He poured three cups of coffee and slid a plate of cookies across the table.

"Help yourself, fellas," he said. "My wife's recipe. Won't find any better."

The judge sat and looked at Paul and the sheriff. "Okay, let's see what you have."

Paul pulled his laptop out of his backpack and placed it on the table facing the judge. He slid his chair closer and pulled up the video. He pressed play and sat back. The judge watched the video, then asked him to run it again.

"Horrendous," he said. "The things we humans do to each other."

Paul opened the cell tower dump and explained what they were looking at. The judge studied the map with a bony finger and then looked at the two phone numbers Paul had written on a separate note. He compared the numbers to the ones on the screen and then asked Paul to open the video again. He compared the time stamp on the video to the one on the tower dump.

"So, you think Clive Bechtel and this Harrison fella were talking to each other after the beating?"

"Yes sir, Your Honor. We don't know who called who, but we assume, since the beating was not premeditated, that Harrison was calling Bechtel for directions," said Paul.

The judge looked up. "Mike, what do you think?"

"I think that the beating was horrendous, as you stated, and I think we need to find out how much Bechtel knew. It might be the only way to stop this sniper. The answers might be in his phone."

The judge sipped his coffee and ate a cookie from the plate. "I agree with you fellas, but I'm worried this might look like a fishing expedition. Clive's got a lot of powerful friends, and he brings a lot of money into this county. I would hate to see us suffer the consequences if you're wrong. That being said, I also understand the need for swift action. This sniper has caused enough damage."

He was quiet for a minute, and Paul enjoyed several cookies while they waited. The judge looked at the sheriff.

"Mike, write up the warrant application. I'll give you his phone, but nothing else until you can prove his involvement. You can use the computer and printer in the office. Paul and I will sit here and finish our coffees and eat some more of these wonderful cookies, so take your time."

For the first time that night, the judge smiled.

Chapter Forty-Four

Paul and Sheriff Drucker slid into the sheriff's SUV and noted the clock on the dash.

"You think he's asleep?" asked the sheriff.

"It's nine thirty. I doubt it, but if he is, let's go wake him up."

The sheriff started the SUV and drove towards the resort. They pulled up to the gate and signed in with the night security guard, who pushed a button inside the guard shack and activated the gate. The sheriff drove through and followed a long, sweeping curve that ended at Clive Bechtel's driveway. The house, a huge log home, was lit like it was daylight. Every one of the massive windows was bright, and it lit up the forest around the house.

The sheriff pulled into the driveway and parked.

"Looks like he's awake," said Paul. He pushed open the door and, followed by the sheriff, approached the massive double-wide front door. Paul pushed the doorbell, and they heard a chime from inside the house.

Clive Bechtel answered the door holding a glass of brown liquid and stared at the sheriff and Paul.

"Whatever this is, it couldn't wait until morning?" Bechtel's red face revealed his anger at being disturbed. The words came out garbled.

Paul held up the search warrant. "Clive Bechtel, we have a warrant to collect your phones. Please step aside so we can enter."

"What the fuck do you mean you have a warrant? I'm the victim here. Why are you persecuting me?"

Bechtel stood rigid in the doorway and didn't budge. Paul looked at him, but the sheriff spoke first. "Come on, Clive. No one is persecuting you. Now, please step out of the way before this goes someplace none of us want to go."

"Let me see the warrant," he said, spittle running down his chin.

Paul handed him the warrant.

"You got that fucking old man to sign this? Who the fuck does he think he is?" asked Bechtel. "I'll tell you this, when he comes up for reelection, you can bet I'll do everything in my power to crush him. His days are numbered, as are yours, Sheriff. I won't forget what a shitty job you and your friends have done with this investigation. You mark my words. I will destroy you."

Paul had heard enough, and he pushed Bechtel out of the way and entered the spacious foyer. Bechtel was pushed up against the wall, and his drink spilled on his shirt. He leaned away from the wall.

"Who the fuck?" yelled Bechtel.

Paul pushed him against the wall and got in his face. "We've asked you twice to step back and let us in. I'm not asking again. So shut up and stand there or I'll cuff you and lock you in the sheriff's SUV for interfering with a police investigation."

While Paul was leaning on Bechtel, the sheriff had stepped in and walked into the great room off to the left side. There was a fire in the fireplace, and the logs looked like honey in the warm glow. The sheriff found Bechtel's phone sitting on a large wooden end table next to a huge leather couch and picked it up. He pushed the button, and a password request came on the screen.

The sheriff walked back to where Paul and an angry Bechtel were standing and held up the phone.

"Is this your only phone, Clive?" asked the sheriff.

"That's none of your business, you little piss-ant public servant. You work for me, you son of a bitch."

Paul pushed him against the wall harder, and the glass fell from his hand and smashed on the granite tile entry floor. Bechtel opened his mouth, and Paul spun him around and slapped his handcuffs on him. He then led him by the arm into the living room and pushed him onto the leather couch.

Paul took the phone from the sheriff and leaned in close to Bechtel, who sunk into the couch, the bravado gone.

"The sheriff asked you a question. Is this your only phone?" asked Paul.

Bechtel stared at Paul and shook his head.

"Good," said Paul. "Where do we find your other phone?"

"In the office; the desk drawer is locked. The key is on my key ring hanging in the kitchen."

"See," said Paul. "That wasn't so hard, was it? What's your password?"

"If I give you the password, will you take off the

cuffs?" asked Bechtel.

Paul stood and towered over him. "You're in no position to negotiate. We gave you every opportunity to cooperate, but you chose a different route. Now, what's the password?"

"One, two, three, four, five," said Bechtel.

Paul looked at him, shook his head and entered the numbers into the phone. The phone opened, and Paul entered the call log. From the amount of memory used, it didn't look like the log had ever been cleaned up. He scrolled through to the date and time they had gotten from Buck, and Paul smiled.

He showed the screen to Bechtel. "Do you remember this call?" asked Paul.

Bechtel looked at the date and time and laughed. "That was over two years ago. How the fuck would I remember a call from that long ago?"

Paul reached into his backpack, which he had set on the floor next to the couch, and pulled out his laptop. He opened the video file they had shown the judge, and he turned the screen so Bechtel could see and hit the play button.

"Note the time and date stamp on the video, and then look at the time and date on your call log."

Whether Bechtel heard him wasn't clear, but his eyes were glued to the screen, and all the color drained from his face. Paul stopped the video as Harrison was making the call. Paul left the picture on the screen.

"This is Harrison's phone number on your call log at this exact moment. Why was Harrison calling you?"

Bechtel stared at the screen. Tears ran down his face. He looked up at Paul.

"This isn't real. You did some kind of AI generation," said Bechtel, but Paul could tell his heart wasn't in the fight.

"Did Harrison tell you how bad they had beaten that young man?" asked Paul.

The sheriff stepped up behind him holding four burner phones. He looked at Bechtel.

Bechtel shook, and he looked like he wanted to vomit. "He didn't tell me they beat the guy. He told me one activist had come to the construction office drunk and had gotten mouthy. He asked me what I wanted him to do. I told him to let the kid go, and if he was that drunk, maybe he'd run off the road."

Paul pushed the button, and the video played. Bechtel watched as Dawson left the screen and came back a few seconds later with a bottle, and they poured whatever was in the bottle into the kid's mouth. The kid was a bloody mess, and he was as limp as a rag doll as they poured the contents into his mouth. Paul stopped the video as the two SUVs drove away from the construction trailer.

"So, you had no idea what they did?" asked Paul.

"God no," said Bechtel. "I believed Harrison when he told me the kid was drunk. That's why I fought the lawsuit so hard. I had nothing to do with this!"

"You could have saved yourself a hell of a lot of problems if you had bothered to find out what happened to the kid. By the way, that kid they beat to death was the brother of the sniper who is trying to destroy you."

Bechtel looked at him through tear-filled eyes. "What? That can't be."

"It is," said Paul. "When the family lost their last appeal, the sister did what the courts wouldn't. This whole mess is your fault."

Paul looked at the sheriff and the four phones. He looked back at Bechtel. "What's with the four burner phones?"

As Bechtel was explaining about the four burners, Paul was looking through call and text logs. The same password worked on each phone. Three of the phones were empty, but the fourth one had several texts and a call. He scrolled through until he found the same date and time and scrolled as he read. He stopped and read the text string. He held out the phone, and the sheriff read the texts.

"Fuck," said the sheriff.

Paul nodded. He held the text screen so Bechtel could read it.

Text from burner: **Is it done?**

Text from Harrison's phone: **Yes.**

Text from burner: **Good. Clean up and call 911. I'll make sure the cop is a friendly. Bonus coming.**

Text from Harrison's phone: **Thanks**

Paul opened the call log and looked at the call dated later that day. He showed it to the sheriff. "Wanna bet this number goes to a state police accident investigator?"

The sheriff shook his head. "Nope, that would just be throwing money away."

Paul smiled. "Well, Mr. Bechtel. Isn't it a bitch when you get caught in a lie?"

Bechtel objected, but Paul stopped him. He pulled out his Miranda warning card and read Bechtel his rights.

"Clive Bechtel, you are under arrest for conspiracy to commit murder, and a shitload of other stuff that we'll let the DA figure out."

Paul pulled his phone out of his pocket and dialed.

"Hey, Paul. What's up?" asked Mel.

"Hi, Mel. I'm texting you a number from a burner phone we found in Clive Bechtel's office. I need to know who the number belongs to, and then we need a warrant to get phone records and run a background on whoever you find."

Paul pushed send and heard a chime through the phone. "Got it. We'll get on it right away. You want to give me any details?"

"I just arrested Bechtel for his part in the murder of Tyler Nelson. I think the number I sent you is for a state patrol accident investigator."

"No worries," said Mel. "We'll see what we can find." The call disconnected.

Paul put his laptop away, pulled out five evidence bags and placed each phone in a bag, sealed and signed the bags and placed them on his laptop. He pulled out his phone, dialed Franklin and asked him to mobilize the forensic team.

The sheriff lifted Bechtel by the arm, walked him to a hall closet and pulled a coat off the rack. He draped the coat over his shoulders and led Bechtel through the door to the waiting SUV. Paul grabbed the keys the sheriff had hung back on the kitchen wall, locked the front door and put the keys in his backpack. He pulled out his phone and called Buck.

Chapter Forty-Five

Bax packed up her go bag, checked the hotel room one last time and opened the door. The snow had stopped late, and Mack had called her to tell her he would fly up before dawn and pick her up. He wanted to catch the window between storms.

Bax stepped through the front door just as the first rays of dawn were coming over the hills to the east. The sky was leaden, but there were pockets where the clouds had pulled apart.

Bax turned towards her car, which was parked in the first row, and stopped as a person in a hooded winter coat approached. Bax's right hand was on her pistol, but she froze as the person pulled back the hood.

Angela Nelson held up her hands as she approached. "Didn't mean to sneak up on you, Agent Baxter."

"Angela, what are you doing here, and what's with the suitcase?" asked a surprised Bax.

"Detective Villareal said you were leaving this morning. I'd like to go with you to see if I can help talk Abigail down."

"Does Caleb know about this?" asked Bax.

"No," said Angela. "He was asleep when I left." Tears rolled down her cheeks. "My son died all alone. If it comes to it, I don't want the same thing to happen to my daughter, and if I can get her to lay her gun down, I would like to try."

Bax could see how deep this mother's love ran for her daughter. Even faced with the prospect that Abigail would end up in prison for the rest of her life, Angela was willing to step up and try to keep her from getting killed.

Bax nodded and headed for her rental car. Angela threw her suitcase in the back and slid into the passenger seat. Bax started the car and headed for the airport.

Bax pulled in front of the FBO, and she and Angela slid out and entered the building. She spotted Mack chatting up the night receptionist and introduced him to Angela.

"We're all set to go," said Mack. "We've got a clear window between here and Lake City, so we should get there with no issues."

He grabbed his worn leather flight jacket off the back of a couch and grabbed Angela's bag. She tried to protest, but he told her it was all part of the service. He pushed open the door to the tarmac and walked towards the plane. The fuel truck was just finishing topping off the wing tanks, and Mack signed the receipt and placed Angela's suitcase and Bax's go bag into the small cargo hold. He helped them into the plane and took his place in the cockpit.

Mack didn't have to deice, since he had just flown in, so he called the tower and received clearance for immediate takeoff. He taxied to the runway, revved the engines, made one last cockpit check and took off.

The flight to Lake City was smooth, and Mack set the plane onto the runway. He taxied to the FBO as the sun crested the mountains. Mack parked, pulled out the luggage and headed for the office. He followed the women through the door and set their bags down.

"Angela, it was nice to meet you," he said. "Hope everything works out with your daughter."

Angela nodded and stepped away. Mack turned to Bax. "Well, young lady, you know where to find me if you need me again." He gave Bax a hug and stepped back. "Be careful," he said.

Bax nodded and watched as he checked in at the counter, filed his flight plan to Grand Junction and headed into the morning sky.

Bax led Angela to the parking lot. She unlocked her Jeep and threw in the bags, cleaned off the snow that had accumulated, slid in and pulled out of the lot. She pulled out her phone and dialed Buck.

Buck sounded half asleep when he answered.

"Hey," she said. "You awake?"

"Yeah," said Buck. "Where are you?"

"Abigail's mom, Angela, came with me. We just landed."

"Okay, give me fifteen minutes," said Buck, "and I'll meet you at the restaurant on the plaza."

Buck disconnected the call, and Bax turned in at the gate to the resort, stopped at the guardhouse, signed in with the two troopers on duty and headed for the plaza. She parked next to the plaza, slid out and scanned the valley. Angela slid out of the Jeep, and they headed for the Mexican restaurant. Bax was on high alert.

Bax pulled open the door to the condo lobby, and they entered the warm, inviting space and spotted Paul and the sheriff eating breakfast. She pulled over two chairs and introduced Angela. They took off their coats and sat, and the owner approached and filled the two extra cups with coffee. He gave them a minute to look at the menu and took their order.

"So, what did I miss?" asked Bax.

Paul looked up from his breakfast. "We arrested Clive Bechtel this morning."

Bax set her coffee cup on the table. "What's the charge?"

Paul was hesitant to talk with Angela there, and Bax got the message. She changed the subject just as Buck walked in. He stripped off his jacket, pulled over a chair and shook hands with Angela. The owner appeared at the table and set a large glass of Coke in front of him. Buck ordered the breakfast burrito and looked at Angela.

"So, Bax says you'd like to see if you can talk your daughter down. Do you think she will listen to you?" asked Buck.

Angela sat back as her breakfast was set in front of her. She picked up her fork and looked at Buck. "I have to try. I can't lose another child. We have a good relationship, and all I can do is hope that's enough."

"Ma'am, I can appreciate that," said Buck. "But you need to understand. I cannot guarantee your safety. I am going to tell you something because I don't want you going into this blind. Overnight, your daughter attempted to place explosives on the gas valves for all ten buildings in the resort. Luckily, with the information Bax found in your daughter's house, we got ahead of her for the first time and forced her to change her plans. Instead of placing them on the valves, which would have been devastating, our actions forced her to attach the explosives to each door, which could have still caused significant damage. The sheriff collected those devices. Your daughter intended to burn the entire resort to the ground. She is unpredictable."

Angela's hand moved towards her mouth. She was stunned. Buck continued.

"Those devices are now sitting in the middle of the county garbage dump, and a team of bomb disposal experts from the state patrol are working on disarming them. I want you to understand that besides the damage and the deaths your daughter has already caused, her intention is to destroy this resort."

Buck took a bite of his burrito and a sip of Coke. "Those devices were set to go off in three hours. We have no idea where your daughter is, but we know she is prepared to turn this resort into a cinder pile. We are all here to stop her. That's our jobs. You do not need to be here, and I cannot minimize the danger you will put yourself in if you stay.

"I also want you to know that yesterday we arrested the men responsible for your son's death, and late last night, we arrested the owner of this resort for his part in the conspiracy to cover up that murder."

Tears flowed down Angela's cheeks, and she

looked around the table. "That's all we ever wanted, for someone to be held responsible. It was never about the money. That was just to get their attention. We always believed he was murdered, but no one would believe us."

Buck pushed his plate aside. "I was going to broadcast that information across the resort in the hope it will get your daughter to lower her weapons and come out. If you feel up to it, I'd like you to deliver that message. Do you think you can do that?"

Angela wiped her eyes. "I can try."

Buck nodded. "All right, folks. We stopped the bombs, but if she has more incendiary rounds, she can still make a mess. Let's see if we can end this without any more death or damage."

They all stood and put their coats on and headed for the door. Buck took the bill up to the manager and handed him the money from the table. "I want you to close up the restaurant now and get whoever is working with you into town, so they are someplace safe."

The owner nodded, thanked him and disappeared into the kitchen. He could hear a lot of commotion and conversation as the staff shut everything down. Buck hoped they would have someplace to come back to when this was all over.

Chapter Forty-Six

Abigail woke from a restless sleep and looked at her watch. The condo unit she had been hiding in was warm and comfortable, with beige walls and rustic furnishings. The heat was still working, so the space was warm as compared to sleeping outside. She had snuck into the condo after the cops cleared the building.

So far, no one had come back to do any follow-up checks. She had propped a chair against the door to prevent anyone from entering the space. She hoped it would be enough, but she knew she needed to sleep. She was tired, and she was afraid that would hurt her aim. She also needed to rest her ankle. The throbbing was making it difficult to rest, but she hadn't found any painkillers in the condo.

The resort was empty, so she ran some water in the kitchen sink, stripped down and washed herself. She dressed in her winter gear, laid her weapons out on the kitchen table and did a quick inventory. She assumed the authorities had discovered the bombs she placed on the valve room doors, but she had more than enough incendiary bullets and was confident she could still cause a huge amount of damage.

She put all her gear in her backpack, slung it and her rifle over her shoulder and opened the door a crack. The hall was empty, and she pulled open the door and headed for the rear exit. She opened the exit door a crack, checked her surroundings and slipped into the forest. She would circumvent the parking lot to get to the nest she had scoped out the day before.

The forest was quiet from the newly fallen snow and with no moon was as dark as a cave. Abigail had scoped out her route, and she knew she could navigate without using a light.

Her route took her around behind the complex, and at one point she stopped and crouched. She had a feeling she was being watched, but as she scanned the mountain behind her, she couldn't see any signs that someone was there. She figured it was just nerves, so she stood and kept moving. She crossed the small stream that separated the village from the lift area, walked past the lift and disappeared behind the old maintenance building. She stopped, checked her surroundings and entered the forest.

She kept to the densest part of the forest until she had gotten just below the ridge she would use as her nest, and then she started climbing, keeping well back in the trees. The earliest glow of the sun was painting the tops of the mountains above the resort a rich gold color, and she checked her watch. She was right on schedule.

By the time she reached her nest, the sun was just cresting the mountains, and she settled in and unloaded her gear. She pulled out a couple of energy bars and drank from her water bottle. The resort below was empty except for the cops, who had been there since the beginning. She scanned the village and noticed that the Mexican restaurant was closed. That was odd, since they'd been the only ones open since her first attack on the resort. That seemed like a long time ago.

Using her backpack as a solid base, she set her rifle into the slight crease she created and lay flat behind the scope. She zoomed in on the flag at the lift area, made some calculations in her ever-present notebook and adjusted her scope. She pulled the full magazines from her backpack, laid them next to her and inserted the first fifteen-round clip into the rifle. She charged the rifle and put her eyes behind the scope.

The sky was turning a beautiful shade of blue, and there were no clouds and almost no breeze. It was a great day, and she was ready to make Clive Bechtel pay. She checked her watch.

The crackling sound from the speakers startled her, and she twisted deeper into her nest. She had no idea what the hell was going on, but then a voice she recognized filled the air in the valley.

"Abby, it's Mom. I hope you can hear me. Abby, we are all proud of you for trying to help our family, but it's time to stop this before anyone else gets hurt. We've lost your brother. We don't want to lose you. Please put down your weapons and come out. Agent Taylor has guaranteed your safety. No one will hurt you. They want me to tell you they arrested the men responsible for your brother's murder, and yes, according to Agent Taylor, it was murder. We can finally get justice for your brother. Remember, we always told the lawyers this wasn't about the money, it was about justice. We now have the chance to get that, and then Tyler can rest easy, but none of that will be possible if you don't come out. We all know you've done some bad things here, but we love you, and we will face those things as we always have. As a family.

Please, Abby, please lower your weapon and come out from wherever you are. You don't have to do this anymore."

Abby wiped the tears from her eyes, got behind the scope and scanned the area. She couldn't see her mom anywhere. This was the last thing she needed. She couldn't risk hurting or God forbid killing her mother. She wanted to scream for her to get away, but she had no idea where she was. She thought about what her mom had said. If it was true, then her brother had been murdered just like they always said, and if the men responsible had all been arrested, then they could get justice. But she was on a mission, and she still believed that Clive Bechtel had to pay a price for Tyler's death.

She was torn between continuing the fight or giving up. She knew if she gave up, her life wouldn't be worth spit. She had killed or injured dozens of people. There was no coming back from that. She would spend the rest of her life in a Colorado prison, far from her parents and her life in Cody. She was in too deep, but she loved her mother, and she wanted to believe everything she said was true.

Abigail checked her watch. There was still an hour before the bombs were set to go off. She decided that would be her signal. If the bombs had not been compromised or disarmed and they went off, then she would finish what she started and she would burn this resort to the ground. If the bombs failed to go off, she would lay down her rifle and surrender. She thought that was fair, and in her mind, it left the decision up to someone else.

Chapter Forty-Seven

It had been a long time since Taylor Robinson had spent the night behind his rifle scope, and the cold was gnawing through his clothes. He was cold and stiff and he needed to pee, but he wasn't gonna take his eyes off the scope. He closed his eyes for just a few seconds, but that was all it took, and he fell asleep.

He woke with a start as the voice filled the valley below. He wiped the sleep out of his eyes and positioned himself behind the scope. He scanned the ridges on the other side of the valley, concentrating on the rock outcropping, which would make for great sniper hides.

The voice was a woman, and she was asking Abby to lay down her weapons and come out. "So, the sniper is a woman," he said to himself. "That's crazy. Women don't have the skills to shoot those kinds of distances, and they don't have the nerve."

He was getting into a heated argument with himself over the merits of female snipers. He had been out of the military for a long time, and he knew times had changed, but being a sniper was the last bastion of man. He couldn't believe that a woman could do the job he had trained so long and hard to do.

Besides, what woman could endure the things he had endured for the last seven hours? The lack of sleep, the cold, the hunger, the need to pee—those were things he had been trained to deal with. No, the cops must be playing some psychological game on the sniper. That must be it. But the woman sure sounded convincing. If he was getting paid a huge amount of money, he might give himself up after listening to her pleading. He shook off the doubts and scanned the ridges again.

The sun was coming over the mountains, and it looked like they were in for a Colorado bluebird sky. Bright blue and no clouds. It was a good day to be a sniper. He checked his calculations, adjusted his scope and waited. He could feel the tension in the air. He needed to be ready. If she surrendered, she would stand and show herself. Since Bechtel had made no distinctions other than wanting the sniper dead, then her surrendering would give him the best chance of completing the mission. It would be like shooting fish in a barrel.

***

Marty Whitcomb was back in his element. Nestled deep in his hiding spot, just him, his rifle and his scope. He felt good, calm even, for the first time in a long time. Melody had been right when he told her he felt a strong need to help. She had encouraged him, knowing as well as he did that sooner or later, he would need to pick up a rifle again. He knew he would never be an elite sniper again, but the feeling that he was doing the right thing made him feel like a man again.

He adjusted his position. The scars from his surgery were small, but they still felt tight when he stayed in one position too long, and he hadn't moved in hours. He took a sip of water and a bite from his trail mix. There was enough light in the sky that he could now get a better view of the ridges and rock outcroppings on the other side of the valley. He glued his eye to the scope and scanned the areas that looked most promising.

He picked out a few spots that he would use if the situation was reversed and he was the sniper. There were still a lot of shadows and dark recesses visible, and he hoped he wouldn't let the rest of the team down.

His radio crackled in his ear. "Buck to Marty, over."

Marty keyed the mic, never taking his eyes off the scope. "Go ahead, Buck."

"Anything look promising?" asked Buck.

"Too many places. I'm scanning them all. Hopefully, the sniper will make a mistake."

"Okay. Be aware," said Buck. "We are getting ready to put the sniper's mom on the loudspeaker system. We're hoping she'll surrender, but who knows, so keep your eyes peeled for anything that looks like a surrender or the start of her attack. We want to take her alive if she surrenders."

"No problem, Buck."

"Also, Paul and two deputies are making their way through the forest behind the houses below the ridge, hoping to come in behind her. Make sure your target is clear. Buck out."

Marty scanned the ridges again, and then a booming voice filled the valley. "Abby, it's Mom."

Marty scanned slowly, tuning out the noise. He had a job to do, and he wasn't about to let a moment's lapse or distraction compromise that job.

He moved his view to the houses below the ridge

and spotted movement in the trees. He tightened his zoom and identified Paul and the two deputies. They were three hundred yards from the area he had been scanning. Something in his peripheral vision caught his eye, and he swung his rifle. He thought he saw a shadow, but as he looked closer, nothing appeared out of place. Besides, the movement was on the ski slope side. If the sniper was there, she would be facing the wrong direction to do any damage to the resort.

"Probably an elk," he said out loud.

He moved the rifle back to the ridge and continued to scan.

Chapter Forty-Eight

Bax and Sheriff Drucker moved across the ski lift area and headed into the trees. They had their rifles up, and they were ten feet apart and moving as quietly as they could. The snow under their feet crunched as they moved, but they moved steadily towards the ridge, staying in the shadows.

Buck had asked them to flank the right side of the ridge as Paul and the two deputies flanked the left side. They had moved out before Angela had made her plea to Abigail. The hope was that if she gave up, Buck would have units close enough to affect the arrest, and if she completed her mission, then he would have units close enough to stop her. He had scattered state troopers and SWAT officers around the resort, on the ground and on rooftops. He felt good that they could contain her if she started shooting.

He was relying on Marty, hiding behind the resort buildings, to keep his people safe.

Bax and the sheriff moved slowly, and then Bax froze. She slowly looked around. Mike moved closer to her.

"What's up?" he whispered.

"I feel like we're being watched," she said.

"Yeah," he said. "Marty is monitoring us."

Bax looked at him. "No, this is different. I feel like there's someone behind us."

Bax had learned over the years to trust her feelings.

Buck always paid attention to what he called the little bug in his brain that moved around depending on how the investigation was going. Bax had worked on paying attention to those odd little feelings, and she was sensing one right now.

She nodded at the sheriff. "Let's keep moving."

They separated and moved higher up the slope, but Bax couldn't shake the feeling.

***

Paul and Deputies Walt Cummings and Kevin Rhodes put on their ballistic vests and checked their weapons. They dashed across the parking lot and entered the woods behind Bechtel's office building. They followed a trail that had been worn in the snow and entered the forest. They separated and moved out but found the going slow because of the amount of snow the resort had received since this mess started.

Paul was moving ahead when Cummings called him on his radio.

"Paul. I've got fresh footprints up here."

Paul spotted Cummings up the ridge twenty yards away. He moved up the hill and stopped next to Cummings, who was kneeling and pointing at a spot on the ground. Paul kneeled and examined the boot prints.

"It hasn't snowed since last night. If these were made before that, they would be filled with snow. These are fresh today," said Cummings.

"Okay," said Paul. "You follow the tracks; we'll follow behind and cover your flanks."

Cummings nodded and moved out. The sun was casting long shadows from the trees as it came over the mountains. They moved carefully, and then Cummings stopped. Paul moved to his position. Cummings pointed to a rock outcropping. The footprints stopped at the rocks.

Paul signaled for Rhodes to stay where he was and keep an eye on the rock outcropping, while he and Cummings moved farther up the slope. They moved their way above and behind the rocks and then moved down the slope.

Paul moved in from one side, and Cummings moved in from the other, rifles at the ready. The nest was empty, except for an old leather backpack. Paul stepped into the nest, removed his glove and placed his hand on the ground.

"It's still warm. She can't be too far."

Paul left the backpack where it was and marked the GPS coordinates on his phone. He would return later with the state patrol bomb squad.

"What do you think?" asked Rhodes, as he joined them crouched down in the nest.

"I think we need to move away from the backpack and hunker down," he said. "Buck will have the mom on the speaker system in a few minutes. Let's see if it gets a response."

The three men spread out and hunkered down in the rocks, watching the ridge above them.

***

Bax moved through the trees with her rifle at the

ready. As she came into a small clearing, she stopped and kneeled. Sheriff Drucker slid next to her.

"What have you got?" he asked.

Bax pointed. "Those are fresh tracks. We're not alone."

"Could they be the sniper's tracks?" asked the sheriff.

"Not likely," she responded. "These are larger, and they are heading away from the ridge. She'd have no sight line to the resort from up there."

Bax pulled out her radio.

"Bax to Buck."

"Go ahead, Bax."

"We may have a problem. We just came across fresh tracks in the snow, but they are heading away from the ridge."

"Could the sniper be circling around you?" asked Buck.

"These tracks look too big to be a female. I think we have company."

"Buck to Marty."

"Go ahead."

"Marty, can you see anything from your position?" asked Buck.

"Bax, this is Marty. Can you flash something so I can pinpoint your location?"

"Hold on," said Bax.

There were a few seconds of silence while Bax and the sheriff looked for something shiny. The sheriff opened his jacket and unclipped his badge from his shirt. Bax smiled, and the sheriff held his badge and moved it around.

"Marty, this is Bax. Look for a flash above and to the left of the ski lift base building."

"Got it. Which way are the tracks heading?" asked Marty.

"We're in the trees about fifty yards from the ski run, and the tracks almost follow that line," said Bax.

There was silence, and Bax figured Marty was scanning his way up the slope.

"This is Marty, nothing visible from my position, but I'll keep scanning."

"Bax," said Buck. "Stay where you are and keep your head on a swivel. I'm about to put Angela on the speakers again."

"Will do," said Bax. "Over and out."

Chapter Forty-Nine

Abigail had been focused on her mother's voice and hadn't realized how close to her nest the cops were. She heard the crunch of hard snow and knew she needed to move to her second location farther up the ridge. She slid out of the nest with her rifle and ammo bag and left her leather backpack in the nest. She hoped they'd think it might be a booby trap and it would occupy their attention for a bit.

She stayed low and moved over the rocks like a cat, trying to leave as little evidence as possible of her travel directions. She reached the escape path she had made earlier and followed it up into the trees and towards the top of the ridge. It was farther from the resort, but she knew she didn't need to be as accurate with the incendiary rounds. They would still be effective even if her aim was off by a couple of feet.

She slid down the slope and into her backup nest. She had placed a blanket on the rocks to act as a benchrest, and she placed her rifle on the blanket and zeroed in her scope on the main building. She checked her calculations in her notebook and made her adjustments. She was ready. She checked her watch. Ten minutes to go.

Her mom's voice echoed through the valley again. "Abby, it's Mom. I need you to come out now, dear. You've made your point, and I don't want anything bad to happen to you. I have spoken with your father, and he is calling around to get you the best attorney possible. You are making a lot of people nervous, and

Agent Taylor doesn't want anything to happen to you. Please, Abby. Lay down your rifle and come out. Agent Taylor asked me to tell you that the bombs you placed around the resort have all been neutralized. Abby, I'm scared I will never see you again. Please, lower your weapon and come down."

Abigail wiped tears from her eyes. If her mom was telling the truth, then her plan to burn down the resort had been scuttled. She lay back in her nest. She had accomplished part of what she wanted to do. She had hoped someone would take a serious look at her brother's death and do something about it, and it looked like that was going to happen. She knew Bechtel would never pay her the money she wanted, especially with his arrest. She looked at her watch as the minute hand moved one minute past the hour. There were no explosions. Her mom had been right. It was time to end her war.

Abby set her rifle aside and steeled herself for what was to come. She knew she could be seen from this nest, so she stood up and waved her arms.

"This is Marty. I have movement on the ridge about a hundred yards above and three hundred yards north of Paul's position. She appears to be unarmed and is waving her arms."

"This is Paul. We have a visual and we are moving to intercept."

The rifle crack echoed through the valley, and Abigail fell behind the rocks she was standing on.

"This is Buck. Who fired?"

"Sniper!" came several voices.

Chapter Fifty

Taylor Robinson waited, scanning the ridgeline for any movement. He was also observing two people who were now hiding several hundred yards below him. He had spotted them earlier and wondered what they had stopped to look at. Not that it mattered. He didn't want to kill any of the cops, but a million and a half dollars was a lot of money, and he would do what he had to do to collect.

The speakers below crackled as the woman's voice echoed through the valley, pleading with her daughter to come out of hiding. He was fascinated by the fact that she had planted explosives around the village. This girl had a lot of spunk. He could have used someone like that on his team when they were fighting terrorists around the world.

He scanned the ridge and spotted movement to his left. He scanned back, and there she was, standing on top of a rock pile, waving her arms. His goose was about to lay its golden egg. He lined up his shot, let out half a breath and fired. He watched through the scope as she fell behind the rocks. He thought he had seen a red cloud appear as she fell.

He switched his focus down the slope to where the two people were earlier and spotted a blond woman working her way up the slope. He sighted in on the logo on her vest and let out half a breath. He never felt the bullet slam into his left ear.

***

Marty watched as the sniper fell back onto the rocks. He had seen a splash of red through his scope when she fell, and he knew she was hit. Bax had been right. There was another sniper. There was a lot of noise coming through the earpiece, so he pulled it out and swung his rifle around to where he believed the noise had come from. He knew where to look.

The movement was subtle, but he knew he had seen it this time, and he knew it was no elk. He lined up his shot and squeezed the trigger. The rifle bucked, and he saw a red mist appear above the snow.

Marty clicked the mic on his collar. "Sniper neutralized."

He scanned down the hill and saw Bax and the sheriff racing up the hill as fast as they could go in the deep snow. He waited until he saw Bax step around the shooter's nest and wave her arms. He lowered his rifle and sat up. His body ached as he stretched his legs, and he struggled to stand. He sat on the big rock he had spent the past twelve hours behind and took a deep breath. He took off his gloves and held his hands flat out in front of him. The shaking was gone.

Marty stripped down his rifle and placed it in the case, grabbed his backpack and the gun case and headed down the hill towards the resort.

***

Angela finished her speech, wiped the tears from her eyes and left the security office. Buck was right behind her. They walked out onto the plaza and stood, watching the ridge on the other side of the resort.

"This is Marty. I have movement on the ridge about a hundred yards above and three hundred yards north of Paul's position. She appears to be unarmed and is waving her arms."

"This is Paul. We have a visual and we are moving to intercept."

Angela ran out onto the plaza to get a better view. She spotted Abigail and waved her hands, hoping her daughter would see her. She looked back at Buck, a smile forming between the teardrops.

The rifle crack echoed through the valley, and Abigail fell behind the rocks she was standing on.

Angela stood for a second, stunned, and then she screamed.

"This is Buck. Who fired?"

"Sniper!" came several voices.

Buck heard the second shot and looked towards the ski area. With the way the valley sat, it was difficult to get a solid direction on the shooter, but then he heard the words. "Sniper neutralized."

He held up his radio. "Paul, sitrep."

Angela ran back to Buck and stood next to him, waiting to hear.

Buck keyed the mic. "Paul, come in."

"Buck, we just got to her. We're gonna need air evacuation, ASAP. She's hurt bad. Cummings is working on her."

"Roger, Paul."

Buck pulled his phone off his belt and speed-dialed a number.

"Buck, what's going on?" asked the director.

"Sir, we're gonna need immediate air evac. Abigail surrendered but was shot by another sniper."

"I'm making the call now," said the director, and the line went dead.

A minute later, his phone chimed.

"Sir."

"Evac en route, Buck. They figure five to seven minutes. They are coming from Durango. I've told them to head for the hospital in Colorado Springs, and I'll meet them there. Tell me about the second sniper."

"No idea, sir. There was no sign of a second sniper. As soon as I know something, I'll fill you in."

"Are our people safe, Buck?"

"Yes, sir."

"Good, I'll call you from the hospital." The director disconnected the call.

Buck keyed the mic. "Bax, come in."

"Bax here. We're good."

Buck heard the chopper coming up the valley and walked to the middle of the parking lot. He had Angela stay by his side. The chopper flew over, and he waved them down. The side door opened, and Buck helped Angela inside. He pointed towards Paul, who was standing on the ridge, and the chopper lifted off and headed across the valley.

Buck watched as they lowered the basket, and then a minute later, they pulled Abigail into the chopper. They lowered the basket and then pulled Paul up. The helicopter turned and headed towards the hospital.

Chapter Fifty-One

Buck sat at a table in Clive Bechtel's office building. He sipped from his bottle of Coke and waited for the team. Marty arrived first, and Buck shook his hand.

"You okay?" asked Buck.

Marty set his gear down next to the wall and grabbed the chair opposite Buck.

"Yeah," he said. "I'm good. I called Melody on the walk down and told her I'd be home soon."

"You were a tremendous help today," said Buck.

Marty smiled. "I won't lie. I was pretty nervous this morning lying in the snow and thinking about what might happen, but I'm glad I did it. I had no idea if I could still take the shot. It felt good to be back in the field."

Buck nodded. "Well, Bax and the sheriff are glad you took the shot. They might have been next."

"Any ID on the other shooter? I feel bad that I couldn't locate him this morning."

Bax and the sheriff walked in and dropped their gear. Buck introduced Bax to Marty.

"We have an ID on the second shooter. Taylor Robinson," said Bax.

Marty looked stunned. "Taylor?"

Buck reviewed the pictures on Bax's phone and then looked at her and the sheriff.

"Any idea how he got involved? Didn't you guys talk to him?"

The sheriff nodded. "We did, and there was no sign he was part of this. I'm at a loss."

Bax had put on nitrile gloves and pulled Robinson's phone out of the evidence bag.

"This might be something," she said. "His last call yesterday was from Clive Bechtel, and he's had five calls and seven texts from his wife wanting to know where he is."

"Bax, why don't you and Mike head over to his house and make the notification and see what she can tell us?"

Bax put the phone back in the evidence bag and placed it in her backpack. She and Sheriff Drucker grabbed their gear and headed out the door.

Deputies Cummings and Rhodes walked in looking wiped out. Buck thought about the last time anyone had gotten any actual sleep. It had been a while.

They set Paul's backpack and rifle on the table and set Abigail's rifle and gear on the floor along the wall. Buck waited until they sat.

"How bad?" he asked.

Rhodes opened a bag of trail mix and placed a handful in his mouth. He swallowed. "She was hurt bad. The bullet entered to the right of her midline. If it missed her heart, it was by a fraction of an inch. Walt was able to slow the bleeding while we waited for the chopper. She was in shock and had lost a lot of blood by the time we got to her. The cold might have helped slow down the bleeding. Do we know who the second sniper was and why he took her out instead of all of us?"

"The second sniper was Taylor Robinson," said Buck.

Cummings looked surprised. "I saw Taylor in town yesterday. He was picking up some groceries."

"Mike and Bax are on the way to talk to his wife. His last call was from Bechtel."

Cummings shook his head. "Taylor and Bechtel had a live and let live agreement, since Taylor's property bordered the resort. Taylor accepted the resort because Bechtel let him hunt on his land, otherwise he couldn't stand the guy."

"Well," said Buck. "Something changed yesterday afternoon. We'll talk to Bechtel and figure it out. Why don't you guys call it a day and go grab some sleep?"

Buck looked at Marty. "You might as well head home."

"I'll do that," said Marty. He held out his hand, and Buck shook it. "Thanks, Buck. You letting me be a part of this made me feel like a man again. I'm sad about shooting Taylor. He was good people, but I'm glad I could be of service."

He picked up his backpack and rifle case and walked out the door. Buck leaned back in the chair and sipped his Coke. He pulled out his phone and called Franklin. They had two more crime scenes to process and a shitload of paperwork to get done before they wrapped this up.

He grabbed his backpack and Paul's gear, along with Abigail's rifle and gear bag, locked up the office with the keys he had taken off Bechtel and walked towards his Jeep. The paperwork could wait until tomorrow.

Epilogue

Buck walked into the kitchen of the B&B, pulled a bottle of Coke out of the refrigerator and sat down at the table opposite Bax. She slid a plate of breakfast burritos towards him, and he picked one up.

In the two days since they had arrested Abigail Nelson, a lot had changed around the resort. With Bechtel in jail awaiting arraignment, Guy Pembroke, the resort manager, called all his employees back to work to get the resort ready to open. After discussion with Buck and Sheriff Drucker, he had reopened the restaurant that morning, and guests and owners had started to arrive. Buck had released all the state troopers and the SWAT team. Their presence at the resort had been a huge help.

When Buck was in the plaza with Franklin, as they wrapped up the forensic investigation of the two sniper locations, many of the shops, restaurants and bars were coming back to life and getting ready for the first wave of guests. Buck was glad to see that the last few days hadn't dampened the enthusiasm for the resort. The locals were excited to see the visitors return to the valley.

"How did you make out with Mrs. Robinson?" asked Buck.

Bax looked up from her laptop. "We interviewed her for a couple of hours. I'm convinced she had no idea what her husband was up to or why he was in the resort. She knew nothing about the call from Bechtel. She's pretty broken up with her husband's death, but she is cooperating. Franklin and his team are going through the house and the outer buildings, and he expects to be done in the next few hours. How did things go with Bechtel and Harrison?"

Buck had spent the better part of the day before in Denver at the federal lockup, interviewing Harrison.

"It was a slow process," said Buck. "Even when we showed him the video of the beating, he still sat there stone-faced and refused to answer any of our questions. I turned him over to army CID, figured I'd give them a day or two to break him. Maybe he'll be more cooperative. CID arrested a colonel, a couple of junior officers and several enlisted men and women at Fort Carson. They have been supplying Harrison with weapons for years. CID thinks most of them ended up with the cartels in Mexico. He's facing a long time in prison."

"Where's Paul?" asked Bax.

"He's interviewing Bechtel this morning," said Buck. "He refused to admit anything about anything, and he wouldn't even acknowledge he had called Taylor Robinson, but he'll crack. I spoke to the director last night, and the governor had already received five phone calls from friends of Bechtel, pushing to get him released."

Bax sipped her coffee while Buck finished his burrito. She looked up. "Any word on Abigail?"

"Yeah," said Buck. "We have agents on her around the clock. She's in an induced coma, and the doctors aren't sure when they will bring her out of it. The bullet did a lot of damage, and according to the director, she's lucky to be alive. She lost a lot of blood and was in surgery for almost nine hours. Her parents are with her, and we'll arrest her as soon as she wakes up. I heard her family hired Danny Jefferson."

"Wow!" said Bax. "Jefferson is one of the best criminal defense attorneys in the state. He rarely loses."

Buck laughed. "Only when he's come up against us."

Bax finished her coffee and closed her laptop. "What do you want me to do?"

Buck stood and washed his plate in the sink. He dried the plate, turned and faced her.

"Pack up and head home. I was planning to head out later today. Take a few days off, and let's meet up at the office next week and box everything up for the DA."

Bax stood, walked over and gave him a hug. "Go home and rest. You did a good job hiding it, but I can see you're hurting."

Buck stepped back and nodded. Since his hospitalization, Bax had been watching him like a hawk, and he wondered if his daughter, Cassie, had put her up to it. He smiled. He was glad he had those two in his life.

Buck walked to the front door and grabbed his coat from the rack next to the door. He opened the door and looked at a perfect Colorado morning. There was a trace of fresh snow on the ground from an overnight storm, and the sky was clear blue and cloudless. He zipped up his coat and put on his sunglasses. The sheriff's office was six streets over, and it was a perfect morning for a walk.

Bax was packing her go bag and looked out the window. She spotted Buck walking away from the house, and she laughed. She picked up her phone and dialed.

"Hey," she said.

"Hey yourself," said Cassie. "How's he doing?"

Bax smiled. "You know your father. Nothing can stop him."

Acknowledgments

A special thank-you to my daughter Christina J. Morgan, my unofficial collaborator.

Thanks to my editor, Laura Dragonette, whose efforts helped turn my manuscript into a polished novel. Her help is greatly appreciated. Any mistakes the reader may find are solely the responsibility of the author.

Special thanks to my daughter Stephanie Morgan, my beta reader. Stephanie has read every novel in its rough stages and rarely gets to see the completed product. Her insight and critique have been critical to making sure the stories make sense.

Also, I would like to thank my family for their encouragement. I have been telling them stories since they were little, and I always told them that someone should be writing this stuff down. I decided to write it down myself.

I want to thank my closest friend, Trish Moakler-Herud. She has been encouraging me for years to write my stories down. I hope this will make her proud.

A special thanks to my late wife, Jane. She pushed me for years to become a writer, and my biggest regret is that she didn't live long enough to see it happen. I love her with all my heart and miss her every day. I think she would be pleased.

Finally, thanks to the readers. Without you, none of this would be important.

About the Author

2019 Pacific Book Awards Best Mystery Finalist . . . *Crime Delayed*

2020 Pacific Book Awards Best Mystery Winner . . . *Crime Denied*

2020 Chanticleer International Book Awards: 1st Place Blue Ribbon, CLUE Book Awards for Suspense, Thriller Fiction . . . *Crime Denied*

2021 Chanticleer International Book Awards Finalist, CLUE Book Awards for Suspense, Thriller Fiction . . . *Crime Conspiracy*

2021 Chanticleer International Book Awards Finalist, Book Series, CLUE Book Awards for Suspense, Thriller Fiction . . . Crime Series, The Buck Taylor Novels

2022 Chanticleer International Book Awards Finalist, CLUE Book Awards for Suspense, Thriller Fiction . . . *Crime Exploded*

2022 Chanticleer International Book Awards Finalist, CLUE Book Awards for Suspense, Thriller Fiction . . . *Crime Spree*

2023 Chanticleer International Book Awards Finalist, CLUE Book Awards for Suspense, Thriller Fiction . . . *Crime Scene*

2023 Chanticleer International Book Awards Series Finalist, Mystery & Mayhem Book Awards . . . *Crime Series*

Chuck Morgan attended Seton Hall University and Regis College and spent thirty-five years as a construction project manager. He is an avid outdoorsman, an Eagle Scout and a licensed private pilot. He enjoys camping, hiking, mountain biking and fly-fishing.

He is the author of the Crime series, featuring Colorado Bureau of Investigation Agent Buck Taylor. The series includes *Crime Interrupted, Crime Delayed, Crime Unsolved, Crime Exposed, Crime Denied, Crime Conspiracy, Crime Unknown, Crime Exploded, Crime Spree, Crime Family, Crime Scene, Crime Victims* and *Crime Unraveled.* He is also the author of *The Assassin's Heart,* a romantic thriller, and *Preserve, Protect, and Defend,* a political thriller.

He is also the author of *Her Name Was Jane*, a memoir about his late wife's nine-year battle with breast cancer. He has three children and four grandchildren. He resides in Lone Tree, Colorado, with his Siberian husky.

Other Books by the Author

Dear Reader, thank you for reading this novel. Please enjoy the other books in this series and follow Colorado Bureau of Investigation Agent Buck Taylor and his team as they investigate new and sometimes unusual crimes in the Colorado mountains. Each novel is a separate story, and they can be read in any order, but you might find it more enjoyable to read them in order.

Happy Reading,

Chuck Morgan

"*Crime Interrupted: A Buck Taylor Novel* by Chuck Morgan is a gripping, edge-of-the-seat novel. *Right from page one, the action kicks off and never stops, gaining pace as each chapter passes." Reviewed by Anne-Marie Reynolds for Readers' Favorite.*

Finalist . . . 2019 Pacific Book Awards Best Mystery

"This crime novel reads like a great thriller. The writing is atmospheric, laced with vivid descriptions that capture the setting in great detail while allowing readers to follow the intensity of the action and the emotional and psychological depth of the story." Reviewed by Divine Zape for Readers' Favorite.

"Professionally written in the style of a best-selling crime novelist, such as Tom Clancy, Crime Unsolved: A Buck Taylor Novel by Chuck Morgan is a spellbinding suspense novel with an environmental flair. Intriguing subplots of fraud, survivalist paranoia, and murder weave their way through the fabric of the plot, creating a dynamic story. This is an action-filled, stimulating tale which contains fascinating details that are relevant in our present climate." Reviewed by Susan Sewell for Readers' Favorite.

"Chuck Morgan has a unique gift for plot, one that makes Crime Exposed: A Buck Taylor Novel a hard-to-put-down book. *From the start, readers know what happens to Barb, but they become curious as they follow the investigation, wondering if the characters will find out what happened to her. The descriptions are filled with clarity, and they offer readers great images. The prose is elegant, and it captures both the emotional and psychological elements of the novel clearly while offering vivid descriptions of scenes and characters. This is a fast-paced thriller with memorable characters and a criminal investigation that is so real readers will believe it could happen." Reviewed by Romuald Dzemo for Readers' Favorite.*

Winner . . . 2020 Pacific Book Awards Best Mystery

2020 Chanticleer International Book Awards: 1st Place Blue Ribbon, CLUE Book Awards for Suspense, Thriller Fiction

"It's really progressive to see a female serial killer portrayed with such intelligent writing and depth of character, and the cat and mouse chase dynamic is thrown off nicely by the switching of genders. What results is a really enjoyable thriller and crime mystery novel, and overall Crime Denied is certain to please fans of both hard-boiled detective tales and action/adventure crime novels." Reviewed by K.C. Finn for Readers' Favorite.

2021 Chanticleer International Book Awards Finalist, CLUE Book Awards for Suspense, Thriller Fiction . . . *Crime Conspiracy*

"This makes for a truly dynamic story where anything is possible, and a hero you can root for even when it looks like all is lost." Reviewed by K.C. Finn for Readers' Favorite.

"This is a book you can't put down, which will entertain you on many levels, and at times make your skin crawl; the kind of book that remains in your thoughts long after you

finish reading.” *Reviewed by Steven Robson for Readers' Favorite.*

“I read Crime Unknown in one sitting. The plot is intense and the main character, Agent Buck Taylor, is a hero like no other. *This book has everything a thriller needs to be and more. I thought I knew the story at the beginning. Buck will solve a tricky murder case, I thought. But Chuck Morgan adds a twist to this story that expands it and makes it one of the most enjoyable books I've read in this genre. I loved that the lead was such an awesome well-rounded fellow but that he also had a support team who were just as important to the story.” Reviewed by Maureen Dangarembizi for Readers' Favorite.*

“Crime Unknown is a thoroughly enjoyable read and I would not hesitate to recommend this book to fans of the crime genre and those looking for a gateway in.” *Reviewed by K.C. Finn for Readers' Favorite.*

2022 Chanticleer International Book Awards Finalist, CLUE Book Awards for Suspense, Thriller Fiction . . . *Crime Exploded*

*"**Action-packed and fast-paced, I was sucked into the story the moment I opened the novel.** The author built the story to perfection. Chuck Morgan gave just the right amount of suspense, mystery and action to keep readers' attention on Buck and his team. There was never a dull moment in the story. The narrative ran smoothly until the end; it followed the development of the story and the pace set by the characters. I enjoyed the twists and turns. What I loved more than anything else in the plot was how calculating Buck was. He was smart; he didn't let the FBI discourage him and kept his head in the game. The action gave me an adrenaline rush. Absolutely brilliant!" Reviewed by Rabia Tanveer for Readers' Favorite.*

2022 Chanticleer International Book Awards Finalist, CLUE Book Awards for Suspense, Thriller Fiction . . . *Crime Spree*

"It is one of the best crime novels I have read in a long while, with real characters developed in a way to let you get to know them intimately, understand them, and appreciate their strengths and weaknesses. The plot is tight, exciting, and tense, with plenty of action, and it will grip you from the start. The bizarre storyline is enthralling, written in descriptive prose that lands you right in the middle of the action. Forget sleep; once you pick this book up, you won't want to put it down until it's finished. Fantastic story, and highly recommended for fans of high-octane crime thrillers." Reviewed by Anne-Marie Reynolds for Readers' Favorite.

"Crime Family is the tenth book in the Buck Taylor series. Chuck Morgan had me hooked from the first page until the end. *There was never a dull moment with all the action; one chapter flowed into the next. The story was fast-paced and kept me on the edge of my seat. I kept turning the pages to find out what would happen next. I was intrigued, and with all the twists and turns, I could not predict what was looming. The characters were well-developed. Each had a background description, and it was fun getting to know some of them. The story was excellently written with a fitting ending." Reviewed by Alma Boucher for Readers' Favorite.*

"Crime Scene is a must-read for lovers of mystery sleuth and

murder tales with a touch of conspiracy." *Reader's Favorite review.*

"Crime Scene has a carefully designed intrigue that deepens with every unforeseeable turn of events and a dynamic narrative." *Reader's Favorite review.*

"This is a great book. Holds your attention and you don't want to put it down. I would recommend this book to anyone who loves a good crime novel." *Amazon review.*

"Spellbinding, gripping, powerful, and relevant are just a few words that come to mind after turning the last page of Crime Scene: A Buck Taylor Novel, Book 11, by Chuck Morgan." *Amazon Review.*

"A riveting plot and good pacing keep the reader in suspense as Buck Taylor and his team establish evidence beyond a reasonable doubt. *The author sustains interest by skillfully showing the art and intuition involved in crime investigation and the science behind it, as well as the elements that can delay or confound it. There are a lot of quirky characters in the novel and the author gives them mannerisms, voices and descriptions that make them distinctive and realistic. The details and descriptions of the work and everyday life of the players are both pleasantly appealing and revolting, depending on the scenario. What's most captivating and intriguing about the character development is the backstory of the unhinged characters and how the author uses them as part of the perplexing trail of a horrendous crime. Themes of sadism, cruelty, grief, forensics, police procedures, and even a little bit of romance can be found in this installment of the Buck Taylor series. Highly recommended for crime story fans who especially enjoy the information as well as the twists, turns, and the untangling of intricate and cold case crime sprees." Reviewed by Carmen Tenorio for Readers' Favorite.

⭐ ⭐ ⭐ ⭐ ⭐ If you are looking for a mystery murder novel with a touch of crime, Chuck Morgan's Crime Unraveled is just what you should be looking for.

⭐ ⭐ ⭐ ⭐ ⭐ Chuck Morgan took me on a roller coaster ride with Crime Unraveled. The action started on the first page and continued until the last.

⭐ ⭐ ⭐ ⭐ ⭐ Filled with suspense and action, Crime Unraveled: A Buck Taylor Novel, Book 13, by Chuck Morgan delivers a compelling and realistic story with historical and legal elements.

⭐ ⭐ ⭐ ⭐ ⭐ The 13th book in the Buck Taylor series, Crime Unraveled by Chuck Morgan is a fantastic addition to the series. I've read a few books in this series and they never fail to leave me in awe. This is the type of high-octane, fast-paced thriller I've come to expect from this author.

Delia Cahill is one of the world's elite assassins, but her next assignment has gotten into her head. Will Delia carry out her assignment or risk everything, including her life, to protect her intended victim?

⭐ ⭐ ⭐ ⭐ ⭐ *If you are looking for a thriller with brains, heart, and just the right amount of edge, this one is a must read. 5 stars, no doubt.*

⭐ ⭐ ⭐ ⭐ ⭐ *Chuck Morgan's The Assassin's Heart will keep the reader's heart thumping from the first page to the last.*

⭐ ⭐ ⭐ ⭐ ⭐ *Overall, I enjoyed the novel very much. If you're craving a fast-paced, action-packed thriller, you will not be disappointed!*

"Preserve, Protect, and Defend by Chuck Morgan was intricate and enthralling, grabbing my attention from start to finish. This fast-paced, action-packed story had me turning the pages as quickly as possible, afraid to miss a single detail. With each twist and turn, the plot kept me on my toes, continually surprising me

with its unpredictability. The suspense had me sitting on the edge of my seat, making it hard to set the book aside. The engaging writing style made it easy to immerse myself fully in the story, and the characters felt incredibly genuine and relatable. Mike was a powerful force, and Stevenson had no idea what was headed his way. This book was masterfully written and maintained my interest throughout. It surpassed all my expectations, and I enjoyed every moment." Reviewed by Alma Boucher for Readers' Favorite.